PENGUIN BOOKS
1170
PIGS HAVE WINGS
P. G. WODEHOUSE

PIGS HAVE WINGS

P. G. Wodehouse

PENGUIN BOOKS

Penguin Books Ltd, Harmondsworth, Middlesex
CANADA: Penguin Books (Canada) Ltd, 178 Norseman Street,
Toronto 18, Ontario
AUSTRALIA: Penguin Books Pty Ltd, 762 Whitehorse Road,
Mitcham, Victoria
SOUTH AFRICA: Penguin Books (S.A.) Pty Ltd, Gibraltar House,
Regent Road, Sea Point, Cape Town

—

First published 1952
Published in Penguin Books 1957

All the characters in this book
are purely imaginary and have no relation
whatsoever to any living person

Made and printed in Great Britain
by C. Nicholls & Company Ltd

CHAPTER ONE

BEACH the butler, wheezing a little after navigating the stairs, for he was not the streamlined young under-footman he had been thirty years ago, entered the library of Blandings Castle, a salver piled with letters in his hand.

'The afternoon post, m'lord,' he announced, and Lord Emsworth, looking up from his book – he was reading Whiffle on *The Care Of The Pig* – said: 'Ah, the afternoon post? The afternoon post, eh? Quite. Quite.' His sister, Lady Constance Keeble, might, and frequently did, complain of his vagueness – ('Oh, for goodness sake, Clarence, don't *gape* like that!') – but he could on occasion be as quick at the uptake as the next man.

'Yes, yes, to be sure, the afternoon post,' he said, fully abreast. 'Capital. Thank you, Beach. Put it on the table.'

'Very good, m'lord. Pardon me, m'lord, can you see Sir Gregory Parsloe?'

'No,' said Lord Emsworth, having glanced about the room and failed to do so. 'Where is he?'

'Sir Gregory telephoned a few moments ago to say that he would be glad of a word with your lordship. He informed me that he was about to walk to the castle.'

Lord Emsworth blinked.

'Walk?'

'So Sir Gregory gave me to understand, m'lord.'

'What does he want to walk for?'

'I could not say, m'lord.'

'It's three miles each way, and about the hottest day we've had this summer. The man's an ass.'

To such an observation the well-trained butler, however sympathetic, does not reply 'Whoopee!' or 'You said it, pal!' Beach merely allowed his upper lip to twitch slightly by way of indication that his heart was in the right place, and Lord Emsworth fell into a reverie. He was thinking about Sir Gregory Parsloe-Parsloe, Bart, of Matchingham Hall.

To most of us, casual observers given to snap judgements, the lot of an Earl dwelling in marble halls with vassals and serfs at his side probably seems an enviable one. 'A lucky stiff,' we say to ourselves as we drive off in our charabanc after paying half a crown to be shown over the marble halls, and in many cases, of course, we would be right.

But not in that of Clarence, ninth Earl of Emsworth. There was a snake in his Garden of Eden, a crumpled leaf in his bed of roses, a grain of sand in his spiritual spinach. He had good health, a large income and a first-class ancestral home with gravel soil, rolling parkland and all the conveniences, but these blessings were rendered null and void by the fact that the pure air of the district in which he lived was polluted by the presence of a man like Sir Gregory Parsloe – a man who, he was convinced, had evil designs on that pre-eminent pig, Empress of Blandings.

Empress of Blandings was the apple of Lord Emsworth's eye. Twice in successive years winner in the Fat Pigs class at the Shropshire Agricultural Show, she was confidently expected this year to triumph for the third time, provided – always provided – that this Parsloe, who owned her closest rival, Pride of Matchingham, did not hatch some fearful plot for her undoing.

Two years before, by tempting him with his gold, this sinister Baronet had lured away into his own employment Lord Emsworth's pig man, the superbly gifted George Cyril Wellbeloved, and it was the opinion of the Hon. Galahad Threepwood, Lord Emsworth's younger brother, strongly expressed, that this bit of sharp practice was to be considered just a preliminary to blacker crimes, a mere flexing of the muscles, as it were, preparatory to dishing out the real rough stuff. Dash it all, said Galahad, reasoning closely, when you get a fellow like young Parsloe, a chap who for years before he came into the title was knocking about London without a bean in his pocket, living God knows how and always one jump ahead of the gendarmerie, is it extravagant to suppose that he will stick at nothing? If such a man has a pig entered for the Fat Pigs contest and sees a chance of making the thing a certainty for his own candidate by nobbling the favourite, he is dashed well going to jump at it. That was the view of the Hon. Galahad Threepwood.

'Parsloe!' he said. 'I've known young Parsloe since we were both in the early twenties, and he was always so crooked he sliced bread with a corkscrew. When they saw Parsloe coming in the old days, strong men used to wince and hide their valuables. That's the sort of fellow he was, and you can't tell me he's any different now. You watch that pig of yours like a hawk, Clarence, or before you know where you are, this fiend in human shape will be slipping pineapple bombs into her bran mash.'

The words had sunk in, as such words would scarcely have failed to do, and they had caused Lord Emsworth to entertain toward Sir Gregory feelings similar to, though less cordial than, those of Sherlock Holmes toward Professor Moriarty. So now he sat brooding on him darkly, and would probably have gone on brooding for some considerable time, had not Beach, who wanted to get back to his pantry and rest his feet, uttered a significant cough.

'Eh?' said Lord Emsworth, coming out of his coma.

'Would there be anything further, m'lord?'

'Further? Oh, I see what you mean. Further. No, nothing further, Beach.'

'Thank you, m'lord.'

Beach withdrew in that stately, ponderous way of his that always reminded travellers who knew their Far East of an elephant sauntering through an Indian jungle, and Lord

Emsworth resumed his reading. The butler's entry had interrupted him in the middle of that great chapter of Whiffle's which relates how a pig, if aiming at the old mid-season form, must consume daily nourishment amounting to not less than fifty-seven thousand eight hundred calories, these calories to consist of barley meal, maize meal, linseed meal, potatoes, and separated buttermilk.

But this was not his lucky afternoon. Scarcely had his eye rested on the page when the door opened again, this time to admit a handsome woman of imperious aspect in whom – after blinking once or twice through his pince-nez – he recognized his sister, Lady Constance Keeble.

2

He eyed her apprehensively, like some rat of the underworld cornered by G-men. Painful experience had taught him that visits from Connie meant trouble, and he braced himself, as always, to meet with stout denial whatever charge she might be about to hurl at him. He was a great believer in stout denial and was very good at it.

For once, however, her errand appeared to be pacific. Her manner was serene, even amiable.

'Oh, Clarence,' she said, 'have you seen Penelope anywhere?'

'Eh?'

'Penelope Donaldson.'

'Who,' asked Lord Emsworth courteously, 'is Penelope Donaldson?'

Lady Constance sighed. Had she not been the daughter of a hundred Earls, she would have snorted. Her manner lost its amiability. She struck her forehead with a jewelled hand and rolled her eyes heavenward for a moment.

'Penelope Donaldson,' she said, speaking with the strained sweetness of a woman striving to be patient while conversing with one of the less intelligent of the Jukes family, 'is the younger daughter of the Mr Donaldson of Long Island City in the United States of America whose elder daughter is married to your son Frederick. To refresh your memory, you have two sons – your heir, Bosham, and a younger son, Frederick. Frederick married the elder Miss Donaldson. The younger Miss Donaldson – her name is Penelope – is staying with us now at Blandings Castle – this is Blandings Castle – and what I am asking you is ... Have you seen her? And I do wish, Clarence, that you would not let your mouth hang open when I am talking to you. It makes you look like a goldfish.'

It has already been mentioned that there were moments when Lord Emsworth could be as quick as a flash.

'Ah!' he cried, enlightened. 'When you say Penelope Donaldson, you mean Penelope Donaldson. Quite. Quite. And have I seen her, you ask. Yes, I saw her with Galahad just now. I was looking out of the window and they came past. Going for a walk or something. They were walking,' explained Lord Emsworth, making it clear that his brother and the young visitor from America had not been mounted on pogo-sticks.

Lady Constance uttered a sound which resembled that caused by placing a wet thumb on a hot stove lid.

'It's too bad of Galahad. Ever since she came to the castle he has simply monopolized the girl. He ought to have more sense. He must know that the whole point of her being here is that I wanted to bring her and Orlo Vosper together.'

'Who – ?'

'Oh, Clarence!'

'What's the matter now?'

'If you say "Who is Orlo Vosper?", I shall hit you with something. I believe this vagueness of yours is just a pose. You put it on simply to madden people. You know perfectly well who Orlo Vosper is.'

Lord Emsworth nodded intelligently.

'Yes, I've got him placed now. Fellow who looks like a screen star. He's staying here,' he said, imparting a valuable piece of inside information.

'I am aware of it. And Penelope seems to be deliberately avoiding him.'

'Sensible girl. He's a dull chap.'

'He is nothing of the kind. Most entertaining.'

'He doesn't entertain me.'

'Possibly not, as he does not talk about pigs all the time.'

'He's unsound on pigs. When I showed him the Empress, he yawned.'

'He is evidently very much attracted by Penelope.'

'Tried to hide it behind his hand, but I saw it. A yawn.'

'And it would be a wonderful marriage for her.'

'What would?'

'This.'

'Which?'

'Oh, Clarence!'

'Well, how do you expect me to follow you, dash it, when you beat about the bush like – er – like someone beating about the bush? Be plain. Be clear. Be frank and straightforward. Who's marrying who?'

Lady Constance went into her wet-thumb-on-stove routine again.

'I am merely telling you,' she said wearily, 'that Orlo Vosper is obviously attracted by Penelope and that it would please Mr Donaldson very much if she were to marry him. One of the oldest families in England and plenty of money, too. But what can he do if she spends all her time with Galahad? Still, I am taking her to London to-morrow, and Orlo is driving us in his car. Something may come of that. Do *listen*, Clarence!'

'I'm listening. You said Penelope was going to London with Mr Donaldson.'

'Oh, Clar-*ence*!'

'Or rather with Vosper. What's she going to London for in weather like this? Silly idea.'

'She has a fitting. Her dress for the County Ball. And Orlo has to see his lawyer about his income tax.'

'Income tax!' cried Lord Emsworth, staring like a war horse at the sound of the bugle. Pigs and income tax were the only two subjects that really stirred him. 'Let me tell you – '

'I haven't time to listen,' said Lady Constance, and swept from the room. These chats with the head of the family nearly always ended in her sweeping from the room. Unless, of course, they took place out of doors, when she merely swept away.

Left alone, Lord Emsworth sat for awhile savouring that delicious sense of peace which comes to men of quiet tastes when their womenfolk have said their say and departed. Then, just as he was about to turn to Whiffle again, his eye fell on the pile of correspondence on the table, and he took it up and began glancing through it. And he had read and put aside perhaps half a dozen of the dullest letters ever penned by human hand, when he came upon something of quite a different nature, something that sent his eyebrows shooting up and brought a surprised 'Bless my soul!' to his lips.

It was a picture postcard, one of those brightly coloured picture postcards at which we of the intelligentsia click our tongues, but which afford pleasure and entertainment to quite a number of the lower-browed. It represented a nude lady, presumably Venus, rising from the waves at a seashore resort with a cheery 'I'm in the pink, kid' coming out of her mouth in the form of a balloon, and beneath this figure, in a bold feminine hand, were the words 'Hey hey, to-day's the day, what, what? Many happy returns, old dear. Love and kisses. Maudie.'

It puzzled Lord Emsworth, as it might have puzzled an

even deeper thinker. To the best of his knowledge he was not acquainted with any Maudie, let alone one capable of this almost Oriental warmth of feeling. Unlike that *beau sabreur* and man about town, his brother Galahad, who had spent a lifetime courting the society of the breezier type of female and in his younger days had never been happier than when knee deep in barmaids and ballet girls, he had always taken considerable pains to avoid the Maudies of this world.

Recovering his pince-nez, which, as always in times of emotion, had fallen off and were dangling at the end of their string, he slipped the card absently into his pocket and reached out for his book. But it was too late. The moment had passed. What with butlers babbling about Parsloes and Connies babbling about Vospers and mystery women sending him love and kisses, he had temporarily lost the power to appreciate Whiffle's mighty line.

There was only one thing to be done, if he hoped to recover calm of spirit. He straightened his pince-nez, and went off to the piggeries to have a look at Empress of Blandings.

3

The Empress lived in a bijou residence not far from the kitchen garden, and when Lord Emsworth arrived at her boudoir she was engaged, as pretty nearly always when you dropped in on her, in hoisting into her vast interior those fifty-seven thousand and eight hundred calories on which Whiffle insists. Monica Simmons, the pig girl, had done her well in the way of barley meal, maize meal, linseed meal, potatoes, and separated buttermilk, and she was digging in and getting hers in a manner calculated to inspire the brightest confidence in the bosoms of her friends and admirers.

Monica Simmons was standing at the rail as Lord Emsworth pottered up, a stalwart girl in a smock and breeches who looked like what in fact she was, one of the six daughters of a rural Vicar all of whom had played hockey for Roedean. She was not a great favourite with Lord Emsworth, who suspected her of a lack of reverence for the Empress. Of this fundamental flaw in her character she instantly afforded ghastly proof.

'Hullo, Lord Emsworth,' she said. 'Hot, what? Have you come to see the piggy-wiggy? Well, now you're here, I'll be buzzing off and getting my tea and shrimps. I've a thirst I wouldn't sell for fifty quid. Cheerio.'

She strode off, her large feet spurning the antic hay, and Lord Emsworth, who had quivered like an aspen and was supporting himself on the rail, gazed after her with a smouldering eye. He was thinking nostalgically of former custodians of his pig supreme – of George Cyril Wellbeloved, now in the enemy's camp; of Percy Pirbright, George Cyril's successor, last heard of in Canada; and of Edwin Pott, who, holding portfolio after Percy, had retired into private life on winning a football pool. None of these would have alluded to Empress of Blandings as 'the piggy-wiggy'. Edwin Pott, as a matter of fact, would not have been able to do so, even had he wished, for he had no roof to his mouth.

Ichabod, felt Lord Emsworth, and was still in a disturbed state of mind, though gradually becoming soothed by listening to that sweetest of all music, the sound of the Empress restoring her tissues, when there appeared at his side, leaning on the rail and surveying the champ through a black-rimmed monocle, a slim, trim, dapper little gentleman in his late fifties, whom he greeted with a cordial 'Ah, Galahad.'

'Ah, to you, Clarence old bird, with knobs on,' responded the newcomer, equally cordial.

The Hon. Galahad Threepwood was the only genuinely distinguished member of the family of which Lord Emsworth was the head. The world, it is said, knows little of its greatest men, but everyone connected with the world of clubs, bars, theatres, restaurants, and race courses knew

Gally, if only by reputation. He was one of that determined little band who, feeling that London would look better painted red, had devoted themselves at an early age to the task of giving it that cheerful colour. A pain in the neck to his sister Constance, his sister Julia, his sister Dora, and all his other sisters, he was universally esteemed in less austere quarters, for his heart was of gold and his soul overflowing with the milk of human kindness.

As he stood gazing at the Empress, something between a gulp and a groan at his side caused him to transfer his scrutiny to his elder brother, and he was concerned to note that there was a twisted look on those loved features, as if the head of the family had just swallowed something acid.

'Hullo, Clarence!' he said. 'The old heart seems a bit bowed down. What's the matter? Not brooding on that incident at the Emsworth Arms, are you?'

'Eh? Incident? What incident was that?'

'Has no word of it reached your ears? I had it from Beach, who had it from the scullery maid, who had it from the chauffeur. It appears that that butler of Parsloe's – Binstead is his name, I believe – was swanking about in the tap room of the Emsworth Arms last night, offering five to one on Parsloe's pig.'

Lord Emsworth stared.

'On Pride of Matchingham? The fellow's insane. How can Pride of Matchingham possibly have a chance against the Empress?'

'That's what I felt. It puzzled me, too. The simple explanation is, I suppose, that Binstead had got a snootful and was talking through his hat. Well, if that's not what's worrying you, what is? Why are you looking like a bereaved tapeworm?'

Lord Emsworth was only too glad to explain to a sympathetic ear what had caused the resemblance.

'That girl Simmons upset me, Galahad. You will scarcely credit it, but she called the Empress a piggy-wiggy.'

'She did?'

'I assure you. "Hullo, Lord Emsworth," she said. "Have you come to see the piggy-wiggy?"'

Gally frowned.

'Bad,' he agreed. 'The wrong tone. If this is true, it seems to show that the child is much too frivolous in her outlook to hold the responsible position she does. I may mention that this is the view which Beach takes. He has put a considerable slice of his savings on the Empress's nose to cop at the forthcoming Agricultural Show, and he is uneasy. He asks himself apprehensively is La Simmons fitted for her sacred task? And I don't blame him. For mark this, Clarence, and mark it well. The girl who carelessly dismisses Empress of Blandings as a piggy-wiggy to-day is a girl who may quite easily forget to give her lunch to-morrow. Whatever induced you, my dear fellow, to entrust a job that calls for the executive qualities of a Pierpont Morgan to the pop-eyed daughter of a rural vicar?'

Lord Emsworth did not actually wring his hands, but he came very near to it.

'It was not my doing,' he protested. 'Connie insisted on my engaging her. She is some sort of protégé of Connie's. Related to someone she wanted to oblige, or something like that. Blame Connie for the whole terrible situation.'

'Connie!' said Gally. 'The more I see of this joint, the more clearly do I realize that what Blandings Castle needs, to make it an earthly Paradise, is fewer and better Connies. Sisters are a mistake, Clarence. You should have set your face against them at the outset.'

'True,' said Lord Emsworth. 'True.'

Silence fell, as nearly as silence could ever fall in the neighbourhood of a trough at which Empress of Blandings was feeding. It was broken by Lord Emsworth, who was peering about him with the air of a man who senses something missing in his surroundings.

'Where,' he asked, 'is Alice?'

'Eh?'

'Or, rather, Penelope. Penelope Donaldson. I thought you were out for a walk together.'

'Oh, Penny? Yes, we have been strolling hither and thither, chewing the fat. There's a nice girl, Clarence.'

'Charming.'

'Not only easy on the eye and a conversationalist who holds you spellbound on a wide variety of subjects, but kind-hearted. I happened to express a wish for a whisky-and-soda, and she immediately trotted off to tell Beach to bring me one, to save me trudging to the house.'

'You are going to have a whisky-and-soda?'

'You follow me like a bloodhound. It will bring the roses back to my cheeks, which is always so desirable, and it will enable me to drink Beach's health with a hey-nonny-nonny and a hot-cha-cha. It's his birthday.'

'Beach's birthday?'

'That's right.'

'God bless my soul.'

Lord Emsworth was fumbling in his pocket.

'By the afternoon post, Galahad, I received an extraordinary communication. Most extraordinary. It was one of those picture postcards. It said "Many happy returns, old dear. Love and kisses", and it was signed Maudie. Now that you tell me it is Beach's birthday, I am wondering ... Yes, as I thought. It was intended for Beach and must have got mixed up with my letters. Look.'

Gally took the card and scrutinized it through his monocle. On the reverse side were the words:

Mr Sebastian Beach,
Blandings Castle,
Shropshire

16

A grave look came into his face.

'We must inquire into this,' he said. 'How long has Beach been at the castle? Eighteen years? Nineteen? Well, the exact time is immaterial. The point is that he has been here long enough for me to have grown to regard him as a son, and any son of mine who gets picture postcards of nude Venuses from girls named Maudie has got to do some brisk explaining. We can't have Sex rearing its ugly head in the butler's pantry. Hoy, Beach!'

Sebastian Beach was approaching, his customary measured step rather more measured than usual owing to the fact that he was bearing a tall glass filled to the brim with amber liquid. Beside him tripped a small, slender girl with fair hair who looked as if she might have been a wood nymph the butler had picked up on his way through the grounds. Actually, she was the younger daughter of an American manufacturer of dog biscuits.

'Here come the United States Marines, Gally,' she said, and Gally, having replied with a good deal of satisfaction that he could see them with the naked eye, took the glass and drank deeply.

'Happy birthday, Beach.'

'Thank you, Mr Galahad.'

'A sip for you, Penny?'

'No, thanks.'

'Clarence?'

'Eh? No, no thank you.'

'Right,' said Gally, finishing the contents of the glass. 'And now to approach a painful task. Beach!'

'Sir?'

'Peruse this card.'

Beach took the postcard. As his gooseberry eyes scanned it, his lips moved the fraction of an inch. He looked like a butler who for two pins, had he not been restrained by the rigid rules of the Butlers' Guild, might have smiled.

'Well, Beach? We are waiting. Who is this Maudie?'

'My niece, Mr Galahad.'

'That is your story, is it?'

'My brother's daughter, Mr Galahad. She is what might be termed the Bohemian member of the family. As a young girl she ran away from home and became a barmaid in London.'

Gally pricked up his ears, like a specialist whose particular subject has come up in the course of conversation. It was as if razor blades had been mentioned in the presence of Mr Gillette.

'A barmaid, eh? Where?'

'At the Criterion, Mr Galahad.'

'I must have known her, then. I knew them all at the Criterion. Though I don't remember any Maudie Beach.'

'For business purposes she adopted the *nom de guerre* of Montrose, sir.'

Gally uttered a glad cry.

'Maudie Montrose? Is that who she was? Good heavens, of course I knew her. Charming girl with blue eyes and hair like a golden bird's nest. Many is the buttered rum I have accepted at her hands. What's become of her? Is she still working the old beer engine?'

'Oh no, Mr Galahad. She married and retired.'

'I hope her husband appreciates her many sterling qualities.'

'He is no longer with us, sir. He contracted double pneumonia, standing outside a restaurant in the rain.'

'What on earth did he do that for?'

'It was in pursuance of his professional duties, sir. He was the proprietor of a private investigation bureau, Digby's Day and Night Detectives. Now that he has passed on, my niece conducts the business herself, and I believe gives general satisfaction.'

Penny gave an interested squeak.

'You mean she's a sleuth? One of the bloodstain and magnifying glass brigade?'

'Substantially that, miss. I gather that she leaves the rougher work to her subordinates.'

'Still she's a genuine private eye. Golly, it takes all sorts to make a world, doesn't it?'

'So I have been given to understand, miss,' said Beach indulgently. He turned to Lord Emsworth, who, finding the Maudie topic one that did not grip, had started to scratch the Empress's back with a piece of stick. 'I should have mentioned, m'lord, that Sir Gregory has arrived.'

'Oh, dash it. Where is he?'

'I left him in the morning-room, m'lord, taking off his shoes. I received the impression that his feet were paining him. He expressed a desire to see your lordship at your lordship's earliest convenience.'

Lord Emsworth became peevish.

'What on earth does the man want, coming here? He knows that I regard him with the deepest suspicion. But I suppose I shall have to see him. If I don't, it will only mean an unpleasant scene with Connie. She is always telling me I must be neighbourly.'

'Thank goodness I don't have to be,' said Gally. 'I can look young Parsloe in the eye and make him wilt. That's the advantage of not having a position to keep up. That was interesting, what Beach was telling us, Clarence.'

'Eh?'

'About Maudie.'

'Who is Maudie?'

'All right, master-mind, let it go. Trot along and see what that thug wants.'

Lord Emsworth ambled off, followed at just the right respectful distance by his faithful butler, and Gally looked after them musingly.

'Amazing,' he said. 'Do you know how long I have known

Beach? Eighteen years, or it may have been nineteen, ever since I was a slip of a boy of forty. And only to-day have I discovered that his name is Sebastian. The same thing happened with Fruity Biffen. I don't think you met my old friend Fruity Biffen, did you? He was living down here at a house along the Shrewsbury road till a short time ago, but he left before you arrived. In the old days he used to sign his I.O.U's George J. Biffen, and it was only after the lapse of several years, one night when we were having supper together at Romano's and he had lost some of his reserve owing to having mixed stout, *crème de menthe,* and old brandy, to see what it tasted like, that he revealed that the J. stood for – '

'Gally,' said Penny, who for some moments had been tracing arabesques on the turf with her shoe and giving other indications of nerving herself to an embarrassing task, 'can you lend me two thousand pounds?'

4

It was never an easy matter to disconcert the Hon. Galahad. For half a century nursemaids, governesses, tutors, schoolmasters, Oxford dons, bookmakers, three-card-trick men, jellied eel sellers, skittle sharps, racecourse touts and members of the metropolitan police force had tried to do it, and all had failed. It was an axiom of the old Pelican Club that, no matter what slings and arrows outrageous fortune might launch in his direction, Gally Threepwood could be counted upon to preserve the calm insouciance of a pig on ice. But at these words a spasm definitely shook him, causing his black-rimmed monocle to leap as nimbly from his eye as the pince-nez had ever leaped from the nose of his brother Clarence. His look, as he stared at the girl, was the look of a man unable to believe his ears.

'Two thousand pounds?'

'It's sorely needed.'

Gally gave a little sigh. He took her hand and patted it.

'My child, I'm a pauper. I'm a younger son. In English families the heir scoops in the jackpot and all the runners-up get are the few crumbs that fall from his table. I could no more raise two thousand pounds than balance that pig there on the tip of my nose.'

'I see. I was afraid you mightn't be able to. All right, let's forget about it.'

Gally looked at her, astounded. Did she really think that Galahad Threepwood, one of the most inquisitive men who ever knocked back a Scotch and soda, a man who wished he had a quid, or even ten shillings, for every time he had been called a damned old Nosey Parker, was as easily put off as this?

'But, good heavens, aren't you going to explain?'

'Shall I? It depends whether you can keep a secret.'

'Of course I can keep a secret. Why, if I were to reveal one tithe of the things I know about my circle of acquaintance, it would rock civilization. You can confide in me without a tremor.'

'It would be a relief, I must say. Don't you hate bottling things up?'

'I prefer unbottling them. Go on. What's all this about two thousand pounds? What on earth do you want it for?'

'Well, it isn't exactly for me. It's for a man I know. It's the old, old story, Gally. I'm in love.'

'Aha!'

'Aha to you. Why shouldn't I be in love? People do fall in love, don't they?'

'I've known of cases.'

'Well, I'm in love with Jerry.'

'Jerry what?'

'Jerry Vail.'

'Never heard of him.'

21

'Well, I don't suppose he's ever heard of you.'

Gally was indignant.

'What do you mean, he's never heard of me? Of course he's heard of me. England's been ringing with my name for the last thirty years. If you weren't a benighted Yank on your first visit to the British Isles, you would have my life history at your finger-tips and treat me with the respect I deserve. But to return to the dream man. From the fact that you are going about trying to bite people's ears on his behalf, I deduce that he is short of cash. A bit strapped for the ready, eh? What is sometimes called an impecunious suitor?'

'Well, he gets by. He's self-supporting.'

'What does he do?'

'He's an author.'

'Good heavens! Oh, well, I suppose authors are also God's creatures.'

'He writes thrillers. But you know the old gag. "Crime doesn't pay . . . enough." We couldn't possibly get married on what he makes, even in a good year.'

'But your father, the well-to-do-millionaire. Won't he provide?'

'Not for an impecunious suitor. If I were to write and tell Father I wanted to marry someone with an annual income of about thirty cents, he would whisk me back to America by the next boat, and I should be extremely lucky if I didn't get interned at my old grandmother's in Ohio.'

'Stern parent stuff, eh? I thought all that sort of thing went out in the eighties.'

'Yes, but they forgot to tell Father. And anyway, Jerry's much too full of high principles and what have you to let himself be supported by his wife.'

'You could talk him out of that.'

'I wouldn't want to. I admire him for it. If you'd seen some of the fortune-hunting dead-beats I've had to keep off

22

with a stick since I ripened into womanhood, you could understand my thinking it's a pleasant change to meet someone like Jerry. He's swell, Gally. He has to be seen to be believed. And if only he can get this two thousand pounds...'

'You might give me the inside stuff on that. Does he want it for some particular reason, or is it just that he likes two thousand pounds?'

'He has a friend, a doctor, who wants to start one of those health places. Did you ever hear of Muldoon's in America?'

'Of course. I was always popping in and out of America in the old days.'

'This would be something on the same sort of lines, only, being in England, more ... what's the word?'

'Posh?'

'I was going to say plushy. It would cater for tired Dukes and weary millionaires, all paying terrific fees. There's a place like it up in Wales, Jerry tells me, which simply coins money. This would be the same sort of thing, only easier to get at because the house Jerry's doctor friend has his eye on is in Surrey or Sussex or somewhere, much nearer London. The idea is that if Jerry could raise this two thousand pounds and buy in, he would become a junior partner. The boy friend would feel the patients' pulses and prescribe diets and so on, and Jerry would take them out riding and play tennis and golf with them and generally be the life and soul of the party. It's the sort of thing that would suit him down to the ground, and he would be awfully good at it. And he would have time to write his great novel.'

'Is he writing a great novel?'

'Well, naturally he hasn't been able to start it yet, being so busy winning bread, but he says it's all there, tucked away behind the frontal bone, and give him a little leisure, he says, a few quiet hours each day with nothing to distract him, and he'll have it jumping through hoops and snapping sugar off its nose. Why are you looking like a stuffed frog?'

'If you mean why am I looking like Rodin's *Le Penseur*, I was wondering how the dickens you ever managed to get acquainted with this chap. Connie met you when you landed at Southampton, and after a single night in London brought you down here, where you have been ever since. I don't see where you fitted in your billing and cooing.'

'Think, Gally. Use the bean.'

'No, it beats me.'

'He was on the boat, chump. Jerry's got vision. He realized that the only way for a writer to make a packet nowadays is to muscle in on the American market, so he took time off and dashed over to study it.'

'How do you study an American market?'

'I suppose you ... well, study it, as it were.'

'I see. Study it.'

'That's right. And when he had finished studying it, he hopped on the boat and came home.'

'And who should be on the boat but you?'

'Exactly. We met the second day out, and never looked back. Ah, those moonlight nights!'

'Was there a moon?'

'You bet there was a moon.'

Gally scratched his chin. He removed his monocle and polished it thoughtfully.

'Well, I don't know quite what to say. You have rather stunned your grey-haired old friend. You really love this chap?'

'Haven't you been listening?'

'But you can't have known him for more than about four days?'

'So what?'

'Well, I was just thinking ... Heaven knows I'm not the man to counsel prudence and all that sort of thing. The only woman I ever wanted to marry was a music-hall serio who sang songs in pink tights. But – '

'Well?'

'I think I'd watch my step, if I were you, young Penny. There are some queer birds knocking around in this world. You can't always go by what fellows say on ocean liners. Many a man who swears eternal devotion on the boat deck undergoes a striking change in his outlook when he hits dry land and gets among the blondes.'

'Gally, you make me sick.'

'I'm sorry. Just thought I'd mention it. Facts of life and all that sort of thing.'

'If I found Jerry was like that, I'd give him the air in a second, though it would break my heart into a million quivering pieces. We Donaldsons have our pride.'

'You betcher.'

'But he isn't. He's a baa-lamb. And you can't say a baa-lamb isn't a nice thing to have around the house.'

'Nothing could be nicer.'

'Very well, then.'

The Empress uttered a plaintive grunt. A potato, full of calories, had detached itself from the rest of her ration and rolled outside the sty. Gally returned it courteously, and the noble animal thanked him with a brief snuffle.

'But if he's a baa-lamb, it makes it all the worse. I mean, it must be agony for you being parted from such a paragon. Here you are at Blandings, and there he is in London. Don't you chafe?'

'I did until to-day.'

'Why until to-day?'

'Because this morning sunshine broke through the clouds. Lady Constance told me she is taking me to London to-morrow for a fitting. Lord Vosper is driving us in his car.'

'What do you think of Vosper?'

'I like him.'

'He likes you.'

'Yes, so I've noticed.'

'Good-looking chap.'

'Very. But I was telling you. The expedition arrives in London to-morrow afternoon, so to-morrow night I shall be dining with my Jerry.'

Gally gazed at her in amazement. Her childish optimism gave him a pang.

'With Connie keeping her fishy eye on you? Not a hope.'

'Oh yes, because there's an old friend of Father's in London, and Father would never forgive me if I didn't take this opportunity of slapping her on the back and saying hello. So I shall dine with her.'

'And she will bring your young man along?'

'Well, between us girls, Gally, she doesn't really exist. I'm like the poet in Shakespeare, I'm giving to airy nothing a local habitation and a name. Did you ever see The Importance Of Being Earnest?'

'Don't wander from the point.'

'I'm not wandering from the point. Do you remember Bunbury, the friend the hero invented? This is his mother, Mrs Bunbury. You can always arrange these things with a little tact. Well, I must be going in. I've got to write to Jerry.'

'But if you're seeing him to-morrow – '

'Really, Gally, for an experienced man, you seem to know very little about these things. I shall read him the letter over the dinner table, and he will read me the one he's probably writing now. I sent him a telegram this morning, saying I was coming up and staying the night with Lady Garland – your sister Dora, in case you've forgotten – and telling him to meet me at the Savoy at eight.'

Penny hurried away, walking on the light feet of love, and Gally, whose youth had been passed in a world where girls, except when working behind bars or doing *entrechats* at the Alhambra, had been less resourceful, gave himself up to meditation on the spirit and enterprise of their present-day successors. There was no question that the current younger generation knew how to handle those little problems with which the growing girl is so often confronted. This was particularly so, it appeared, if their formative years had been passed in the United States of Northern America.

Having reached the conclusion that the advice of an elderly greybeard counselling prudence and look-before-you-leap-ing would be something of a drug on the market where the younger daughter of Mr Donaldson of Donaldson's Dog Joy was concerned, he was resuming his study of the Empress, when a bleating noise in his rear caused him to turn. Lord Emsworth was approaching, on his face that dying duck look which was so often there in times of stress. Something, it was plain to him, had occurred to upset poor old Clarence.

5

His intuition had not deceived him. Poor old Clarence was patently all of a doodah. Eyeing him as he tottered up, Gally was reminded of his old friend Fruity Biffen on the occasion when that ill-starred sportsman had gone into Tattersall's ring at Hurst Park wearing a long Assyrian beard in order to avoid identification by the half-dozen bookmakers there to whom he owed money, and then the beard had fallen off. The same visible emotion.

'Strike me pink, Clarence,' he exclaimed, 'you look like something out of a Russian novel. What's on your mind? And what have you done with Parsloe? Did you murder him, and are you worried because you don't know how to get rid of the body?'

Lord Emsworth found speech.

'I left him in the morning-room, putting on his shoes. Galahad, an appalling thing has happened. I hardly know how to tell you. Let me begin,' said Lord Emsworth, groping his way to the rail of the sty and drooping over it like a wet sock, 'by saying that Sir Gregory Parsloe is nothing short of a rogue and a swindler.'

'We all knew that. Get on.'

'Don't bustle me.'

'Well, I want to hear what all the agitation's about. When last seen, you were on your way to the house to confront this bulging Baronet. Right. You reached the house, found him in the morning-room with his shoes off, gave him a cold look and said stiffly: "To what am I indebted for the honour of this visit?", to which Parsloe, twiddling his toes, replied . . . what? To what *were* you indebted for the honour of his visit?'

Lord Emsworth became a little calmer. His eyes were resting on the Empress, and he seemed to draw strength from her massive stolidity.

'Do you ever have presentiments, Galahad?'

'Don't ramble, Clarence.'

'I am not rambling,' said Lord Emsworth peevishly. 'I am telling you that I had one the moment I entered the morning-room and saw Parsloe sitting there. Something seemed to whisper to me that the man was preparing an unpleasant surprise for me. There was a nasty smirk on his face, and I didn't like the sinister way he said "Good afternoon, Emsworth." And his next words told me that my presentiment had been right. From an inside pocket he produced a photograph and said: "Cast an eye on this, old cock."'

'A photograph? What of?'

Lord Emsworth was obliged to fortify himself with another look at the Empress, who was now at about her fifty-fourth thousandth calorie.

'Galahad,' he said, sinking his voice almost to a whisper, 'it was the photograph of an enormous pig! He thrust it under my nose with an evil leer and said: "Emsworth, old cocky-wax, meet the winner of this year's Fat Pig medal at the Shropshire Agricultural Show." His very words.'

Gally found himself unable to follow this. It seemed to him that he was in the presence of an elder brother who spoke in riddles.

'You mean it was a photograph of Pride of Matchingham?'

'No, no, no. God bless my soul, no. This animal would make two of Pride of Matchingham. Don't you understand? This is a new pig. He imported it a day or two ago from a farm in Kent. Queen of Matchingham, he calls it. Galahad,' said Lord Emsworth, his voice vibrating with emotion, 'with this Queen of Matchingham in the field, Empress of Blandings will have to strain every nerve to repeat her triumphs of the last two years.'

'You don't mean it's fatter than the Empress?' said Gally, cocking an eye at the stable's nominee and marvelling that such a thing could be possible.

Lord Emsworth looked shocked.

'I would not say that. No, no, I certainly would not say that. But the contest will now become a desperately close one. It may be a matter of ounces.'

Gally whistled. He was fully alive at last to the gravity of the situation. Apart from his fondness for old Clarence and a natural brotherly distaste for seeing him in the depths, the thing touched him financially. As he had told Penny, he was not a rich man, but, like Beach, he had his mite on the Empress and it appeared now that there was a grave peril that his modest investment would go down the drain.

'So that's why Binstead was going about the place with his five to one! He knew something. But is this hornswoggling high-binder allowed to import pigs? I thought the competition was purely for native sons?'

'There has always been an unwritten law to that effect, a gentleman's agreement, but Parsloe informs me that there exists no actual rule. Naturally the possibility of such a thing happening never occurred to those who drew up the conditions governing these contests. It's abominable!'

'Monstrous,' agreed Gally with all the warmth of a man who, having slapped down his cash on what he supposed to be a sure thing, finds the sure thing in danger of coming unstuck.

'And the ghastliest part of it all is that, faced with this hideous menace, I am forced to rely on the services of that Simmons girl to prepare the Empress for the struggle.'

A stern look came into Gally's face. A jellied eel seller who had seen it would have picked up his jellied eels and sought refuge in flight, like one who fears to be struck by lightning.

'Simmons must go!' he said.

Lord Emsworth blinked.

'But Connie – '

'Connie be blowed! We can't afford to humour Connie's whims at a time like this. Leave Connie to me. I'll see that she ceases to bung spanners into the machinery by loading you up with incompetent pig girls when there are a thousand irreproachable pig men who will spring to the task of fattening the Empress for the big day. And while I'm about it, I'll have a word with young Parsloe and warn him that anything in the nature of funny business on his part will not be tolerated for an instant. For don't overlook that aspect of the matter, Clarence. Parsloe, with this new pig under his belt, is certain to get ideas into his head. Unless sternly notified that his every move will be met with ruthless reprisals, he will leave no stone unturned and no avenue unexplored to nobble the Empress.'

'Good heavens, Galahad!'

'But don't worry. I have the situation well in hand. My first task is to put the fear of God into Connie. Where is she? At this time of day, poisoning her system with tea, I suppose. Right. I'll go and talk to her like a Dutch uncle.'

Lord Emsworth drew a deep breath.

'You're such a comfort, Galahad.'

'I try to be, Clarence, I try to be,' said Gally.

He screwed the monocle more firmly into his eye, and set off on his mission, resolution on his every feature. Lord Emsworth watched him out of sight with a thrill of admiration. How a man about to talk to Connie like a Dutch uncle could be looking like that, he was unable to understand.

But Galahad was Galahad.

CHAPTER TWO

Up at the castle, Sir Gregory Parsloe, having put on his shoes, was standing at the window of the morning-room, looking out.

If you like your baronets slender and willowy, you would not have cared much for Sir Gregory Parsloe. He was a large, stout man in the middle fifties who resembled in appearance one of those florid bucks of the old Regency days. Like Beach, he had long lost that streamlined look, and the fact that, just as you could have made two pretty good butlers out of Beach, so could you have made two quite adequate baronets out of Sir Gregory was due to the change in his financial position since the days when, as Gally had put it, he had knocked about London without a bean in his pocket.

A man with a fondness for the fleshpots and a weakness for wines and spirits who, after many lean years, suddenly inherits a great deal of money and an extensive cellar finds himself faced with temptations which it is hard to resist. Arrived in the land of milk and honey, his disposition is to square his elbows and let himself go till his eyes bubble. He remembers the days when he often did not know where his next chump chop was coming from, and settles down to make up leeway. This is what had happened to Sir Gregory Parsloe. Only an iron will could have saved him from accumulating excess weight in large quantities, and he had not an iron will. Day by day in every way he had got fatter and fatter.

Outside the morning-room window the terrace shimmered in the afternoon sun, but at the farther end of it a spreading tree cast its shade, and in this cool retreat a tea-table had been set up. Presiding over it sat Lady Constance Keeble, reading a letter, and an imperative urge to join her came over Sir Gregory. After his gruelling three-mile hike, a cup of tea was what he most needed.

As he made for the terrace, limping a little, for he had a blister on his right foot, it might have been supposed that his thoughts would have been on the impending refreshment, but they were not. A week or two ago he had become engaged to be married, and he was thinking of Gloria Salt, his betrothed. And if anyone is feeling that this was rather pretty and touching of him, we must reluctantly add that he was thinking of her bitterly and coming very near to regretting that mad moment when, swept off his feet by her radiant beauty, he had said to her 'I say, old girl – er – how about it, eh, what?' It would be too much perhaps to say that the scales had fallen from his eyes as regarded Gloria Salt, but unquestionably he had had revealed to him in the past few days certain aspects of her character and outlook which had materially diminished her charm.

Sighting him on the horizon, Lady Constance put down the letter she was reading, one of a number which had come for her by the afternoon post, and greeted him with a bright smile. Unlike her brothers Clarence and Galahad, she was fond of this man.

'Why, Sir Gregory,' she said, beaming hospitably, 'how nice to see you. I didn't hear your car drive up.'

Sir Gregory explained that he had walked from Matchingham Hall, and Lady Constance twittered with amazement at the feat.

'Good gracious. Aren't you exhausted?'

'Shan't be sorry to rest for a bit. Got a blister on my right foot.'

'Oh, dear. When you get home, you must prick it.'

'Yes.'

'With a needle.'

'Yes.'

'Not a pin. Well, sit down and I'll give you a cup of tea. Won't you have a muffin?'

Sir Gregory took the muffin, gave it a long, strange, sad look, sighed and put it down on his plate. Lady Constance picked up her letter.

'From Gloria,' she said.

'Ah,' said Sir Gregory in a rather guarded manner, like one who has not quite made up his mind about Gloria.

'She says she will be motoring here the day after to-morrow, and it's all right about the secretary.'

'Eh?'

'For Clarence. You remember you said you would ring her up and ask her to get a secretary for Clarence before she left London.'

'Oh, yes. And she's getting one? That's good.'

It was a piece of news which would have lowered Lord Emsworth's already low spirits, had he been present to hear it. Connie was always encouraging ghastly spectacled young men with knobbly foreheads and a knowledge of shorthand to infest the castle and make life a burden to him, but there had been such a long interval since the departure of the latest of these that he was hoping the disease had run its course.

'She says she knows just the man.'

This again would have shaken Lord Emsworth to his foundations. The last thing he wanted on the premises was anyone who could be described as just the man, with all that phrase implied of fussing him and bothering him, and wanting him to sign things and do things.

'Clarence is so helpless without someone to look after his affairs. He gets vaguer every day. It was sweet of Gloria to bother. What a delightful girl she is.'

'Ah,' said Sir Gregory, again in that odd, guarded manner.

'I do admire those athletic girls. So wholesome. Has she been winning any tennis tournaments lately?'

Sir Gregory did not reply. His eyes were on the muffin, as it swam in butter before him, and once more he heaved that heavy sigh. Following his gaze, Lady Constance uttered a concerned cry. The hostess in her had been piqued.

'Why, Sir Gregory, you are eating nothing. Don't you like muffins?'

This time the sound that emerged from the Baronet, seeming to come up from the very soles of his feet, was nothing so mild as a sigh. It was unmistakably a groan, the sort of groan that might have been wrung from the reluctant lips of a Red Indian at the stake.

'I love 'em,' he said in a low voice that shook with feeling. 'But Gloria says I've got to cut them out.'

'Gloria? I don't understand.'

Until this moment, like the Spartan boy who allowed the fox to gnaw his vitals without mentioning it to a soul, Sir Gregory had kept his tragedy a secret from the world. Rightly or wrongly, he thought it made a fellow look such an ass. Chaps, he felt, chaps being what they were, would, if informed that he was mortifying the flesh at the whim of a woman, be inclined to laugh their silly heads off at a chap. But now the urge to confide in this sympathetic friend was too strong for him.

'She says I'm too fat, and if I don't reduce a bit the engagement's off. She says she positively refuses to stand at the altar rails with someone who looks like ... well, she was definitely outspoken about it. You know what girls are, especially these athletic girls who dash about tennis courts shouting "Forty love" and all that. They're all for the lean, keen, trained-to-the-last-ounce stuff. Dam' silly, of course, the whole thing. I put it to her straight. I said: "Dash it, old girl, what's all this about? I'm not proposing to enter for the six-day bicycle race or something," but nothing would move her. She said unless I ceased to resemble a captive balloon poised for its flight into the clouds, those wedding bells would not ring out. She said she was as fond of a laugh as the next girl, but that there were limits. I quote her verbatim.'

'Good gracious!'

Now that he had started to pour out his soul, Sir Gregory found it coming easier. His hostess was gazing at him wide-eyed, as if swearing, in faith, 'twas strange, 'twas passing strange, 'twas pitiful, 'twas wondrous pitiful, and there came upon him something of the easy fluency which had enabled Othello on a similar occasion to make such a good story of his misfortunes.

'So, the upshot is no butter, no sugar, no bread, no alcohol, no soups, no sauces, and I'm not allowed to swallow so much as a single potato. And that's not all. She's mapped out a whole chart of bally exercises for me. Up in the morning. Breathe deeply. Touch the toes. Light breakfast. Brisk walk. Chop down a tree or two. Light lunch. Another brisk walk. That's the one I'm taking now, and how I'm to get home under my own steam with this blister ... Ah well,' said Sir Gregory, summoning all his manhood to his aid, 'I mustn't bore you with all this stuff. Merely observing that I am going through hell, I will now withdraw. No, no more tea, thanks. She specifies a single cup.'

He rose heavily and made his way across the terrace. As he walked, he was thinking of that new pig of his. Pretty dashed ironical, he was feeling, that whereas he was under these strict orders to get thinner and thinner, Queen of Matchingham was encouraged – egged on with word and gesture, by gad – to get fatter and fatter. Why should there be one law for pigs and another for Baronets?

Musing thus, he had reached the top of the drive and was congratulating himself on the fact that from there onwards for the next three-quarters of a mile it would be all downhill, when he heard his name called in a sharp, imperious voice and, turning, perceived the Hon. Galahad Threepwood.

2

Gally was looking cold and stern.

'A word with you, young Parsloe,' he said.

Sir Gregory's full height was six foot one. He drew himself to it. Even in the days when they had been lads about town together, he had never like Gally Threepwood, and more recent association with him had done nothing to inaugurate a beautiful friendship.

'I have no desire to speak to you, my good man,' he said.

Gally's monocle flashed fire.

'Oh, you haven't? Well, I'm dashed well going to speak to *you*. Parsloe, it was the raw work of slippery customers of your kidney that led to the destruction of the cities of the plain and the decline and fall of the Roman Empire. What's all this about your new pig?'

'What about it?'

'Clarence says you imported it from Kent.'

'Well?'

'A low trick.'

'Perfectly legitimate. Show me the rule that says I mustn't.'

'There are higher things than rules, young Parsloe. There is an ethical code.'

'A what?'

'Yes, I thought you wouldn't know what that meant. Let it pass. You are really proposing to enter this porker of yours in the Fat Pigs class at the Agricultural Show?'

'I have already done so.'

'I see. And now, no doubt, your subtle brain is weaving plots and schemes. You're getting ready to start the funny business, just as you used to do in the old days.'

'I don't know what you're talking about.'

Gally gave a short, hard, unpleasant laugh.

'He doesn't know what I'm talking about! I will ask you, Parsloe, to throw your mind back a number of years to a certain evening at the Black Footman public-house in Gossiter Street. You and I were young then, and in the exuberance of youth I had matched my dog Towser against your dog Banjo for a substantial sum in a rat contest. And when the rats were brought on and all should have been bustle and activity on Towser's part, where was he? Dozing in a corner with his stomach bulging like an alderman's. I whistled him . . . called him . . . Towser, Towser . . . No good. Fast asleep. And why? Because you had drawn him aside just before the starting bell was due to go and filled him up past the Plimsoll mark with steak and onions, thus rendering his interest in rats negligible and enabling your Banjo to win by default.'

'I deny it!'

'It's no good standing there saying "I deny it". I am perfectly aware that I am not able to prove it, but you and I know that that is what happened. Somebody had inserted steak and onions in that dog – I sniffed his breath, and it was like opening the door of a Soho chop-house on a summer night – and the verdict of History will be that it was you. You were the world's worst twister in the old days, a man who would stick at nothing to gain his evil ends. And . . . now I approach the nub . . . you still are. Even as we stand here, you are asking yourself "How can I nobble the Empress and leave the field clear for my entry?" Oh, yes, you are. I remember saying to Clarence once, "Clarence," I said, "I have known young Parsloe for thirty years and I solemnly state that if his grandmother was entered in a competition for fat pigs and his commitments made it desirable for him to get her out of the way, he would dope her bran mash and acorns without a moment's hesitation." Well, let me tell you that that is a game two can play at. Your every move will be met with ruthless reprisals. You try to nobble our pig, and we'll nobble yours. One poisoned potato in the Empress's dinner pail, and there will be six poisoned potatoes in Queen of Matchingham's. That is all I wanted to say. A very hearty good afternoon to you, Parsloe,' said Gally, turning on his heel.

Sir Gregory, who had been gulping, recovered speech.

'Hey!'

'Well?'

'Come back!'

'Who, me? Certainly not. I have no desire to speak to you, my good man,' said Gally, and continued his progress in the direction of the terrace.

Lady Constance was dipping her aristocratic nose in her tea cup as he approached the table. At the sound of his footsteps, she looked up.

'Oh, it's you?' she said, and her tone made it abundantly clear that no sudden gush of affection had caused her to alter the opinion she had so long held that this brother of hers was a blot on the Blandings scene. 'I thought it was Sir Gregory. Have you seen Sir Gregory?'

'The man Parsloe? Yes. He has just slunk off.'

'What do you mean, slunk off?'

'I mean slunk off.'

'If you are referring to the fact that Sir Gregory was limping, he has a blister on his foot. There was something I was going to tell him. I must wait and telephone when he gets home. Do you want tea?'

'Never touch the muck.'

'Then what do you want?'

Gally screwed his monocle more firmly into his eye.

'To talk to you, Constance,' he said. 'To talk to you very seriously about this Simmons disaster, this incompetent ex-Roedean hockey-knocker whom you have foisted upon Clarence in the capacity of pig girl. Clarence and I have been discussing it, and we are in complete agreement that Simmons must be given the old heave-ho. The time has come to take her by the seat of her breeches and cast her into outer darkness where there is wailing and gnashing of teeth. Good God, are you prepared to stand before the bar of world opinion as the woman who, by putting up with your bally Simmonses, jeopardized the Empress's chance of performing the unheard of feat of winning the Fat Pigs medal for the third year in succession? A pig man, and the finest pig man money can procure, must place his hand upon the tiller in her stead. No argument, Constance. This is final.'

3

It is always a disturbing thing to be threatened. In an unpublished story by Gerald Vail there is a scene where a character with a criminal face sidles up to the hero as he pauses on Broadway to light a cigarette and hisses in his ear 'Say, listen, youse! Youse'll get out of this town if youse knows what's good for youse!', and the hero realizing from this that Louis The Lip's Black Moustache gang have become aware of the investigations he has been making into the bumping off of the man in the green fedora, draws in his breath sharply and, though a most intrepid young man, is conscious of a distinct chill down the spine.

Precisely the same sort of chill was cooling off the spine of Sir Gregory Parsloe as he limped back to Matchingham Hall. His encounter with Gally had shaken him. He was not an imaginative man, but a man did not have to be very imaginative to read into Gally's words the threat of unilateral action against Queen of Matchingham. True, the fellow had spoken of 'reprisals', as though to imply that hostilities would not be initiated by the Blandings Castle gang, but Sir Gregory's mental retort to this was 'Reprisals my left eyeball'. The Galahad Threepwood type of man does not wait politely for the enemy to make the first move. It acts, and acts swiftly and without warning, and the only thing to do is to mobilize your defences and be prepared.

His first act, accordingly, on arriving at Matchingham Hall, sinking into an arm chair and taking off his shoes, was to ring the bell and desire his butler to inform George Cyril Wellbeloved, his pig man, that his presence was desired for a conference. And in due season a rich smell of pig came floating in, closely followed by George Cyril in person.

George Cyril Wellbeloved was a long, lean, red-haired man with strabismus in the left eye. This rendered his left eye rather unpleasant to look at, and as even the right eye was nothing to cause lovers of the beautiful to turn handsprings, one can readily understand why Sir Gregory during the chat which followed preferred to avert his gaze as much as possible.

But, after all, what is beauty? Skin deep, you might say. His O.C. Pigs had a mouth like a halibut's, a broken nose acquired during a political discussion at the Emsworth Arms and lots of mud all over him, but when you are engaging a pig man, Sir Gregory felt, you don't want a sort of male Miss America, you want someone who knows about pigs. And what George Cyril Wellbeloved did not know about pigs could have been written on one of Maudie Montrose's picture postcards.

In terse, nervous English Sir Gregory related the substance of his interview with Gally, stressing that bit about the poisoned potatoes, and George Cyril listened with a gravity which became him well.

'So there you are,' said Sir Gregory, having completed his tale. 'What do you make of it?'

George Cyril Wellbeloved was a man who went in for a certain verbal polish in his conversation.

'To speak expleasantly, sir,' he said, 'I think the old — means to do the dirty on us.'

It would perhaps have been more fitting had Sir Gregory at this point said 'Come, come, my man, be more careful with your language,' but the noun — expressed so exactly what he himself was thinking of the Hon. Galahad Threepwood that he could not bring himself to chide and rebuke. As a matter of fact, though — is admittedly strong stuff, he had gone even farther than his companion, labelling Gally in his mind as a ****** and a !!!!!!.

'Precisely what I think myself,' he agreed. 'From now on, Wellbeloved, ceaseless vigilance.'

'Yes, sir.'

'We cannot afford to relax for an instant.'

'No, sir. The Hun is at the gate.'

'The what's where?'

'The Hun, sir. At the gate, sir. Or putting it another way,' said George Cyril Wellbeloved, who had attended Sunday School in Market Blandings as a boy and still retained a smattering of what he had learned in the days when he was trailing clouds of glory, 'See the troops of Midian prowl and prowl around.'

Sir Gregory thought this over.

'Yes. Yes, I see what you mean. Troops of Midian, yes. Nasty fellers. You did say Midian?'

'Yes, sir. Midian, troops of. Christian, dost thou hear them on the holy ground? Christian, up and smite them!'

'Quite. Yes. Precisely. Just what I was about to suggest myself. You will need a shot-gun. Have you a shot-gun?'

'No, sir.'

'I will give you one. Keep it beside you, never let it out of your hands, and if the occasion arises, use it. Mind you, I am not saying commit a murder and render yourself liable to the extreme penalty of the law, but if one of these nights some bally bounder – I name no names – comes sneaking around Queen of Matchingham's sty, there's nothing to prevent you giving him a dashed good peppering in the seat of the pants.'

'Nothing whatever, sir,' assented George Cyril Wellbeloved cordially.

'If he asks for it, let him have it.'

'I will, sir. With both barrels.'

The conference had gone with such a swing up to this point, overlord and vassal being so patently two minds with but a single thought, that it was a pity that Sir Gregory should now have struck a jarring note. A sudden idea had occurred to him, and he gave it utterance with all the relish of a man whose betrothed has put him on a strict teetotal regimen. Misery loves company.

'And another thing,' he said. 'From this moment you abstain from all alcoholic beverages.'

'Sir!'

'You heard. No more fuddling yourself in tap rooms. I want you keen, alert, up on your toes.'

George Cyril Wellbeloved swallowed painfully, like an ostrich swallowing a brass door-knob.

'When you say alcoholic beverages, sir, you don't mean beer?'

'I do mean beer.'

'No beer?'

'No beer.'

'No *beer*?'

'Not a drop.'

George Cyril Wellbeloved opened his mouth, and for a moment it seemed as if burning words were about to proceed from it. Then, as though struck by a thought, he checked himself.

'Very good, sir,' he said meekly.

Sir Gregory gave him a keen glance.

'Yes, I know what you're thinking,' he said. 'You're thinking you'll be able to sneak off on the sly and lower yourself to the level of the beasts of the field without my knowing it. Well, you won't. I shall give strict orders to the landlords of the various public-houses in Market Blandings that you are not to be served, and as I am on the licensing board, I think these orders will be respected. What beats me,' said Sir Gregory virtuously, 'is why you fellers want to go about swilling and soaking. Look at me. I never touch the stuff. All right, that's all. Push off.'

Droopingly, like a man on whose horizon there is no ray of light, George Cyril Wellbeloved, having given his employer one long, sad, reproachful look, left the room, taking some, but not all, of the pig smell with him. A few moments after the door had closed behind him, Lady Constance's telephone call came through.

'Matchingham 8-30?'

'Yes.'

'Sir Gregory?'

'Yes.'

'Are you there?'

'Yes.'

'Is your blister still painful?'

'Yes.'

'I did tell you to prick it, didn't I?'

'Yes.'

'With a needle. Not a pin. Pins are poisonous. I think they are made of brass, though I must say they don't *look* as if they were made of brass. But what I rang up about was this other trouble of yours. Gloria, you know. The dieting, you know. The exercises, you know.'

Sir Gregory said he knew.

'All that sort of thing cannot be good for you at your age.'

Sir Gregory, who was touchy on the subject, would have

liked to ask what she meant by the expression 'your age', but he was given no opportunity to do so. Like most female telephonists, Lady Constance was not easy to interrupt.

'I couldn't bear to think of you having to go through all that dieting and exercising, because I do think it is so dangerous for a man of your age. A man of your age needs plenty of nourishing food, and there is always the risk of straining yourself seriously. A distant connexion of ours, one of the Hampshire Wilberforces, started touching his toes before breakfast, and he had some sort of a fit. Well, I don't know how I came to forget it when you were here this afternoon, but just after you had left, I suddenly remembered seeing an advertisement in the paper the other day of a new preparation someone had just invented for reducing the weight. Have you heard of it? Slimmo they call it, and it sounds excellent. Apparently it contains no noxious or habit-forming drugs and is endorsed by leading doctors, who are united in describing it as a safe and agreeable medium for getting rid of superfluous flesh. It seems to me that, if it is as good as they say, you would be able to do what Gloria wants without all that dieting and exercising which had such a bad effect on that distant connexion of ours. Rupert Wilberforce it was – a sort of second cousin I suppose you would have called him – he married one of the Devonshire Fairbairns. He was a man getting on in years – about your age – and when he found he was putting on weight, he allowed himself to be persuaded by a thoughtless friend to touch his toes fifty times before breakfast every morning. And on the third morning he did not come down to breakfast, and they went up to his room, and there he was writhing on the floor in dreadful agonies. His heart had run into his liver. Slimmo. It comes in the small bottles and the large economy size. I do wish you would try it. You can get it in Market Blandings, for by an odd coincidence the very day I read about it in the paper I saw some bottles in Bulstrode's window, the chemist in the High Street. It's curious how often that happens, isn't it? I mean, seeing a thing and then seeing it again almost directly afterwards. Oh, Clarence! I was speaking to Clarence, Sir Gregory. He has just come in and is bleating about something. What *is* it, Clarence? You want what? He wants to use the telephone, Sir Gregory, so I must ring off. Good-bye. You won't forget the name, will you. Slimmo. I suggest the large economy size.'

Sir Gregory removed his aching ear from the receiver and hung up.

For some moments after silence had come like a poultice to heal the blows of sound, all that occupied his mind was the thought of what pests the gentler sex were when they got hold of a telephone. The instrument seemed to go to their heads like a drug. Connie Keeble, for instance. Nice sensible woman when you talked to her face to face, never tried to collar the conversation and all that, but the moment she got on the telephone, it was gab, gab, gab, and all about nothing.

Then suddenly he was asking himself whether his late hostess's spate of words had, after all, been so devoid of significance as in his haste he had supposed. Like most men trapped on the telephone by a woman, he had allowed his attention to wander a good deal during the recent monologue, but his subconscious self had apparently been drinking it in all the time, for now it brought up for his inspection the word Slimmo and then a whole lot of interesting stuff about what Slimmo was and what it did. And it was not long before it had put him completely abreast of the thing.

The idea of achieving his ends by means of an anti-fat specific had not previously occurred to Sir Gregory. But now that this alternative had presented itself, it became more attractive the longer he mused on it. The picture of himself, with a tankard of Slimmo at his elbow, sailing into the starchy foods with impunity intoxicated him.

There was but one obstacle in the way of this felicity. Briefly, in order to start filling the wassail bowl with Slimmo, you have first to get the bally stuff, and Sir Gregory, a sensitive man, shrank from going into a shop and asking for it. He feared the quick look of surprise, the furtive glance at the waist-line and the suppressed – or possibly not suppressed – giggle.

Then what to do?

'Ha!' said Sir Gregory, suddenly inspired.

He pressed the bell, and a few moments later Binstead, his butler, entered.

We have heard of Binstead before, it will be remembered. He was the effervescent sportsman who electrified the tap room of the Emsworth Arms by bounding in and offering five to one on his employer's pig. It is interesting to meet him now in person.

Scrutinizing him, however, we find ourselves unimpressed. This Binstead was one of those young, sprightly butlers, encountering whom one feels that in the deepest and holiest sense they are not butlers at all, but merely glorified foot-men. He had none of Beach's measured majesty, but was slim and perky. He looked – though, to do him justice, he had never yet actually proceeded to that awful extreme – as if at any moment he might start turning cart-wheels or sliding down the banisters. And when we say that he was often to be found of an evening playing ha'penny nap with George Cyril Wellbeloved and similar social outcasts and allowing them to address him as 'Herb', we think we have said everything.

'Sir?' said this inadequate juvenile.

Sir Gregory coughed. Even now it was not going to be easy.

'Er, Binstead,' he said. 'Have you ever heard of Slimmo?'

'No, sir.'

'It's some sort of stuff you take. Kind of medicine, if you see what I mean, endorsed by leading doctors. A distant connexion of mine . . . one of the Hampshire Wilberforces . . . has asked me to get him some of it. I want you to telephone to Bulstrode in the High Street and tell him to send up half a dozen bottles.'

'Very good, sir.'

'Tell him the large economy size,' said Sir Gregory.

4

There had been a grave, set look on the face of the Hon. Galahad Threepwood as he stumped away from the tea table on the terrace, and it was still there when, after considerable moody meditation in the grounds, he turned into the corridor that led to Beach's pantry. In the battle of wills which had recently terminated he had not come off any too well. The trouble about talking to a sister like a Dutch uncle is that she is very apt to come right back at you and start talking to you like a Dutch aunt. This is what had happened to Gally at his interview with Lady Constance, and an immediate exchange of ideas with Shropshire's shrewdest butler seemed to him essential.

Entering the pantry, he found only Penny there. Her letter finished, she had gone off, as she so often did, to sit at the feet of one whose society, ever since she had come to the castle, had been a constant inspiration to her. Right from the start of her visit to Blandings Castle, the younger daughter of Mr Donaldson of Donaldson's Dog Joy had recognized in Sebastian Beach a soul-mate and a buddy.

In the butler's absence she was endeavouring to fraternize with his bullfinch, a bird of deep reserves who lived in a cage on the table in the corner. So far, however, she had been unsuccessful in her efforts to find a formula.

'Oh, hello, Gally,' she said. 'Listen, what do you say to a bullfinch?'

'How are you, bullfinch?'

'To make it whistle, I mean.'

'Ah, there you take me into deep waters. But I didn't come here to talk about bullfinches, whether whistling or strongly silent. Where's Beach?'

'Gone into Market Blandings. The chauffeur took him.'

'Dash the man. What did he want to go gadding off to Market Blandings for?'

'Why shouldn't he go gadding off to Market Blandings? The poor guy's got a right to see a little life now and then. He'll be back soon.'

'He should never have left his post.'

'Why, what's the matter?'

'This pig situation.'

'What pig situation would that be?'

Gally passed a careworn hand over his brow.

'I'd forgotten you weren't there when Clarence broke the big story. You had left to go and write to that young man of yours ... Dale, Hale, Gale, whatever his name is.'

'Vail.'

'Oh, Vail.'

'One of the Loamshire Vails. You must learn to call him Jerry. So what happened after I left?'

'Clarence appeared, buffeted by the waves and leaking at every seam like the Wreck of the Hesperus. He had just been talking to that hell-hound.'

'What hell-hound?'

'Sir Gregory Parsloe.'

'Oh yes, the character who keeps taking off his shoes. Who is Sir Gregory Parsloe?'

'Good God! Don't you know that?'

'I'm a stranger in these parts.'

'I'd better begin at the beginning.'

'Much better.'

If there was one thing Gally prided himself on – and justly – it was his ability to tell a story. Step by step he unfolded his tale, omitting no detail however slight, and it was not long before Penny had as complete a grasp of the position of affairs as any raconteur could have wished. When, after stressing the blackness of Sir Gregory Parsloe's soul in a striking passage, he introduced the Queen of Matchingham motif into his narrative and spoke of the guerrilla warfare which must now inevitably ensue, fraught with brooding peril not only to Lord Emsworth's dreams and ambitions but to the bank balances of himself and Beach, she expressed her concern freely.

'This Parsloe sounds a hot number.'

'As hot as mustard. Always was. Remind me to tell you some time how he nobbled my dog Towser on the night of the rat contest. But you have not heard the worst. We now come to the Simmons menace.'

'What's that?'

'In your ramblings about the grounds and messuages do you happen to have seen a large young female in trousers who looks like an all-in wrestler? That is Monica Simmons, Clarence's pig girl. Her high mission is to look after the Empress. Until recently the latter's custodian was a gnome-like but competent old buffer of the name of Pott. But he won a football pool and turned in his seal of office, upon which my sister Connie produced the above Simmons out of her hat and insisted on Clarence engaging her. When this Queen of Matchingham thing came up, Clarence and I agreed that it would be insanity to leave the Empress's fortunes in the hands of a girl like that. Simmons must go, we decided, and as Clarence hadn't the nerve to tackle Connie about it, I said I would. I've just been tackling her.'

'With what result?'

'None. She dug her feet in and put her ears back and generally carried on like a Grade A deaf adder. And what do you think?'

'What?'

'Clarence had told me that Connie's interest in this Simmons was due to the fact that she, the Simmons, was tied up in some way with someone Connie wanted to oblige. Who do you suppose that someone is?'

'Not Parsloe?'

'None other. Parsloe himself. In person, not a picture. The girl is his cousin.'

'Gosh!'

'You may well say "Gosh!". The peril would be ghastly enough if we were merely up against a Parsloe weaving his subtle schemes in his lair at Matchingham Hall. But Parsloe with a cousin in our very citadel, a cousin enjoying free access to the Empress, a cousin whose job it is to provide the Empress with her daily bread ... Well, dash it, if you see what I mean.'

'I certainly do see what you mean. Dash it is right.'

'What simpler than for Parsloe to issue his orders to this minion and for the minion to carry them out?'

'Easy as falling off a log.'

'It's an appalling state of things.'

'Precipitates a grave crisis. What are you going to do?'

'That's what I came to see Beach about. We've got to have a staff conference. Ah, here he comes, thank goodness.'

Outside, there had become audible the booming sound of a bulky butler making good time along a stone-flagged corridor. The bullfinch, recognizing the tread of loved feet, burst into liquid song.

But Beach, as he entered, was not taking the bass. A glance was enough to tell them that he was in no mood for singing. His moon-like face was twisted with mental agony, his gooseberry eyes bulging from their sockets. Even such a man so faint, so spiritless, so dead, so dull in look, so woebegone, drew Priam's curtain in the dead of night and would have told him half his Troy was burned – or so it seemed to Penny, and she squeaked in amazement. Hers had been a sheltered life, and she had never before seen a butler with the heeby-jeebies.

'Beach!' she cried, deeply stirred. 'What is it? Tell Mother.'

'Good Lord, Beach,' said Gally. 'Then you've heard, too?'

'Sir?'

'About the Simmons girl being Parsloe's cousin.'

Beach's jaw fell another notch.

'Sir Gregory's cousin, Mr Galahad?'

'Didn't you know?'

'I had no inkling, Mr Galahad.'

'Then what are you sticking straws in your hair for?'

With trembling fingers Beach put a green baize cloth over the bullfinch's cage. It was as if a Prime Minister in the House of Commons had blown the whistle for a secret session.

'Mr Galahad,' he said. 'I can hardly tell you.'

'What?'

'No, sir, I can hardly tell you.'

'Snap into it, Beach,' said Penny. 'Have your fit later.'

Beach tottered to a cupboard.

'I think, Mr Galahad, if you will excuse me, I must take a drop of port.'

'Double that order,' said Gally.

'Treble it,' said Penny. 'A beaker of the old familiar juice for each of the shareholders, Beach. And fill mine to the brim.'

Beach filled them all to the brim, and further evidence of his agitation, if such were needed, was afforded by the fact that he drained his glass at a gulp, though in happier times a sipper who sipped slowly, rolling the precious fluid round his tongue.

The restorative had its effect. He was able to speak.

'Sir . . . and Madam . . . '

'Have another,' said Penny.

'Thank you, miss. I believe I will. I think you should, too, Mr Galahad, for what I am about to say will come as a great shock.'

'Get on, Beach. Don't take all night about it.'

'I know a man named Jerry Vail, a young author of sensational fiction,' said Penny chattily, 'who starts his stories just like this. You never know till Page Twenty-three what it's all about. Suspense, he calls it.'

'Cough it up, Beach, this instant, and no more delay. You hear me? I don't want to be compelled to plug you in the eye.'

'Very good, Mr Galahad.'

With a powerful effort the butler forced himself to begin his tale.

'I have just returned from Market Blandings, Mr Galahad. I went there for the purpose of making a certain purchase. I don't know if you have happened to notice it, sir, but recently I have been putting on a little weight, due no doubt to the sedentary nature of a butler's –'

'Beach!'

'Let him work up to it,' said Penny. 'The Vail method. Building for the climax. Go on, Beach. You're doing fine.'

'Thank you, miss. Well, as I say, I have recently become somewhat worried about this increase in my weight, and I chanced to see in the paper an advertisement of a new preparation called Slimmo, guaranteed to reduce super-fluous flesh, which was stated to contain no noxious or habit-forming drugs and to be endorsed by leading doctors. So I thought I would look in at Bulstrode's in the High Street and buy a bottle. It was somewhat embarrassing walking into the shop and asking for it, and I thought I noticed Bulstrode's young assistant give me a sort of sharp look as much as to say "Oho!" but I nerved myself to the ordeal, and Bulstrode's young assistant wrapped the bottle up in paper and fastened the loose ends with a little pink sealing wax.'

'Beach, you have been warned!'

'Do be quiet, Gally. And that was that, eh?'

A spasm shook Beach.

'If I may employ a vulgarism, miss, you do not know the half of it.'

'More coming?'

'Much, much more, miss.'

'Well, here I am, Beach, with the old ear trumpet right at the ear.'

'Thank you, miss.'

Beach closed his eyes for a moment, as if praying for strength.

'I had scarcely paid for my purchase and received my change when the telephone bell rang. Bulstrode's young assistant went to the instrument.'

'And a dead body fell out?'

'Miss?'

'Sorry. My mind was on Mr Vail's stories. Carry on. You have the floor. What happened?'

'He spoke a few words into the instrument. "Okey-doke", I remember, was one of them, and "Righty-ho", from which I gathered that he was speaking to a customer of the lower middle class, what is sometimes called the burjoisy. Then he turned to me with a smile and observed "Well, that is what I call a proper coincidence, Mr Beach. Never rains but it pours, does it? That was Herbert Binstead. And know what he wants? Six bottles of Slimmo, the large economy size.'"

Gally started as if he had been bitten in the leg by Baronets.

'What!'

'Yes, Mr Galahad.'

'That fellow Binstead was buying Slimmo?'

'Yes, Mr Galahad.'

'Good God!'

Penny looked from one to the other, perplexed.

'But why shouldn't he buy Slimmo? Maybe he's a leading doctor.'

Gally spoke in a voice of doom.

'Herbert Binstead is Gregory Parsloe's butler. And if you have the idea that he may have been buying this anti-fat for his own personal use, correct that view. He's as thin as a herring. His motive is obvious. One reads the man like a book. Acting under Parsloe's instructions, he plans to pass this Slimmo on to the accomplice Simmons, who will slip it privily into the Empress's daily ration, thus causing her to lose weight, thus handing the race on a plate to Queen of Matchingham. Am I right, Beach?'

'I fear so, Mr Galahad. It was the first thought that entered my mind when Bulstrode's young assistant revealed to me the gist of his telephone conversation.'

'No explanation other than the one that I have outlined will fit the facts. I told you Parsloe was mustard, Penny. He moves in a mysterious way his wonders to perform.'

Silence fell, one of those deep, uneasy silences which occur when all good men realize that now is the time for them to come to the aid of the party but are unable to figure out just how to set about doing so.

But it was not in the nature of the Hon. Galahad to be baffled for long. A brain like his, honed to razor-like sharpness by years of association with the members of the Pelican Club, is never at a loss for more than a moment.

'Well, there you are,' he said. 'The first shot of the campaign has been fired, and soon the battle will be joined. We must consider our plan of action.'

'Which is what?' said Penny. 'I don't see where you go from here. I take it the idea is to keep an eye on this Simmons beazel, but how is it to be done? You can't watch her all the time.'

'Exactly. So we must engage the services of someone who can, someone trained to the task, someone whose profession it is to keep an eye on the criminal classes, and most fortunately we are able to lay our hand on just such a person. The guiding spirit of Digby's Day and Night Detectives.'

Beach gave a start which set both his chins quivering.

'Maudie, Mr Galahad? My niece, Mr Galahad?'

'None other. Is she Mrs Digby?'

'No, sir. Mrs Stubbs. Digby is a trade name. But –'

'But what?'

'I am in perfect agreement with what you say with regard to the necessity of employing a trained observer to scrutinize Miss Simmons's movements, Mr Galahad, but you are surely not thinking of bringing my niece Maudie here? Her appearance – '

'I remember her as looking rather like Mae West.'

'Precisely, sir. It would never do.'

'I don't follow you, Beach.'

'I was thinking of Lady Constance, sir. I have known her ladyship to be somewhat difficult at times where guests were concerned. I gravely doubt whether her reactions would be wholly favourable, were you to introduce into the castle a private investigator who is the niece of her butler and looks like Miss Mae West.'

'I am not proposing to do so.'

'Indeed, sir? I gathered from what you were saying – '

'The visitor who arrives at Blandings Castle and sings out to the varlets and scurvy knaves within to lower the portcullis and look slippy about it will be a Mrs Bunbury, a lifelong friend of your father, Penny. You remember that charming Mrs Bunbury?'

Penny drew a deep breath.

'You're a quick thinker, Gally.'

'You have to think quick when a man like Gregory Parsloe is spitting on his hands preparatory to going about seeking whom he may devour. By the way, Beach, not a word of all this to Lord Emsworth. We don't want him worrying himself into a decline, nor do we want him giving the whole thing away in the first ten minutes, as he infallibly would if he knew about it. An excellent fellow, Clarence, but a rotten conspirator. You follow me, Beach?'

'Oh yes, indeed, Mr Galahad.'

'Penny?'

'He shall never learn from me.'

'Good girl. Too much is at stake for us to take any chances. The hopes and dreams of my brother Clarence depend on Maudie, and so, Beach, does the little bit of stuff which you and I have invested on the Empress. Get her on the telephone at once.'

'Is the Empress on the telephone?' asked Penny, surprised, though feeling that something like this might have been expected of that wonder-pig.

Gally frowned.

'I allude to Maudie Beach Montrose Digby Stubbs Bunbury. Get on to her without delay and instruct her to pack her toothbrush and magnifying glass and be with us at her earliest convenience.'

'Very good, Mr Galahad.'

'Pitch it strong. Make her see how urgent the matter is. Play up the attractive aspects of Blandings Castle, and tell her that she will find there not only a loved uncle but one of her warmest admirers of the old Criterion days.'

'Yes, Mr Galahad.'

'I will now go and inform my sister Constance that at the urgent request of Miss Penelope Donaldson I am inviting the latter's father's close crony Mrs Bunbury to put in a week or two with us. I do not anticipate objections on the part of my sister Constance, but should she give me any lip or back chat I shall crush her as I would a worm.'

'Do you crush worms?' asked Penny, interested.

'Frequently,' said Gally, and trotted out, to return a few minutes later beaming satisfaction through his monocle.

'All set. She right-hoed like a lamb. She seems to have an overwhelming respect for your father, Penny, no doubt because of his disgusting wealth. And now,' said Gally, 'now that what you might call the preliminary spadework is completed and we are able to relax for a bit, I think a drop more port might be in order. For you, Penny?'

'Let it flow like water, as far as I'm concerned.'

'And you, Beach?'

'Thank you, Mr Galahad. A little port would be most refreshing.'

'Then reach for the bottle and start pouring. And as you pour,' said Gally, 'keep saying to yourself that tempests may lower and storm clouds brood, but if your affairs are in the hands of Galahad Threepwood, you're all right.'

CHAPTER THREE

ALTHOUGH it is the fashion in this twentieth century of ours to speak disparagingly of the modern machine age, to sneer at its gadgets and gimmicks and labour-saving devices and to sigh for the days when life was simpler, these gimmicks and gadgets unquestionably have their advantages.

If Penny Donaldson had been a princess in ancient Egypt desirous of communicating with the man she loved, she would have had to write a long letter on papyrus, all animals' heads and things, and send it off by a Nubian slave, and there is no telling when Jerry Vail would have got it, for the only time those Nubian slaves hurried themselves was when someone was behind them with a spiked stick. Living in modern times, she had been able to telegraph, and scarcely two hours elapsed before Jerry, in his modest flat in Battersea Park Road, London, SW, received the heart-stirring news that she would be with him on the morrow.

Sudden joy affects different people in different ways. Some laugh and sing. Some leap. Others go about being kind to dogs. Jerry Vail sat down and started writing a story designed for one of the American magazines if one of the American magazines would meet him half-way, about a New York private detective who was full of Scotch whisky and sex appeal and got mixed up with a lot of characters with names like Otto the Ox and Bertha the Body.

He was just finishing it on the following afternoon – for stories about New York private detectives, involving as they do almost no conscious cerebration, take very little time to write – when the telephone bell stopped him in the middle of a sentence.

There is always something intriguing and stimulating about the ringing of a telephone bell. Will this, we ask ourselves, be the girl we love, or will it be somebody named Ed, who, all eagerness to establish communication with somebody named Charlie, has had the misfortune to get the wrong number? Jerry, though always glad to chat with people who got the wrong number, hoped it would be Penny.

'Hullo?' he said, putting a wealth of pent-up feeling into the word, just in case.

'Hullo, Jerry. This is Gloria.'

'Eh?'

'Gloria Salt, ass,' said the voice at the other end of the wire with a touch of petulance.

There had been a time when Jerry Vail's heart would have leaped at the sound of that name. Between Gloria Salt and himself there had been some tender passages in the days gone by, passages which might have been tenderer still if the lady had not had one of those level business heads which restrain girls from becoming too involved with young men who, however attractive, are short of cash. Gloria Salt, though she had little else in common with Mr Donaldson of Donaldson's Dog Joy, shared that good man's aloof and wary attitude toward the impecunious suitor.

But though, like the Fairy Queen in Iolanthe, on fire that glows with heat intense she had turned the hose of common sense, and though on Jerry's side that fire had long since become a mere heap of embers, their relations had remained cordial. From time to time they would play a round of golf together, and from time to time they would lunch together. One of these nice unsentimental friendships it had come to be, and it was with hearty good will that he now spoke.

'Why, hullo, Gloria. I haven't heard from you for ages. What have you been doing with yourself?'

'Just messing around. Playing a bit of tennis. Playing a bit of golf. Ridin' a bit, swimmin' a bit. Oh yes, and I've got engaged,' said Miss Salt as an afterthought.

Jerry was delighted to hear the news.

'Well, well. That's the stuff. I like to see you young folks settling down. Who's the other half of the sketch? Orlo the Ox, I presume?'

'Who?'

'I'm sorry. I was thinking of something else. My lord Vosper, I mean.'

There was a momentary silence. Then Gloria Salt spoke in an odd, metallic voice.

'No, not my lord Vosper, thank you very much. I wouldn't marry Orlo by golly Vosper to please a dying grandmother. If I found myself standing with that pill at the altar rails and the clergyman said to me "How about it, Gloria old sport? Wilt thou, Gloria, take this Orlo?", I would reply "Not in a million years, laddie, not to win a substantial wager. If you were suggesting that I might like to attend his funeral," I would proceed, developing the theme, "that would be another matter, but if, as I think, the idea at the back of your mind is that I shall become his wedded wife, let me inform you, my dear old man of God, that I would rather be dead in a ditch." Orlo Vosper, egad! I should jolly well say not.'

Jerry was concerned. Here was tragedy. Mystery, too. Like most of her circle, he had always supposed that it was only a matter of time before these twain sent out the wedding announcements. Affinities, they had seemed to be, always being 'seen' together at Cannes or 'glimpsed' together at Ascot or 'noticed' together playing in the mixed doubles at some seaside tennis tournament. To hear Gloria Salt talking in this acid strain about Orlo, Lord Vosper, was as surprising as if one had heard Swan knocking Edgar or Rodgers saying nasty things about Hammerstein.

'But, good Lord, I always thought –'

'I dare say you did. Nevertheless, the facts are as I have stated. I have returned Orlo Vosper to store and shall

61

shortly – wind and weather permitting – become the bride of Sir Gregory Parsloe, Bart, of Matchingham Hall, Much Matchingham, in the county of Shropshire.'

'But what happened?'

'It's too long to go into over the phone. I'll tell you when we meet, which will be to-night. I want you to give me dinner at Mario's.'

'To-night, did you say?'

'To-night. Are you getting deaf in your old age?'

Jerry was not deaf, but he was deeply agitated, and in the circumstances the toughest baa-lamb might have been excused for being so. This night of nights was earmarked for his dinner with Penny. He had been counting the minutes to that sacred reunion, scrutinizing his boiled shirts, sorting out his white ties, seeing to it that the patent leather shoes and the old top hat had the perfect gloss which such an occasion called for, and what he was thinking now was that, if you have been torn from the only girl that matters and have got an utterly unforeseen chance of having a bite to eat with her at the Savoy, of gazing into her eyes at the Savoy and holding her little hand at the Savoy, it is a pretty state of things when other girls, however old friends they may be, come muscling in, wanting to divert you to Mario's.

'But listen, old thing. I can't possibly manage to-night. Won't to-morrow do?'

'No, it won't. I'm leaving for the country to-morrow. I don't want to see you just for the pleasure of your society, stupendous though that is. I want to do you a good turn. Do you remember telling me once that you were trying to raise two thousand pounds to buy in on some private loony-bin?'

The actual project for which Jerry required the sum mentioned was not, as we have seen, the securing of a share in the management of a home for the mentally unbalanced, but this was no moment for going into long explanations. He gasped, and the room flickered before his eyes.

'You don't mean –?'

'Yes, I think I can put you in the way of getting it.'

'Good Lord! Gloria, you're a marvel. When pain and anguish rack the brow, a ministering angel thou. Let's have full details.'

'To-night. It's much too long to tell you now. Eight sharp at Mario's. And I'm going to dress. Because if you aren't dressed at Mario's, they shove you up in the balcony, a thing my proud spirit would never endure. Have you a dickey and celluloid cuffs?'

'But, Gloria, half a second –'

'That's all there is, there isn't any more. Good-bye. I must rush. Got to see a man about a tennis racquet.'

For some time after the line had gone dead, an observer, had one been present in Flat Twenty-three, Prince of Wales Mansions, Battersea Park Road, would have been able to see what a young man standing at the crossroads looked like, for during that period Gerald Anstruther Vail sat wrestling with himself, torn this way and that, a living ganglion of conflicting emotions.

The thought of cancelling his dinner with Penny, of not seeing her after all, of not gazing into her eyes, of not holding her little hand, was about as unpleasing a thought as had ever entered his mind. It is not too much to say that it gashed the very fibres of his being.

On the other hand, if Gloria had meant what she said, if by conferring with her at Mario's, there was really a chance of learning a method of getting his hooks on that two thousand, would it not be madness to pass it up?

Aeons later he decided that it would. The money was his passport to Paradise, and he knew Gloria Salt well enough to be aware that, though a girl of kind impulses, she was touchy. Spurn her, and she stayed spurned. To refuse to meet her at Mario's and hear her plan for conjuring two thousand pounds out of thin air, which seemed to be what she had in mind, would mean pique, resentment and dudgeon. She would drop the subject entirely and decline to open it again.

Heavily, for the load on his heart weighed him down, he rose and began to turn the pages of the telephone book. Chez Lady Garland, whoever she might be, Penny had said she would be during her brief stay in the great city, and there was a Garland, Lady with a Grosvenor Square address among the G's. He dialled the number, and hooked what sounded like a butler.

'Could I speak to Miss Donaldson?'

He could not. Penny, it appeared, was out having a fit. A what? Oh, a fitting? Yes, I see. Any idea when she will be back? No, sir, I am unable to say. Would you care to leave a message, sir?

'Yes. Will you tell Miss Donaldson that Mr Gerald Vail is terribly sorry but he will be unable to give her dinner tonight owing to a very important business matter that has come up.'

'Business matter, sir?'

'That's right. A most important business matter.'

'Very good, sir.'

And that was that. But oh, the agony of it. Replacing the receiver, Jerry slumped into a chair with a distinct illusion that mocking fiends were detaching large portions of his soul with red-hot pincers.

At Wiltshire House, Grosvenor Square, residence of Dora, relict of the late Sir Everard Garland, K.C.B., Lady Constance Keeble was not feeling any too good herself. Jerry had made his call at the moment when Riggs, the butler, was bringing tea for herself and Lord Vosper, who had looked in hoping for buttered toast and a chat with Penny, and it had taken her attention right off the pleasures of the table.

'Sinister' was the word that flashed through Lady Constance's mind. 'Sir,' Riggs had said, indicating that the mysterious caller was of the male sex, and she was at a loss to comprehend how – unless the girl had told him – any mysterious male could know that Penny was in London. And if she had told him, it implied an intimacy which froze her blood.

'Who was that, Riggs?'

'A Mr Gerald Vail, m'lady, regretting his inability to entertain Miss Donaldson at dinner to-night.'

Training tells. 'Ladies never betray emotion, Connie dear,' an early governess of Lady Constance's had often impressed upon her, and the maxim had guided her through life. Where a woman less carefully schooled might have keeled over in her chair, possibly with a startled 'Golly!' she merely quivered a little.

'I see. Thank you, Riggs.'

She picked up the cake with jam in the middle which had fallen from her nerveless fingers and ate it in a sort of trance. The discovery that on the pretext of dining with her father's old friend Mrs Bunbury, Penelope Donaldson had been planning to sneak off and revel with a young man who, from the fact that she had never mentioned his name, must be somebody quite impossible appalled her. It revealed the child as what her brother Galahad would have called a hornswoggling highbinder, and anyone who has anything to do with highbinders knows that that is the very worst sort.

It was with relief that she remembered that by to-morrow evening Penelope Donaldson would be safely back at Blandings Castle, well away from the Vail sphere of influence.

What a haven and refuge Blandings Castle was, to be sure, felt Lady Constance. It seemed to her to have everything.

Bracing air, picturesque scenery, old world peace and – best of all – not a Vail to be seen for miles.

2

When girls like Gloria Salt, planning dinner with an old friend, say they are going to dress, they use the word in its deepest and fullest sense, meaning that they propose to extend themselves and that such of the populace as are sharing the *salle-à-manger* with them will be well advised to wear smoked glasses. Jerry, waiting in the lobby of Mario's restaurant some three hours later, was momentarily stunned by what came floating in through the revolving door twenty minutes or so after the time appointed for the tryst. Owing to the fact that their meetings for some years had been confined to the golf links and the luncheon table, he had forgotten how spectacular this girl could be when arrayed for the evening meal.

Gloria Salt was tall and slim and the last word in languorous elegance. Though capable of pasting a golf ball two hundred yards and creating, when serving at tennis, the illusion that it was raining thunderbolts, her dark beauty made her look like a serpent of old Nile. A nervous host, encountering her on her way to dine, might have been excused for wondering whether to offer her a dry martini or an asp.

He would have been wrong in either case. She would have declined the asp, and she now declined Jerry's suggestion of a cocktail.

'Never touch 'em. Can't keep fit if you put that foul stuff into you. That's what I told my future lord and master,' said Gloria, as they seated themselves at their table. 'Lay off those pink gins, Greg, I said, avoid those whisky sours, and while you're about it cut out the starchy foods and take regular daily exercises, because a girl who marries

66

a man who looks like you do at moment of going to press is going to have an uneasy feeling that she's committing bigamy.'

'How did he take that?'

'He laughed at the wit. The satire didn't go so well.'

'He is stout, this Parsloe?'

'He certainly gets his pennyworth out of a weighing machine.'

Jerry was not unnaturally anxious to condense preliminaries to a minimum and come to the real business of the evening, but a host must be civil. He cannot plunge into business over the smoked salmon. He was, moreover, extremely curious to learn the inside story of the rift within the lute at which his guest had hinted – if hinted is the word – when speaking earlier in the day of Orlo, Lord Vosper. Jerry, who had known that handsomest ornament of the Peerage from boyhood days and was very fond of him, had been saddened by her tale of sundered hearts.

'A bit of a change from the old Wasp,' he ventured.

'What old wasp?'

'Boyish nickname for Vosper. I was at school with him.'

'You were, were you? Borstal, I presume? Did you kick him?'

'Of course I didn't kick him. I loved him like a brother.'

'The chance of a lifetime thrown away,' said Miss Salt with bitterness. 'If Orlo Vosper in his formative years had been thoroughly kicked twice a day, Sundays included, he might not have grown up the overbearing louse he has become.'

'Would you call him an overbearing louse?'

'I did. To his face.'

'When was this?'

'On the tennis court at Eastbourne, and again when entering the club house. I'd have done it in the dressing-room, too, only he wasn't there. They separate the sexes.

Of all the overbearing lice that ever overbore, I told him, you are the undisputed champion, and I gave him back his ring.'

'Oh, you were engaged?'

'Don't rub it in. We all make mistakes.'

'I didn't see anything about it in the papers.'

'We were going to announce it just before Wimbledon.'

'What did he do to incur your displeasure?'

'I'll tell you. We were playing in the mixed doubles, and I admit that I may have been slightly off my game, but that was no reason why, after we had dropped the first set, he should have started barging into my half of the court, taking my shots for me as if I were some elderly aunt with arthritis in both legs who had learned tennis in the previous week at a correspondence school. "Mine!" he kept yelling. "Mine, mine!", and where was Gloria? Crouching in a corner, looking at him with wide, admiring eyes and saying "My hero!"? No, sir. I told him that if he didn't stop his damned poaching, I would brain him, if he had a brain. That held him for awhile. After that, he kept himself to himself, as it were. But every time I missed a shot, and a girl with an emotional nature couldn't be expected not to miss a few after an ordeal like that, he raised his eyebrows in a superior kind of way and gave a sort of nasty dry snigger and kept saying "Too bad, too bad." And when it was over and we had lost – two six, three six – he said what a pity it all was and if only I had left it to him . . . Well, that was when we parted brass rags. Shortly afterwards I got engaged to Greg Parsloe.'

Jerry clicked his tongue, and when his guest inquired with some asperity why he was making that idiotic noise, and did he think he was riding in the Grand National and encouraging his horse to jump Becher's Brook, explained that her story had distressed him. As, indeed, it had. Nobody likes to hear of these rifts between old friends. He had been devoted to Lord Vosper since the days when they had thrown inked darts at one another, while for Gloria Salt he felt that gentle affection which men feel for women who could have married them and didn't.

'Has the Wasp heard about it?'

'I suppose so. It was in *The Times*.'

'It must have given him a jolt.'

'One hopes so.'

'Where is he now?'

'Goodness knows. I don't. And for heaven's sake let's stop talking about him. I should have thought you would have shown some interest in what I said to you over the phone this afternoon. I pictured you running up to me the moment I came in, all full of eager questions. And you haven't so much as mentioned it.'

Jerry was dismayed to think that she should have got so wrong an impression from his gentlemanly reserve.

'Good Lord, of course I'm interested. But I thought you would get around to that when you felt like it. I didn't want you to think that was the only reason I wanted to dine with you.'

'Did you want to dine with me?'

'Of course I did.'

'You didn't sound too pleased.'

'Well, you see, actually I had another date for to-night, and I was feeling it might be awkward breaking it.'

'A girl?'

It was a loose way of describing the divinest of her species, but Jerry let it pass.

'Yes, a girl.'

Gloria Salt's eyes grew soft and sympathetic. She leaned across the table and patted his cheek.

'I'm terribly sorry, Jerry. I didn't know. Is this love? Yes, I can see it is from the way your eyes are goggling. Well, well. When did this happen?'

'Not so long ago. I dashed over to New York the other day, and she was on the boat coming back.'

'When are you going to get married?'

'Never, unless I can raise that two thousand pounds.'

'It's like that, is it? Don't you make anything with your writing?'

'Not half enough.'

'I see. Well, as I say, I'm sorry I had to come butting in, but this was my last chance of getting hold of you. I'm motoring down to Shropshire to-morrow, to stay at a place called Blandings Castle.'

Jerry started.

'Blandings Castle?'

'You know it?'

Jerry hesitated. Should he tell her all about Penny? On the whole, he thought, no. The fewer people who knew, the better.

'I've heard of it,' he said. 'Nice place, I believe.'

'So they all tell me. It's only a mile or two from where Gregory hangs out, so we'll be able to see something of each other. I imagine that's why Lady Constance invited me. Well, keep the words "Blandings Castle" steadily in your mind, because they are the heart of the matter. I will now approach the heart of the matter.'

A waiter brought roast beef, underdone, and she took a thin slice. Jerry took two slices, with potatoes, and Gloria in her austere way advised him to be very careful how he tucked into those things, because she was convinced that it was a lifelong passion for potatoes that had made Sir Gregory Parsloe the man he was ... or, rather, she added, for she was a girl who liked exactness, the two men he was.

'Where were we?' she asked, as the waiter withdrew.

'You were about to approach the heart of the matter.'

'That's right. So I was. Well, here it comes. Listen attentively, for what I have to say will interest you strangely.'

She ate a Brussels sprout. It is the virtue of Brussels sprouts that you can wolf them freely without running any risk of becoming like Sir Gregory Parsloe, Bart, of Matchingham Hall, Much Matchingham.

'I don't know about the flora of Blandings Castle,' she said, 'though no doubt they are varied and beautiful, but its fauna consist of – amongst others – Clarence, ninth Earl of Emsworth, and his sister, Lady Constance. What the relations are between the noble lord and my betrothed I cannot say, but Lady Constance and he appear to be on matey terms, so much so that when the other day she wanted to get a new secretary for Lord Emsworth, she asked if he could do anything to help. "Charmed, dear lady," said Greg, and got me on the phone and told me to attend to it, if it was not giving me too much trouble. "No trouble at all, my king," I said. "As a matter of fact, I know a man." You're the man.'

Jerry gasped. The roast beef swam before his eyes.

'You don't mean –?'

'The job's yours, if you care to take it, and I strongly advise you to take it, because there is more in this than meets the eye and the plot is shortly about to thicken. But I suppose you're going to come over all haughty and say that the Vails don't take jobs as secretaries.'

Jerry laughed. The thought of being too proud to allow himself to be employed in a house which contained Penny, a house probably stiff with rose gardens and other secluded nooks where he and Penny could meet and talk of this and that, was an amusing one. Had it been required of him, he would have accepted office as the boy who cleaned the knives and boots.

'I'll be there. You couldn't have suggested anything that would have suited me better.'

'That's all right, then. And now for the thickening of the plot. About a year ago I ran into a lad I used to go dancing with in the days of Edward the Confessor, a youth named Hugo Carmody, and he gave me lunch and told me all about Blandings Castle. It seems that he was Lord Emsworth's secretary at one time, and he had me in stitches with his diverting stories about the old boy. Are you listening?'

'You bet I'm listening.'

'I had completely forgotten Hugo and his saga till Greg rang me up, and then the word "secretary", taken in conjunction with the words "Blandings Castle", brought it all back to me, and I saw that this was where I could do my day's good deed. The gist of what Hugo had told me was that the old bird – I allude to the ninth Earl – is practically dotty on the subject of pigs. He has a prize pig called Empress of Blandings to which he is devoted. In fact, you might say he thinks of nothing else. Hugo's tenure of his job was very rocky off and on, but he told me he could always stabilize it by talking pig to Lord Emsworth. There were times, he said, when he was at the top of his form as a pig talker, when he got the impression that Lord Emsworth would have given him all he had, even unto half his kingdom. And when Greg told me about this secretary thing and I thought of you, it was because it suddenly struck me that it was quite possible that if you went to Blandings and showed yourself sufficiently pig-conscious, old Emsworth might be induced to advance you that two thousand you require. Naturally I don't say it's a snip. Lots of elderly men, however fond they may have become of an eager youngster, wince and shrink back when the latter shows a disposition to climb on their laps and help himself out of their pockets. But in your case it wouldn't be a straight touch. All you would be asking for would be a loan, and not too risky a loan considering what pots of money these cure places make. You would put it up to him as a business proposition. "Lord Emsworth," you would say, "do you want to make a bit? Because, if so, I

72

can swing it for you," and then you would go into your sales talk and offer him a large interest on his money. An old bird like that probably has all his cash salted away in Government bonds at three per cent, and you would sneer at Government bonds, and ask if he wouldn't prefer a safe ten. I think he would drop. Mind you, I'm not saying that you could walk into Blandings Castle to-morrow and expect to get a cheque for two thousand of the best before bedtime, but after the lapse of some weeks, after you had softened him up with your encyclopaedic knowledge of pigs, I don't see why you shouldn't have a sporting chance. Think it over.'

Jerry was doing so, and now he came up with an objection.

'But I haven't an encyclopaedic knowledge of pigs.'

'There are a million books you can get it from. Good heavens! Go to the British Museum and ask for everything they have on the subject. If I were in your place, I'd guarantee to become an authority in a couple of days. You don't suppose Hugo Carmody knew anything about pigs do you? He had never met a pig except informally over the dish of breakfast bacon. Whenever the sack seemed to him to be looming, when he could hear the beating of its wings, so to speak, he used to sneak down at night to Lord Emsworth's library and bone up on the subject till breakfast time. By then, he tells me, though a little apt to fall asleep where he sat, he did know about pigs. What Hugo could do, you can do. Or are you a spineless worm incapable of honest effort?'

So might the Cleopatra she so closely resembled in appearance have addressed one of her soldiers who seemed in need of a pep talk before the Battle of Actium. And just as this soldier would have sprung to his feet with flashing eyes, so did Jerry Vail leap with flashing eyes from his chair.

'Want to dance?' said Gloria.

Jerry quivered.

'What I really want is to fold you in my arms and cover your upturned face with burning kisses.'

'You can't do that there here. And you seem to be forgetting that we're both engaged to somebody else.'

'You don't get the idea. These would be kisses of gratitude, the sort of kisses a brother would bestow on a sister who deserved well of him. I simply don't know what to say, Gloria, old thing. You spoke of doing your day's good deed. What you have done this night is sufficient to carry you over till a couple of years from now, even if you do no good deeds in the meantime. Well, I suppose all I can say is "Thank you."'

She patted his cheek.

'Don't mention it,' she said. 'Come on, let's dance.'

3

In her bedroom in her neat little house in the suburb of Valley Fields, Maudie Stubbs, *née* Beach, was enjoying a last cigarette before turning in for the night.

All her arrangements for to-morrow's exodus were completed – her packing done, her hair waved, her cat Freddie lodged with a friend down the road, and now she was musing dreamily on something her Uncle Sebastian had said over the telephone yesterday.

The story he had told had of necessity been brief and sketchy, and she had still to learn in detail exactly what was expected of her on arrival at this Blandings Castle of which she had heard so much, but in the course of his remarks Uncle Sebastian had mentioned as the menace to the well-being of himself and associates a Sir Gregory Parsloe.

She wondered if this could possibly be the Tubby Parsloe she had known so well in the days when she had been Maudie Montrose.

CHAPTER FOUR

With the possible exception of Mrs Emily Post, a few of the haughtier Duchesses and the late Cornelia mother of the Gracchi, the British barmaid, trained from earliest years to behave with queenly dignity under the most testing conditions, stands alone in the matter of poise.

It was no timid and fluttering Maudie Stubbs who stepped off the train next day at Market Blandings station. Where another representative of what is sometimes termed the burjoisy might have quailed at the thought of being plunged into so posh – or plushy – a nest of the aristocracy as Blandings Castle, she faced the prospect with equanimity, remaining as calm and composed as she would have been if entering a den of lions like the prophet Daniel or a burning fiery furnace like Shadrach, Meshach and Abednego. In her professional capacity, she had seen far too many members of the Peerage thrown out of the bar over which she presided for blue blood to mean anything to her.

Gally, all eagerness to renew a friendship interrupted by time and change, had walked in to meet the train, and there was an affecting reunion on the station platform. After which, he had taken her off to the Emsworth Arms for a spot of refreshment. He felt she must be in need of it after her long journey, and apart from the altruistic desire to keep an old crony from fainting by the wayside, he thought it would be no bad thing to have a quick run-through before the rise of the curtain, just to make sure that she was letter perfect in her part.

When two old friends get together after long separation, the proceedings always begin with a picking up of threads. The first old friend asks the second old friend for news of Jimmy So-and-so, while the second old friend asks the first old friend what has been heard of Billy Such-and-such. Inquiries are also instituted regarding Tom This, Dick That and Harry The other, with speculations as to whatever became of old Joe What's-his-name, the chap who always used to do an imitation of a cat fight after his third whisky and splash.

These routine preliminaries had been disposed of during the walk from the station, and now, as they sat at a rustic table in the garden behind the inn, sipping the beer for which the Emsworth Arms is so justly renowned, they were at liberty to speak of other things. To a man as gallant as the Hon. Galahad a compliment with reference to his companion's appearance naturally suggested itself first, and he proceeded to pay it.

'Well, well, well,' he said, gazing at her with undisguised admiration. 'Do you know you positively don't look a dashed day older, Maudie? It's amazing.'

And indeed the years had dealt lightly with the erstwhile Maudie Montrose. A little more matronly, perhaps, than the girl with the hourglass figure who had played the Saint Bernard dog to the thirsty wayfarers at the old Criterion, she still made a distinct impression on the eye, and the landlord of the Emsworth Arms, his growing son Percy, and the half dozen Shropshire lads who were propping up the establishment's outer wall had stamped her with the seal of their popeyed approval. Her entrance had been in the nature of a social triumph.

'It's astounding,' said Gally. 'One gasps. Put you in a bathing suit, add you to the line of contestants in any seaside beauty competition, and you would still have the judges whooping and blowing kisses and asking you if you were doing anything next Saturday night.'

It was the sort of tribute a thousand mellowed clients had paid her across the bar in the old days, and Maudie, who had simpered indulgently then, simpered indulgently now.

'Thank you, dear,' she said. 'I call that very nice of you. You don't look so bad yourself,' she added, with that touch of surprise which always came into the voices of those who, meeting Gally after a lapse of years, found him so bright and rosy.

This man's fitness was one of the eternal mysteries. Speaking of him, a historian of Blandings Castle had once written: 'A thoroughly mis-spent life had left the Hon. Galahad Threepwood, contrary to the most elementary justice, in what appeared to be perfect, even exuberantly perfect physical condition. How a man who ought to have had the liver of the century could look as he did was a constant source of perplexity to his associates. It seemed incredible that anyone who had had such an extraordinarily good time all his life should, in the evening of that life, be so superbly robust.'

Striking words, but well justified. Instead of the blot on a proud family which his sister Constance, his sister Julia, his sister Dora and all his other sisters considered him, he might have been a youngish teetotaller who had subsisted from boyhood on yoghurt, yeast, wheat germ and blackstrap molasses. He himself attributed his health to steady smoking, plenty of alcohol and his life-long belief that it was bad form to go to bed before three in the morning.

'I keep pretty well,' he agreed complacently. 'Life in the country suits me.'

'I should have thought you'd have been bored stiff.'

'No, I like it. It's all a matter of taste. Poor old Fruity Biffen, now, he couldn't cope with the local conditions at all. You remember Fruity Biffen? He was down here till a few days ago, but he couldn't take it, and left. A great loss. He would have been of invaluable assistance to us in this task of ours of foiling Parsloe. Your Uncle Sebastian, though a good chap, lacks a certain something. Not the sort of fellow to put in the forefront of the battle. What one wants in a crisis like that through which we are now passing is one of those young, tough, butlers, spitting out of the side of the mouth and ready for anything.'

'How is Uncle Sebastian?'

'Very well, considering everything. Worried, naturally. The dark circles which you will notice under his eyes are due to anxiety regarding the Empress's future. The Agricultural Show is approaching, and he has invested far more on her than he cares to lose. Me too. I also am heavily involved. So we are relying on you, Maudie, to do your bit. Watch the girl Simmons unblinkingly, for it is from that quarter that peril looms. Did your Uncle Sebastian explain the situation fully?'

'Not what you would call fully. But I understand most of it.'

'The pig contest? The danger that threatens? The need for constant vigilance?'

'Yes, all that. But who is this Mrs Bunbury I'm supposed to be?'

'The lifelong friend of a Mr Donaldson, father of a Miss Penelope Donaldson who is a guest at the castle, a merchant prince who provides the American dog with its daily biscuit. So when Connie starts talking about him, don't be like Clarence and say "Who is Mr Donaldson?" Clarence is my brother, Lord Emsworth, and Connie is my sister, Lady Constance Keeble. She is the menace in the treatment.'

'I thought this Sir Gregory Parsloe was the menace.'

'Aided and abetted by Connie. Not that a twister like Tubby Parsloe needs any aiding and abetting.'

Maudie sat up with a jerk.

'Tubby?'

'That's odd,' said Gally. 'I don't suppose I've called him that for thirty years. Meeting you again like this seems to have put the clock back. Tubby was his nickname in the old days, due to his obscene obesity. Did you ever run across him when you were at the Criterion?'

Maudie was breathing emotionally. A strange light had come into her blue eyes.

'Did I ever run across him! Why, I was going to marry him.'

'What!'

'Only he never turned up.'

'Never turned up?'

'Never turned up. I waited an hour and a quarter at the church with my bunch of lilies of the valley in my hand, and then I came away.'

Gally was not one of those monocled men who are always taking their monocle out of their eye and polishing it. He reserved this gesture for occasions when he was much moved, This was one of them. For perhaps half a minute he sat in silence, thoughtfully passing his handkerchief over the crystal, while his guest, her mind back in the past, heaved gently, from time to time drinking beer in a manner that betrayed the overwrought soul.

'Too bad,' he said at length.

'Yes, it annoyed me a good deal, I must say.'

'I'm not surprised. Enough to upset anyone. A rather similar thing happened to Mariana of the Moated Grange, and she was as sick as mud. You really mean he never showed up?'

'Not a sign of him. It's my belief he blew the honeymoon money in at the races and hadn't the nerve to tell me. Because it was all settled. He was living down at Shepperton-on-Thames at that time, and I'd had a letter from him making all the arrangements. I can remember every word of it as if was yesterday. Be at St Saviour's, Pimlico, two o'clock sharp June the seventh, he said. Nothing could be plainer than that, could it? And then all the stuff about going to Paris for the honeymoon. Well, I don't know how you feel about it, but I think there's something not quite nice in telling a girl to meet you at the church and you'll get married and then not showing up,' said Maudie with a touch of austerity. 'That sort of thing sounded funny, I admit, when you heard Vesta Victoria singing about it ... Remember?'

Gally nodded.

'I remember. "There was I, waiting at the church ..." '

'Waiting at the church ...'

'Waiting at the church ...'

'For he'd gone and left me in the lurch. Lord how it did upset me ...'

'—set me.'

'Yes,' said Maudie, suspending the community singing, 'that sort of thing's funny enough in a music hall song, but it's no joke when it happens to you, you can take it from me. Makes a girl feel silly. So he's Sir Gregory Parsloe now?'

'Sir Gregory Parsloe, Bart. A cousin of his died, and he came into the title. Did you ever see him again?'

'No.'

'Did he write?'

'Not a word.'

'Just faded away like a dream at daybreak? Well, that's Parsloe,' said Gally philosophically. 'What else could you expect of a man capable of loading my dog Towser up with steak and onions on the night of the rat contest? But I can readily understand that it must have been an unpleasant experience for you, old girl. Must have given you a jaundiced idea of the male sex. Still, you got over it.'

'Oh, I got over it.'

'You were well out of it, if you ask me. Were you happy with the late Stubbs?'

'Yes, Cedric and I were very happy.'

'There you are, then,' said Gally buoyantly. 'All's well that ends well. No good brooding over what might have been. Let the dead past bury its dead, and all that sort of thing. Well, I'm glad you told me this, Maudie, because it stimulates and encourages me. If young Parsloe did you down in that scurvy fashion, you will be up and doing with a heart for any fate, unremitting in your efforts to get a bit of your own back on the son of a bachelor, straining every nerve to foil his evil schemes. Which is precisely the spirit we want to see in you at this juncture. More beer?'

'No, thanks.'

'Then we might be strolling along and picking up the station taxi, Jno Robinson proprietor. I suppose it's about time I sprang you on the old folks. Keep calm when you meet Connie. And when you see Beach, for goodness sake don't go losing your head and flinging yourself into his arms with a "Hey, hey, Uncle Sebastian!"' said Gally. 'Treat him with distant hauteur, and if you can manage an occasional "Ah, my good man" or "Ha, Beach, my honest fellow," it will help the general composition greatly.'

2

In all properly regulated country houses the hours between tea and dinner are set aside for letter writing. The strength of the company retire to their rooms, heavy with muffins, and settle down to a leisurely disposal of their correspondence. Those who fall asleep try again next day.

Lady Constance Keeble, having a boudoir of her own as well as a bedroom, had gone there as soon as tea on the terrace was over, to relay the latest from Blandings Castle to Mr Donaldson of Long Island City. She had just finished, and was relaxing over a cigarette, when the door opened and her brother Galahad came in.

'Yes?' she said, in a voice in which sisters like her do say 'Yes?' to brothers like Gally. She also raised her eyebrows.

Her intrepid visitor was not the man to be quelled by this sort of thing.

'Step out of the frame, Mona Lisa,' he said briskly. 'I came to hear what you think of this Mrs Bunbury.'

It was a point on which he was most anxious to obtain first-hand information. On presenting Maudie to Lady Constance at the tea table, he had observed the chatelaine of Blandings Castle blink twice, rapidly, rather in the manner of a woman who has been slapped between the eyes with a wet fish, and the spectacle had momentarily disconcerted him. He had not needed Beach to tell him that his sister's standards in the matter of guests were exacting, and there was unquestionably quite a good deal of that passed-for-adults-only stuff about Maudie. He had been forced to ask himself if she had made the grade.

But after that first electric moment it seemed to him that everything had gone with a swing, nor in arriving at this conclusion had he erred. Confronted with Maudie, Lady Constance had certainly blinked, but almost immediately had reminded herself that this guest of hers was American. One always, she knew, has to budget for a touch of the spectacular in the outer crust of the American Society woman. This concession made, she had speedily been won over by the polished elegance of Maudie's deportment, which, as always, was considerable, with the result that the letter to Mr Donaldson now lying on her desk was a definitely enthusiastic one. In her view of the presiding genius of Digby's Day and Night Detectives she was seeing eye to eye with the Shropshire lads, the landlord of the Emsworth Arms and the latter's growing son Percy.

'Nice woman, I thought.'

'Very. I have just been writing to Mr Donaldson to tell him how much I like her.'

'That's fine. That's splendid. That's the way to talk.'

'I don't see why you are so interested.'

Gally gave her a rebuking look.

'My dear Connie,' he said, 'I am interested, as you put

it, because I am extremely fond of Penny Donaldson and would not have liked her to be upset. This Mrs Bunbury is a close friend of her father, and she is naturally anxious for her to get the green light. Picture the poor child's feelings if you had drawn yourself up in that sniffy way of yours and come the *grande dame* over Ma Bunbury. And it might easily have happened. If I've caught you being the haughty English aristocrat once, I've caught you a hundred times. It gets you greatly disliked on all sides.'

'Let me relieve your mind. Mrs Bunbury is a little odd-looking, but I think she is quite attractive.'

'So do I.'

'Not that that matters. Well, good-bye, Galahad.'

'And so does Clarence, by Jove. I've never seen him take to a member of the opposite sex so wholeheartedly. Usually, if you try to make Clarence say What ho to a female of the species, he's off over the horizon like a jack rabbit. But you would not be putting it too strongly if you said that he took this Mrs Bunbury to his bosom. He was all over her. Watching them go off together to see the Empress, I was reminded of a couple of sailors on shore leave at Marseilles. Astounding!'

'I am rather busy, Galahad.'

'Eh?'

'I say I am rather busy.'

'You're not in the least busy. When I came in, you were smoking a gasper with your feet on the mantelpiece.'

'My feet were not on the mantelpiece.'

'And in another minute you'd have been asleep, snoring your head off.'

'How dare you say I snore? I never snore.'

'That is not the point at issue,' said Gally. 'The point at issue is the way you have been behaving since I blew in. Your manner has been most peculiar. It has wounded me a good deal. If your own brother can't come and pay you a friendly visit without having you blinding and stiffing at him like a bargee, things have reached a pretty pass in English family life.'

The conversation was approaching a stage where it might easily have developed into one of those distressing brother-and-sister brawls, for both participants were of high spirit, but at this moment Lord Emsworth appeared, giving tongue immediately in the high, plaintive tenor which he used when he felt ill-treated.

'Stamps!' said Lord Emsworth. 'I am writing a letter and I have no stamps. Have you been taking my stamps, Constance?'

'I have not been taking your stamps,' said Lady Constance wearily. 'You keep letting your box get empty and forgetting to tell Beach to have it filled. You can have one of mine, if you like.'

'Thank you,' said Lord Emsworth, pacified. 'That will be capital, capital. I am writing to the Shropshire, Herefordshire and South Wales Pig-Breeders' Association.'

'Is it their birthday?' asked Gally, interested.

'Eh? No, not that I know of. But I had a letter from them yesterday, asking me to deliver an address on certain aspects of the Empress. Very flattering, I thought it. I am looking forward to ... My God!' said Lord Emsworth in sudden alarm. 'Shall I have to wear a top hat?'

'Of course you will.'

'And a stiff collar?'

'Well, really, Clarence, do you expect to address these people in pyjamas?'

Lord Emsworth considered this.

'No. No, I see what you mean. No, possibly not pyjamas. But a stiff collar in weather like this!'

'*Noblesse oblige*,' said Gally.

'Eh?'

'I presume what Galahad means is that you have a certain position to keep up.'

'Exactly,' said Gally. 'You've got to impress these pig-breeding blighters. Give 'em the morning coat, the sponge-bag trousers, the stiff collar and the old top hat, and you have them saying to themselves "Golly, these Earls are hot stuff!". Whereas, seeing you dressed as you are now, they would give you the bird and probably start a revolution. You must cow them, Clarence, overawe them, make them say "The half was not told me," like the Queen of Sheba when she met King Solomon. This cannot be done in a ten-year-old shooting coat with holes in the elbows.'

'And flannel trousers that have not been pressed for weeks,' added Lady Constance. 'You look like a tramp. I cannot imagine what Mrs Bunbury thought of you.'

Lord Emsworth started. A quick look of concern came into his face.

'Do you think Mrs Bunbury thought I looked like a tramp?'

'Everything turns,' said Gally, 'on whether she thrust a penny into your hand and told you not to spend it on drink. Did she?'

'No. No, I don't remember her doing that.'

'Then all may be well. Nice woman, that, Clarence.'

'Delightful.'

'You seemed to be getting along with her all right.'

'Oh, capitally.'

'Yes,' said Gally. He wandered to the window and stood looking out. 'I was telling Connie that you reminded me of a couple of . . . Hullo.'

'What's the matter?'

'A strange young man is crossing the terrace.'

'A strange young man?'

'Look for yourself.'

Lord Emsworth joined him at the window.

'Where? I don't see any ... Ah yes, I was looking in the wrong direction. That is not a strange young man. That is my new secretary.'

'I didn't know you had a new secretary.'

'Nor did I till just now, dash it.'

'You'd better go and pass the time of day with him.'

'I have passed the time of day with him, and I must say that, much as I resent having these infernal secretaries thrust upon me, this time the outlook seems considerably brighter than usual. By a most happy chance, this fellow turns out to be a mine of information on the subject of pigs, and we got along capitally together. We were exchanging the customary civilities, when he suddenly said "I wonder if you are interested in pigs, Lord Emsworth?" "God bless my soul, yes," I replied. "Are you?" "They are a passion with me," he said. "I'm afraid I'm rather inclined to bore people about pigs," he went on with a little laugh, and then he told me all sorts of things I didn't know myself. He was most informative about pigs in ancient Egypt. It appears that the ancient Egyptians believed that pigs brought good crops and appeased evil spirits.'

'You could hardly ask more of them than that.'

'With regard to the pig in the time of Christopher Columbus –'

Lady Constance rapped the table.

'Clarence!'

'Yes?'

'Go away!'

'Eh?'

'I came to this room to be alone. Am I not to have a moment of privacy?'

'Yes, come along, Clarence,' said Gally. 'Connie is in a strange mood. We are not wanted here, and I am anxious to meet this gifted youth. What's his name?'

'Whose name?'

'The gifted youth's.'

'What gifted youth?'

'Listen, Clarence,' said Gally patiently. 'You have a new secretary. You concede that?'

'Oh, certainly, certainly.'

'Well, I want to know what his name is.'

'Oh, his name? You mean his *name*. Quite. Quite. It's ... no, I've forgotten.'

'Smith? Jones? Brown? Cholmondeley-Marjoribanks? Vavasour-Dalrymple? Ernle-Plunkett-Drax-Plunkett?'

Lord Emsworth stood in thought.

'No ... Ah, I have it. It's Vail.'

'Vail!'

'Gerald Vail. He asked me to call him Jerry.'

The door closed behind them. The sharp, wordless cry which had proceeded from Lady Constance they attributed to a creaking hinge.

2

Having walked as far as the end of the corridor together, in pleasant conversation on such topics as top hats, secretaries and what a pest their sister Constance was, the brothers parted with mutual expressions of good will, Lord Emsworth to go to the library for a quick look at Whiffle on *The Care Of The Pig*, Gally to toddle out into the gloaming for a breath of air.

As he toddled, he was feeling deeply stirred. It was possible, of course, that there were several Gerald Vails in the world and the one now in residence one of the wrong ones, but it seemed unlikely. The way it looked to Gally was that somehow, by the exercise of he knew not what girlish wiles and stratagems, Penny Donaldson had succeeded in smuggling into the home circle the quite unsuitable young man to whom she had given her heart, and he was filled with a profound respect for the resource and enterprise of the present generation. Where the Emmelines and Ermyntrudes of his Victorian youth, parted from ineligible suitors, had merely dropped a tear and eventually married along lines more in keeping with the trend of parental thought, the Pennys of to-day, full of the rebel spirit, pulled up their socks and got things done.

Her behaviour appealed to everything in this deplorable buccaneer of the nineties which made his sister Constance, his sister Julia, his sister Dora, and all his other sisters wince when they saw him and purse their lips when his name was mentioned, and he was still aglow with admiration, proud that such a girl should have honoured him with her friendship, when he bumped into something solid, and saw that it was the dream man in person.

'Oh, sorry,' said Jerry.

'Not at all,' said Gally courteously. 'A pleasure.'

Seeing the object of Penny's affections at close range, he found himself favourably impressed. For an author Jerry Vail was rather nice-looking, most authors, as is widely known, resembling in appearance the more degraded types of fish, unless they look like birds, when they could pass as vultures and no questions asked. His face, while never likely to launch a thousand ships, was not at all a bad sort of face, and Gally could readily picture it casting a spell in a dim light on a boat deck. Looking at him, he found it easy to understand why Penny should have described him as a baa-lamb. From a cursory inspection he seemed well entitled to membership in that limited class.

Jerry, meanwhile, drinking Gally in, had discovered that this was no stranger he had rammed.

'Why, hullo, Mr Threepwood,' he said. 'You won't remember me, but we've met before. I was introduced to you once by Admiral Biffen.'

Gally retained no recollection of this previous encounter,

but the mention of that honoured name stirred him like a bugle.

'You know Fruity Biffen?'

'I've known him all my life. He's a great friend of an uncle of mine. Major Basham.'

Any doubts Gally might have entertained as to the suitability of this young man as a husband for a girl on whom he looked as a daughter were dispelled. The name of Major Basham was equally as honoured as that of Fruity Biffen.

'You mean Plug Basham is your uncle? God bless my soul, as my brother Clarence would say. One of my oldest friends.'

'Yes, I've often heard him speak of you.'

'We've always been like Damon and what's-his-name. I once put a pig in his bedroom.'

'Really? What made you do that?'

'Oh, it struck me as a good idea. It was the night of the Bachelors' Ball at Hammer's Easton. Old Wivenhoe's pig. Puffy Benger and I borrowed it and put it in Plug's room. I had to leave early next morning, so never learned what happened when he met it. No doubt they got together across a round table and threshed things out. Plug Basham, by Jove! I once saw Plug throw a side of beef at a fellow in Romano's. Laid him out cold, and all the undertakers present making bids for the body. How is he these days?'

'Going as strong as ever.'

'Fruity and I were talking about him only a week ago. Fruity was down here. Not staying at the castle – he can't stand my sister Constance, and I don't blame him. I got him to take a little house along the Shrewsbury road not far from here because I met him in London and he seemed a bit run down and I thought a breath of country air would do him good. But he couldn't stick it out. Too much noise. He said there was a bunch of assorted bugs and insects in his front garden which seemed to be seeing the new year in all night, and he went back to Piccadilly, where he said a man could get a bit of peace. I miss him. Did he ever tell about the time when he and I –'

Gally paused. The story he had been about to relate was a good one, but he was a kindly man and realized that this was no time for stories, however entertaining.

'But I mustn't keep you here talking. You'll be wanting to find Penny. Oh, I know all about you and Penny,' said Gally, noticing that his young friend had leaped skywards as if a red-hot iron had been applied to the seat of his trousers. 'She confided in me.'

Jerry became calmer. He was still not sure how he liked the idea of anyone sharing his sacred secret, but this old boy was so obviously friendly that perhaps in his case one could stretch a point.

'I was just thinking, when you came along,' said Gally, 'what a really exceptional girl she must be to have sneaked you in here as Clarence's secretary without my sister Constance entertaining a single suspicion. Good brains there. How the dickens did she work it?'

'But Penny doesn't know I'm here.'

'What! Then how – ?'

'It was a girl called Gloria Salt who got me the job.'

'Gloria Salt? Oh yes, I remember. She's coming here.'

'She's here already. She drove me down in her car. She's an old friend of mine.' Jerry hesitated. Then he decided to keep nothing back. 'She thought that if I became Lord Emsworth's secretary, I might . . . Did Penny ever say anything to you about a scheme I had for –'

'She told me all. In fact, she tried to touch me for that two thousand.'

'Oh, good Lord, she shouldn't have done that.'

'Quite all right. I enjoyed the novel experience of having someone suppose that I had two thousand pounds.

Yes, I know all about that health cure place idea of yours, and I think it's a good one. The problem, as always, is how to get the cash. How are you coming along with regard to that? Any likely prospects in view?'

'I was just going to tell you. Gloria thought – '

'Because if you have nobody on your list who looks like a snip, you could do far worse than consider my brother Clarence.'

'Why, that's just what Gloria – '

'My brother Clarence,' proceeded Gally, 'is a peculiar chap. He eats, sleeps, and dreams pig, and he was telling us just now how extraordinarily pig-minded you were. You positively stunned him with your fund of information on the subject.'

'Yes, you see I – '

'And the thought that crossed my mind was that, if you played your cards right, you might quite easily put yourself in a position where you could go to him, when acquaintance had ripened into friendship, and sting him for the sum you need. Yes, I know,' said Gally catching his audience's eye and observing that it was bulging. 'It seems to you a bizarre idea. Far-fetched. Potty. The picture you are forming in your mind of me is that of a man talking through the back of his neck. But I know Clarence. Not an easy partner in normal circumstances, he would, I am convinced, lend a ready ear to the blandishments of a fellow pig-lover. You wait and see if I'm not right.'

Jerry was looking like the Soul's Awakening. He stammered with emotion.

'What an amazing coincidence!' he said. 'That's exactly what Gloria told me.'

'You mean she suggested touching Clarence?'

'That's why she wanted me to come here as his secretary.'

'So that you could join him in slapping his pig on the

backside and let your light so shine that eventually you would be in a position to put the bite on him?'

'That's right.'

'Sounds an intelligent girl.'

'Oh, she is. Most intelligent. She – '

Jerry broke off. Gally, eyeing him, saw that his face had lighted up as if someone had pressed a switch. Turning, for what had caused this ecstasy was apparently something that was happening behind him, he perceived Penny approaching.

'Ah!' he said, understanding.

The only flaw in what should have been a moment of unalloyed joy was that Penny was not alone. Walking at her side was a tall, superbly built young man whose dark, Byronic beauty made him look like something that had eluded the vigilance of the front office and escaped from the Metro-Goldwyn lot. Having met him at meals for more than two weeks, Gally had no difficulty in identifying him as Orlo, Lord Vosper.

Penny seemed listless. Her eyes, as she walked, were on the ground. It may have been merely maiden meditation, but it looked to Gally more like the pip, and he wondered what was amiss. He whooped welcomingly, and she looked up. Having done so, she stood staring, the colour draining from her face. She reminded Gally of a girl named Mabel something who, walking with him at a Buckingham Palace garden party in the year 1906, had suddenly become aware that there was a beetle down her back.

'Ah, Penny,' he said, subtle as always, 'I want you to meet Clarence's new secretary. His name is – What did you say your name was?'

'Vail,' said Jerry huskily.

'Vail,' said Gally. 'Nice chap. Draw him out on the subject of pigs. Mr Vail, Lord Vosper.'

Lord Vosper, like Penny, seemed not to be in the highest spirits. He nodded dully at Jerry.

'Oh, we know each other. School together. Hullo, Jerry.'

'Hullo, Wasp. You here?'

'That's right. You here, too?'

'Yes.'

'I thought so,' said Lord Vosper, and returned to his meditations.

He was still occupied with them, and the silence which had fallen was still unbroken, when Sebastian Beach appeared, heading in their direction.

'Pardon me, m'lord,' said Beach. 'A Mr Wapshott is on the telephone, desirous of speaking to you. He implied that the matter was of importance – '

Lord Vosper came out of his trance.

'Wapshott?'

'Yes, m'lord. He stated that he represented the firm of Wapshott, Wapshott, Wapshott, and Wapshott.'

'Reminds me,' said Gally, who never let an opportunity like this pass, 'of the story of the chap in New York who rang up the legal firm of Shapiro, Shapiro, Shapiro, and Shapiro. "Hello," he says, "can I speak to Mr Shapiro?" "Mr Shapiro is in court." "Then I'll talk to Mr Shapiro." "Mr Shapiro is in conference with an important client." "Then connect me with Mr Shapiro." "I'm sorry, but Mr Shapiro has taken the day off to play golf." "Oh, all right, then I'll talk to Mr Shapiro." "*Speaking*." Who is this Wapshott?'

'My income tax chap,' said Lord Vosper. 'Fellow who looks after my income tax,' he added, clarifying the situation still further. 'Better go and see what he wants, I suppose.'

He walked away, followed by Beach, and Gally stared after them. It seemed to him that Beach was looking careworn, and it made him uneasy. These were the times that tried men's souls, and at such times one does not like to see a careworn butler, if that butler is a butler with whom one is sitting in on a campaign that calls for alertness and efficiency on the part of all concerned.

Turning, he saw that Penny was still gazing at Jerry in that odd, dumb way. He came to himself with a start.

'Good Lord, I'm sorry,' he said. 'I'm in the way. I see just how it is, Penny. With every fibre of your being you yearn to do a swan dive into this bimbo's arms, but modesty forbids. "How," you are saying, "can I fulfil and express myself with this old image goggling at me through his eyeglass as if he were sitting in the front row at the circus with his all-day sucker and his bag of peanuts?" It's all right. I'll look the other way.'

There is a type of short, sharp, bitter laugh which is like a yelp of agony and does no good to man or beast. Lady Constance sometimes employed it when she heard someone say what a charming man her brother Galahad was. It was a laugh of this kind that now proceeded from Penny Donaldson, and for the first time there began to steal over Jerry a suspicion that he had been mistaken in supposing this the maddest merriest day of all the glad new year and the world in which he moved the best of all possible worlds.

'Please don't bother, Gally,' she said. 'I have not the slightest wish to dive into Mr Vail's arms. I wonder if you would care to hear a little story?'

'Story? Of course, of course. Go ahead. But what's all this "Mr Vail" stuff?'

'You remember me telling you that I was to have had dinner last night with Mr Vail?'

'Certainly. But – '

Penny went on, still speaking in a strange metallic voice that reminded Jerry of Gloria Salt fulfilling and expressing herself on the subject of Lord Vosper.

94

'We had arranged to meet at the Savoy at eight. I had a fitting in the afternoon, and when I came home at about six I found a telephone message waiting for me. It said that Mr Vail regretted that he would be unable to dine to-night as an important business matter had come up. I was naturally disappointed – '

She choked, and a tear stole down her cheek. Jerry, seeing it, writhed with remorse. He realized how a good-hearted executioner at an Oriental court must feel after strangling an odalisque with a bowstring.

'But, Penny – '

'Please!' She gave him a fleeting look, the sort of look a good woman gives a caterpillar on finding it in her salad, and turned back to Gally. 'I was naturally disappointed, of course, because I had been looking forward very much to seeing him, but I quite understood that these things happen – '

Gally nodded.

'Sent to try us.'

'I quite understood that these things happen – '

'Probably meant to make us more spiritual.'

'I say I quite understood that these things happen,' proceeded Penny, raising her voice and giving Gally a look similar in quality to the one she had just given Jerry, 'and I said to myself that naturally, if Mr Vail had important business, he couldn't be expected to neglect it just for me.'

'But, Penny – '

'So, when Lord Vosper, who was there, suggested that he should give me dinner, I thought it would be a nice way of passing the evening. Lord Vosper, it seems, is very fond of a restaurant called Mario's. He took me there.'

She paused again, this time because Jerry, his eyes leaping from their sockets, had uttered a sound not unlike the howl of a trapped timber wolf.

'We didn't dress,' she resumed, 'so they put us up in the balcony. Do you know Mario's, Gally?'

'Since my time.'

'It's quite nice up in the balcony there. You get a good view of the main floor. And one of the first things I saw on that main floor was Mr Vail attending to his important business. It consisted of dining with a girl who looked like a snake with hips and from time to time having his face patted by her.'

Gally's monocle came swinging round at Jerry like the eye of a fire-breathing dragon. His face was hard and set.

'You abysmal young wart-hog!'

'Oh, you mustn't say that, Gally,' said Penny, gently rebuking. 'I'm sure Mr Vail has a perfectly satisfactory explanation. Probably the girl was the editor of some magazine, discussing a series of stories with him. I believe editors always pat contributors' faces. It creates a friendly atmosphere.'

It cost Jerry an effort to raise his chin and square his shoulders, but he did it. The consciousness of being a good man unjustly accused always helps to stiffen the spinal vertebrae.

'I can explain everything.'

'Why is it,' inquired Penny – she seemed to be addressing a passing butterfly, 'that men always say that?'

'I say it,' said Jerry stoutly, 'because it's true. The girl you saw me dining with was Gloria Salt.'

'Pretty name. A friend of yours?'

'A very dear friend of mine.'

'I thought you seemed on good terms.'

'She patted my face twice.'

'I should have said oftener. Of course, I hadn't a score card with me.'

'Twice,' repeated Jerry firmly. 'And I'll tell you why. Let us take these pats in their order. Pat One was a congratulatory pat when I told her how much I loved you. Pat Two occurred when I was thanking her for having suggested a way by which I might be able to raise that two thousand pounds which I need in order to marry you. So much for your face patting! And if,' Jerry went on, addressing the Hon. Galahad, 'you call me an abysmal young wart-hog again, I shall forget the respect due to your grey hairs and haul off and let you have one right on the maxillary bone. Abysmal young wart-hog, indeed! My motives were pure to the last drop. Gloria Salt rang me up in the afternoon to say she wanted me to give her dinner, promising over the meal to spill this scheme of hers for connecting with the cash, because it was too long, she said, to tell me on the phone. Reluctantly, for it made me feel as if my soul were being passed through a wringer, I broke our date. I dined with her at Mario's. She told me her scheme. I thanked her brokenly, and she patted my face. I may mention that when she patted it, it was as though a kindly sister had patted the face of a blameless brother. So I should be much obliged if you would stop looking at me as if you had caught me stealing pennies from a blind man.'

Penny had already done so. Her lips parted, and she was gazing at him, wide-eyed. There was no suggestion in her expression that she had found him enriching himself at the expense of the blind.

'Furthermore,' said Jerry, now thundering, 'if additional proof is required to drive into your nut the fact that the last thing in the minds of either of us was anything in the nature of funny business, I may mention that Miss Salt – besides being, like myself, pure to the last drop, if not further – is engaged to be married. She is shortly to become the bride of a certain Sir Gregory Parsloe, who, I believe, resides in this vicinity.'

Gally's monocle flew from his eye.

'Parsloe!'

'Parsloe.'

Gally recovered his monocle. But as he replaced it, his hand was trembling. He was a man who prided himself on his British fortitude. Come the three corners of the world in arms and we shall shock them, he had said in effect to Beach and Penny when speaking of the Binstead-Simmons threat, and he had been quite prepared to cope gallantly with a pig girl in the Parsloe pay and a Parsloe minion who went about buying bottles of anti-fat, the large economy size. But add to that pig girl and that minion a Parsloe fiancée, and it seemed to him that things were becoming too hot. No wonder, he felt, that Beach just now had looked careworn. The faithful fellow, possibly listening at some key-hole whilst this Salt girl traded confidences with Lady Constance, must just have had the bad news.

'Oh Lord and butter!' he exclaimed, moved to his depths, and without further speech hastened off in the direction of the butler's pantry. It was obvious to him that the crisis called for another of those staff conferences.

'So there you are,' said Jerry. He stepped forward masterfully. 'I shall now kiss you.'

'Oh, heavens, what a mess!' wailed Penny.

Jerry paused.

'Mess? You believe what I was saying?'

'Of course I believe it.'

'You love me?'

'Of course I love you.'

'All right, then. What are we waiting for? Let's go.'

Penny stepped back.

'Jerry darling, I'm afraid things are more complicated than you think. You see, when I saw that girl pat your face – '

'In a sisterly manner.'

'Yes, but the point is that it didn't *look* sisterly, and I got the wrong angle. So when, just as we were finishing dinner,

Orlo Vosper asked me to marry him –'

'Oh, my God!'

'Yes,' said Penny in a small voice. 'He asked me to marry him, and I said I would.'

CHAPTER FIVE

But what, meanwhile, it will be asked, of George Cyril Wellbeloved, whom we left with his tongue hanging out, the future stretching bleakly before him like some grim Sahara? Why is it, we seem to hear a million indignant voices demanding, that no further mention has been made of that reluctant teetotaller?

The matter is susceptible of a ready explanation. It is one of the chief drawbacks to the lot of the conscientious historian that in pursuance of his duties he is compelled to leave in obscurity many of those to whom he would greatly prefer to give star billing. His task being to present a panoramic picture of the actions of a number of protagonists, he is not at liberty to concentrate his attention on any one individual, however much the latter's hard case may touch him personally. When Edward Gibbon, half-way through his Decline and Fall of the Roman Empire complained to Doctor Johnson one night in a mood of discouragement that it – meaning the lot of the conscientious historian – shouldn't happen to a dog, it was to this aspect of it that he was referring.

In this macedoine of tragic happenings in and around Blandings Castle, designed to purge the souls of a discriminating public with pity and terror, it has been necessary to devote so much space to Jerry Vail, Penny Donaldson, Lord Emsworth and the rest of them that George Cyril Wellbeloved, we are fully aware, has been neglected almost entirely. Except for one brief appearance early in the proceedings, he might as well, for all practical purposes, have been painted on the back drop.

It is with genuine satisfaction that the minstrel tuning his harp, now prepares to sing of this stricken pig man.

There is no agony like the agony of the man who wants a couple of quick ones and cannot get them and in the days that followed his interview with Sir Gregory Parsloe, George Cyril Wellbeloved may be said to have plumbed the depths. It would, however, be inaccurate to describe him as running the gamut of the emotions, for he had had but one emotion, a dull despair as there crept slowly upon him the realization of the completeness with which his overlord had blocked all avenues to a peaceful settlement. He was in the distressing position of finding himself foiled at every point.

Although nobody who had met him would have been likely to get George Cyril Wellbeloved confused with the poet Keats, it was extraordinary on what similar lines the two men's minds worked. 'Oh, for a beaker full of the warm South, full of the true, the blushful Hippocrene!' sang Keats, licking his lips, and 'Oh, for a mug of beer with, if possible, a spot of gin in it!' sighed George Cyril Wellbeloved, licking his; and in quest of the elixir he had visited in turn the Emsworth Arms, the Wheatsheaf, the Waggoner's Rest, the Beetle and Wedge, the Stitch in Time, the Jolly Cricketers and all the other hostelries at which Market Blandings pointed with so much pride.

But everywhere the story was the same. Barmaids had been given their instructions, pot boys warned to be on the alert. They had placed at his disposal gingerbeer, ginger ale, sarsaparilla, lime juice and on one occasion milk, but his request for the cup that clears to-day of past regrets and future fears was met with a firm *nolle prosequi*. Staunch and incorruptible, the barmaids and the pot boys refused to serve him with anything that would have interested Omar Khayam, and he had come away parched and saddened.

But it has been well said of pig men as a class that though crushed to earth, they will rise again. You plot and plan and think you have baffled a pig man, but all the while his quick brain has been working, and it has shown him the way out. It was so with George Cyril Wellbeloved. Just when the thought of the Hon. Galahad Threepwood came stealing into his mind, he could not have said, but it did so steal, and it was as though a light had shone upon his darkness. That dull despair gave way to a flaming hope. Glimmering in the distance, he seemed to see the happy ending.

Although during his term of office at Blandings Castle his opportunities of meeting Gally socially had been rather limited, George Cyril knew all about him. Gally, he was aware, was a man with a feeling heart, a man who could be relied upon to look indulgently on such of his fellow men as wanted a gargle and wanted it quick. According to those who knew him best, his whole life since reaching years of what may loosely be called discretion had been devoted to seeing that the other chap did not die of thirst. Would such a man turn his back on even a comparative stranger, if the comparative stranger were in a position to prove by ocular demonstration that his tongue was blackening at the roots? Most unlikely, thought George Cyril Wellbeloved, and if there was even a sporting chance of securing the services of this human drinking fountain, it was his duty, he felt, not to neglect it.

With pig men, to think is to act. Dinner over and his employer safely in his study with his coffee and cigar, he got out his bicycle and started pedalling through the scented summer night.

The welcome he received at the back door of Blandings Castle could in no sense have been termed a gushing one. Beach, informed that there was a gentleman asking for him and finding that the person thus described was a pig man whom he had never liked and who in his opinion smelled to heaven, was at his most formal. He might have been a prominent Christian receiving an unexpected call from one of the troops of Midian.

George Cyril, in sharp contradistinction, was all bounce and breeziness. Unlike most of those who met that godlike man, he stood in no awe of Beach. He held the view, and had voiced it fearlessly many a time in the tap room of the Emsworth Arms, that Beach was an old stuffed shirt.

'Hoy, cocky,' he said, incredible as such a mode of address might seem. 'Where's Mr Galahad?'

Ice formed on the butler's upper slopes.

'Mr Galahad is in the amber drawing-room with the rest of the household,' he replied austerely.

'Then go and hoik him out of it,' said George Cyril Wellbeloved, his splendid spirit unsubdued. 'I want to see him. Tell him it's important.'

2

In stating that Gally was in the amber drawing-room with the rest of the household, Beach had spoken with an imperfect knowledge of the facts. He had been in the amber drawing-room, but he was now just outside it, seated on the terrace with his friend Maudie, and an observer, had one been present, would have received the impression that both he and his companion had much on their minds. In a situation where it might have been expected that reminiscences of the old days would have been flashing merrily to and fro, they had fallen into a silence, busy with their thoughts.

It is possible that there are in the world women of meek and angelic disposition who, deserted by gentlemen friends at the church door, are capable of accepting the betrayal tranquilly, saying to themselves that boys will be boys, but Maudie was not one of them. Hers was a high and mettlesome spirit, and a sense of grievance still burned within her. For years she had been storing up a number of good things which she proposed to say to her faithful lover, should they meet, and it was bitter to think that now, with only three miles separating them, this meeting seemed as far away as ever. Situated as she was, she could hardly ask for the car to drive her over to Matchingham Hall, and she shrank from the thought of walking there in this sultry summer weather, her views on pedestrianism being much the same as those of Sir Gregory Parsloe.

On the premises of Blandings Castle, as of even date, there were to be found stricken souls in large numbers – it would, indeed, have been almost impossible to have thrown a brick without hitting one – and that of Maudie Stubbs, alias Bunbury, came high up on the list.

Gally's moodiness is equally easily explained. With the man Parsloe's cousin closeted daily with the Empress, the man Parsloe's fiancée established in the house and the man Parsloe himself rubbing his hands and singing 'Yo ho ho and a bottle of Slimmo', a consistent cheerfulness on his part was hardly to be expected. Add to this the tragedy which had darkened the lives of Penny Donaldson and this excellent young fellow Vail, and add to that the telephone conversation he had had with Sir Gregory shortly before dinner, and it cannot be wondered at that he was not his usual effervescent self.

How long the silence might have lasted, it is impossible to say. But at this point the spell was broken by the arrival of Lord Emsworth, who came pottering out of the drawing-room with the air of a man looking for somebody. Having observed Maudie making for the terrace, it had seemed to him that here was a capital opportunity of having a quick word with her outside the orbit of his sister Connie's watchful eye. Conditions for such a *tête-à-tête* could scarcely have been more suitable. The moon was riding serenely in the sky, the air was fragrant with the scent of night-blooming flowers, Lord Vosper, who in addition to playing a red-hot game of tennis had a nice tenor voice, was at the piano singing a song with lots of sentimental stomp in it, and what Lord Emsworth felt was that ten minutes of roaming in the gloaming with Maudie, would just about top it off.

Ever since his brother Galahad had introduced him to the relict of the late Cedric Stubbs on this same terrace, strange and novel emotions had been stirring in Lord Emsworth's bosom. He was a man who since the death of his wife twenty years ago had made something of a lifework of avoiding women. He could not, of course, hope to avoid them altogether, for women have a nasty way of popping up at unexpected moments, but he was quick on his feet and his policy of suddenly disappearing like a diving duck had had excellent results. It was now pretty generally accepted by his little circle that the ninth Earl of Emsworth was not a ladies' man and that any woman who tried to get a civil word out of him did so at her own risk.

To Maudie, however, he had felt from the start strangely drawn. He admired her looks. Her personality appealed to him. 'Alluring' was the word that suggested itself. When he caught Maudie's eye, it was as though he had caught the eye of a woman who was silently saying 'Come up and see me some time', and this – oddly enough – struck him as an admirable idea. So now he had pottered out on to the terrace in the hope of a pleasant exchange of views with her.

But these things never work out perfectly. Here was the terrace, bathed in moonlight, and here was she, bathed in moonlight, too, but here in addition, he now saw, was his brother Galahad, also bathed in moonlight, and the sight brought a quick 'Oh, ah' to his lips. The presence of a third party chilled his romantic mood.

'Hullo, Clarence,' said Gally. 'How's the boy?'

'Quite, quite,' said Lord Emsworth, and drifted back into the drawing-room like a family spectre disappointed with the room it had been told off to haunt.

Maudie came out of her thoughts.

'Was that Lord Emsworth?' she said, for from the corner of her eye she seemed to have seen something flickering.

'Yes, there he spouted,' said Gally. 'But he buzzed off, mumbling incoherently. Walking in his sleep, probably.'

'He's absent-minded, isn't he?'

'Yes, I think one could fairly call him that. If he has a mind, it is very seldom there. Did I ever tell you the story of Clarence and the Arkwright wedding?'

'I don't think so.'

'Odd. It happened about the time when I was a regular client of yours at the Criterion and I told it to everybody else. I wonder why I discriminated against you. The Arkwrights lived out Bridgnorth way, and their daughter Amelia was getting married, so Clarence tied a knot in his handkerchief to remind him to send the bride's mother a telegram on the happy day.'

'And he forgot?'

'Oh, no, he sent it. "My heartfelt congratulations to you on this joyous occasion," he said.'

'Well, wasn't that all right?'

'It was fine. Couldn't have been improved on. Only the trouble was that in one of his distrait moments he sent it, not to Mrs Arkwright but to another friend of his, a Mrs Cartwright, and her husband had happened to die that morning. Diabetes. Very sad. We were all very sorry about it, but no doubt the telegram cheered her up. Did I ever tell you about Clarence and the salad?'

'No.'

'I don't seem to have told you any of my best stories. It was in the days when he was younger and used to let me take him about London a bit. Well, of course, even then it wasn't easy to get him absolutely shining and glittering in lively society and being the belle of the ball, but he did have one unique gift. He could mix a superb salad. As his public relations man, I played this up on all occasions. When men came to me and said "Tell me, Gally, am I correct in supposing that this brother of yours you're lugging around town is about as outstanding a dumb brick and fathead as ever broke biscuit?" I would reply "To a certain extent, my dear Smith or Jones, or whatever the name might be, the facts are as you state. Clarence has his limitations as a social ball of fire – except when it comes to mixing salads. You just get him to mix you a salad one of these days." So his fame grew. People would point him out in the streets and say "That's Emsworth, the chap who mixes salads". And came a day when I took him to the Pelican Club, feeling like the impresario of a performing flea on an opening night, and they handed him the lettuce and the tomatoes and the oil and the vinegar and the chives and all the rest of it, and he started in.'

'And made a mess of it?'

'Not at all. He was a sensational success. He had cut his finger that morning and was wearing a finger-stall, and I had feared that this might cramp his style, but no, it didn't seem to hamper him a bit. He chopped and mixed and mixed and chopped, with here a drop of oil and there a drop of vinegar, and in due season the salad was prepared in a lordly bowl and those present flung themselves on it like starving wolves.'

'And they liked it?'

'They loved it. They devoured it to the last morsel. There wasn't so much as a shred of lettuce or a solitary chive left in the bowl. And then, when everyone was fawning on Clarence and slapping his back, it was noticed that he was looking disturbed and unhappy. "What's the matter, old man?" I asked. "Is something wrong?" "Oh, no," he said. "Everything is capital, capital . . . only I seem to have lost my finger-stall." That's Clarence. A sterling fellow whom I love as if he were my own brother, which he

is, of course, but a little on the dreamy side. I remember
my nephew Freddie saying once that if you sent him out to
buy apples, he would come back with an elephant, and
there was considerable justice in the remark. He dodders.
He goes off into trances. And you're seeing him at his worst
these days, for he has much on his mind. He has a speech
to make to-morrow which involves a stiff collar and a top
hat, and he's naturally worried about his pig and the
machinations of the man Parsloe. The shadow of Parsloe
broods over him like a London fog. You've seen that dark
girl with the serpentine figure who's just blown in here?'

'Miss Salt?'

'That's the one. Parsloe's fiancée. Makes you think a
bit, eh? They're closing in on us, old girl, closing in on us.
The iron ring is narrowing. It won't be long now . . . Oh,
dash it, here comes someone else,' said Gally, clicking his
tongue. 'The curse of Blandings Castle, no privacy. Oh,
no, it's all right. I think it's Penny.'

It was Penny. In the amber drawing-room Lord Vosper,
having finished his torch song, had started another with
even more heartbreak to the cubic inch, and it had been too
much for the poor girl. Rising with a stifled sob, she had
made a dive for the French windows and was now coming
towards them, looking like Ophelia.

'Hullo, there,' said Gally. 'Come and join the party.
Nice night.'

Penny sank into a chair.

'Is it?' she said listlessly.

'Come, come,' said Gally. 'Tails up, my child. You
mustn't let yourself get downhearted. There's too much
defeatism in this joint. I've been meaning to speak to you
about that, Maudie. I've noticed in you, too, a dropping of
the spirits. When I told you that story of Clarence and the
salad, which should have had you rolling in the aisle,
gasping with merriment, you were gazing at me

mournfully all the time. What's the matter? Don't you like it here?'

Maudie sighed. Blandings Castle had been a place of enchantment to her.

'It's wonderful. But I feel I'm not doing anything to help. I'm about as much use as a cold in the head.'

'Come, come.'

'It's true. Uncle Sebastian – '

'Not so loud. Castles have ears.'

'Uncle Sebastian,' Maudie went on, lowering her voice, 'was all wrong when he told you about me. He seems to have given you the idea that I was a sort of Sherlock Holmes or something. All I've done since Cedric passed on has been to kind of look after the agency – answer letters and send out the bills and sort of keep an eye on things. I don't do any of the detective work. I wouldn't know how to begin. That's all done by Mr North and Mr Connor and Mr Fauntleroy. I mean, suppose you wanted divorce evidence or something, you would come and see me, and I'd say Okay, we'll attend to it and it'll be so much as a retainer and so much per week and all that, but then I would hand everything over to Mr Fauntleroy and Mr Connor and Mr North. I don't see any point in my staying on here.'

Gally patted her hand.

'Of course you must stay, my dear child. Your moral support is invaluable. And one of these days you're sure to come up with some terrific idea which will solve all our difficulties. A brainy girl like you? Don't tell me. I shouldn't be surprised if there wasn't one fermenting inside you at this very moment.'

'Well, as a matter of fact – '

'I told you so.'

'I was just going to suggest something when Miss Donaldson came along.'

'You may speak freely before Miss Donaldson, who has been associated with me in a number of my cases.'

Maudie looked about her cautiously. They were alone and unobserved. In the drawing-room Lord Vosper was now singing something so full – judging by the sound – of anguish that they were fortunate in not being able to distinguish the words. Even the melody was affecting Penny unpleasantly.

'What I thought was this. Why don't you steal Tubby's old pig?'

'What!'

A momentary fear that she had said something unladylike flitted through Maudie's mind, but she dismissed it. She had known Gally too long to suppose that he was capable of being shocked.

'Well, he seems to be doing everything he can to queer your old pig, so why shouldn't you start? Attack ... what's that thing you hear people say?'

'Attack is the best form of defence?'

'That's right. If I were you, I'd sneak over to his house and wait till there was nobody around – '

Gally patted her hand again.

'What you propose, my dear Maudie,' he said, 'would, of course, be the ideal solution, and the suggestion strengthens the high opinion I had already formed of your resource and intelligence. But there are obstacles in the way. The catch is that there would be somebody around.'

'How do you know that?'

'I have it from an authoritative source. Just before dinner I was called to the telephone. It was young Parsloe. He had rung me up, he said, to warn me that if I was contemplating any off-colour work, I would do well to think twice, because he had provided his pig man, Wellbeloved, with a stout shot-gun and Wellbeloved had a roving commission to blaze away with it at all intruders. So there the matter rests. I don't know how accurate a marksman the blighter is, but I certainly don't propose to ascertain by personal inquiry. It would be foreign to my policy to have to take all my meals standing up for the next few weeks because George Cyril Wellbeloved had planted a charge of small shot in my . . . well, that is neither here nor there. As I was saying, with the broad, general idea of pinching Parsloe's pig I am wholly in sympathy. We could put it in that gamekeeper's shack in the west wood and keep it incommunicado there indefinitely. But things being as they are – '

Maudie nodded.

'I see. Then there's nothing to be done?'

'Nothing, I'm afraid, so long as George Cyril Wellbeloved – '

He broke off. The voice of Sebastian Beach had spoken at his elbow, causing him to leap like a lamb in springtime. Absorbed in his remarks, he had had no inkling that there were butlers present.

'You made me bite my tongue, Beach,' he said reproachfully.

'I am sorry, Mr Galahad. I should have coughed.'

'Or tooted your horn. What is it?'

'A person has called, asking to see you, sir. The man Wellbeloved, Mr Galahad.'

'Wellbeloved?' Gally stiffened formidably. 'You mean that this renegade pig man, this latter-day Benedict Arnold, this degraded specimen of pond life, is *here*?'

'I left him in my pantry, sir. He expressed himself as very desirous of having a word with you. The matter, he said, was one of urgency.'

An idea struck Gally. He slapped his forehead. 'My God! Perhaps he has come to betray Parsloe. Perhaps he wants to change sides again. Like Long John Silver. Did you ever read *Treasure Island*, Beach?'

'No, sir.'

'Ass! Or do you think he is here as a spy? No,' said Gally, having mused a moment, 'it can't be that, or why does he want to see me? Would a spy in the pay of Napoleon Bonaparte have come to the British camp before the battle of Waterloo, asking for a word with the Duke of Wellington? I doubt it. Well, I must certainly hear what he has to say. Lead on, Beach, lead on.'

'If you will step this way, Mr Galahad.'

The departure of the most gifted conversationalist of the little group caused another of those long silences. Maudie was a woman who seldom spoke unless spoken to, and any disposition Penny might have had towards small talk was checked by the wailing of Lord Vosper's reedy tenor. He was now singing something about 'You're breaking my heart, we're drifting apart, as I knew at the start it would be,' and no girl who is headed for the altar with the wrong man can prattle when she hears that sort of thing.

Once again it was Lord Emsworth who broke the spell. Hopeful that by now his brother Galahad might have removed himself, he came out of the drawing-room to have another try for that *tête-à-tête*, only to discover that though the terrace was free from Galahads, it had become all stocked up with Penny Donaldsons. He paused, and said 'Er'.

There was another longish silence.

'The moon,' said Lord Emsworth, indicating it.

'Yes,' said Maudie.

'Bright,' said Lord Emsworth, paying it a well-deserved tribute.

'Yes,' said Maudie.

'Very bright,' said Lord Emsworth. 'Oh, very, very bright,' and seemed for a moment about to converse with easy fluency. But inspiration failed him, and with a 'Quite, quite. Capital', he disappeared again.

Penny regarded his retreating back with a listless eye.

'Do you think he's had a couple?' she asked.

It was precisely what had suggested itself to Maudie. In her Criterion days she had encountered many a customer who had behaved in just such a manner, and her seasoned eye could detect little difference between her host and the scores of exuberant young men whom she had seen in the old days conducted gently from her bar with the bouncer's hand caressing their elbow.

Then a more charitable view supervened.

'Of course, he's very absent-minded.'

'Yes, I believe he is.'

'Gally was saying so only just now.'

'Oh, yes?'

Maudie hesitated.

'Talking of Gally,' she said, 'he was telling me yesterday that you – '

'Yes?'

'He was telling me about you. He said you had gone and got engaged to the wrong young man.'

'Quite true.'

Maudie felt relieved. Like all women, she took a passionate interest in the love lives of other women and was longing for a cosy talk about Penny's and she feared that she might have spoken out of turn and given offence.

'Well, that's how it goes,' she said. 'That happened to me once. Someone rang me up on the telephone one morning and said "Hoy!", and I said "Yes?", and he said "This is Tubby", and I said "Hullo, Tubby", and he said "Hullo, Maudie – I say, will you marry me?", and I said "Rather, of course I will", because I was very much in love with him at the time and quite pleased that he had mentioned it. And it was only after we had made all the plans for the honeymoon that I found it wasn't the Tubby I'd thought it was, but another Tubby whom I didn't like at all. And there I was, engaged to him. I often laugh when I think of it.'

'What did you do?'

'Oh, I gave him the bird. I told him to go fry an egg.'

'Lucky you could.'

'Why, any girl can break off an engagement, can't they?'

'I can't.'

'Why not?'

'Because if I did, Lady Constance would write and tell Father, and Father would have me shipped back to America on the next boat, and I would never see Jerry again. He can't keep coming over to America with ocean liners charging the earth, the way they do.'

'I see what you mean. You would be sundered by the seas.'

'Sundered like nobody's business.'

'Well, that *is* a nice bit of box fruit, isn't it?'

Penny was agreeing that the expression 'A nice bit of box fruit' unquestionably summed up the position of affairs, when out came Lord Emsworth again. For centuries the Emsworths had been noted for their dogged courage, and this time he was resolved that Operation Maudie should be carried through.

'Er,' said Lord Emsworth.

'Er, Mrs Bunbury,' said Lord Emsworth.

'Er, Mrs Bunbury, I – ah – I am just going down to have a look at the Empress,' said Lord Emsworth. 'I wonder if you would care to join me?'

'I'd love to,' said Maudie.

'Capital, capital,' said Lord Emsworth. 'Capital, capital, capital, capital.'

They had scarcely gone, when there was a patter of feet and Gally appeared.

Even in the uncertain light cast by the moon it was easy to see that Gally was in radiant spirits. His eyes were sparkling, his whole demeanour that of a man who has found the blue bird. Whatever had passed between him and George Cyril Wellbeloved, it was plain that it had acted on him like a tonic.

His opening words left no room for doubt on this point.

'I do believe in fairies!' he said. 'There *is* a Santa Claus! Penny, do you know what?'

'What?'

'Listen attentively. This gargoyle Wellbeloved has been pouring out his heart to me. It appears that Parsloe, wishing to keep the fellow alert and on his toes, ruthlessly ordered him to go on the wagon, and furthermore gave instructions to all the pubs in Market Blandings that they weren't to serve him. Did this blot the sunshine from Wellbeloved's life, you ask? It did. The poor chap was in despair. Then he remembered that I was a man with a feeling heart, and he came over here to ask me to do something about it.'

'You mean plead with Parsloe?'

'No, no, no. You can't plead with a hard nut like Parsloe. The man has no bowels of compassion. He wanted me to give him a drink. You see the tremendous significance of this?'

'No.'

'You disappoint me. I'd have thought you would have grasped it in an instant. Why, dash it, it means that the coast is clear. The menace of that shot-gun has ceased to function. I have instructed Beach to lush this Wellbeloved up in his pantry, and he will continue to lush him up till the stuff comes trickling out of the top of his head, while I, taking the car, nip over to Parsloe's lair and remove his pig to that shack in the west wood of which I spoke. Any questions?'

'Yes,' said Penny. 'Isn't Parsloe's pig pretty big?'

'Enormous. It bestrides the narrow world like a Colossus.'

'Then how are you going to remove it?'

'My dear child, pigs have rings through their noses. This facilitates pulling and hauling.'

'You'll never be able to do it.'

'What do you mean, I'll never be able to do it? Of course I'll be able to do it. When Puffy Benger and I stole old Wivenhoe's pig the night of the Bachelors' Ball at Hammer's Easton, we had to get it up three flights of stairs before we could put it in Plug Basham's bedroom, and we found the task an absurdly easy one. A little child could have led it. Why, my nephew Ronald, from motives which I have not the leisure to go into now, once stole the Empress, and I resent the suggestion that I am incapable of performing a task within the scope of a young poop like Ronnie Fish. Never be able to do it, forsooth!' said Gally, burning with honest indignation. 'I can do it on my head. I can do it blindfolded, with one arm tied behind me. So if you wish to be in this, Penny Donaldson, get moving. Come, Watson, come. The game is afoot!'

3

It was some ten minutes later that Gloria Salt, who had been sitting silent and pensive in the amber drawing-room, rose from her chair and said that if Lady Constance didn't mind, she would say good night. One or two things to attend to before turning in, she explained, and glided out.

For a long instant after she had left, Lord Vosper, who had gallantly opened the door for her, stood motionless, the handle in his hand, a strange light in his eyes. The sound of her voice, the scent of her perfume, the sight of her so near to him that he could have slapped her between the shoulder-blades – not that he would have, of course – had affected him powerfully. Standing there, he was wrestling with an almost overmastering urge to dash after her and fold her in his arms and beg her to let bygones be bygones.

It is too often the way. A girl whom we have set on a pedestal calls us an overbearing louse, and love dies. Goodbye to all that, we say to ourselves, wondering what we could ever have seen in her. And then she suddenly pops up out of a trap at the house where we are staying, and before we can say 'What ho!' love has sprung from the obituary column and is working away at the old stand more briskly than ever.

Lord Vosper became calmer. What a writer of radio drama would have called the moment of madness, sheer madness, passed and Reason returned to her throne. He rebuked himself for having allowed his thoughts to wander in such a dubious direction. He had received his early education at Harrow, and Old Harrovians, he reminded himself, when they have plighted their troth to Girl A, do not go about folding Girl B in their arms. Old Etonians, yes. Old Rugbeians, possibly. But not Old Harrovians. With a sigh and a gesture of resignation he closed the door and returned to the piano. Resuming his seat on the music stool, he began to sing once more.

'The sun is dark (*tiddle-om*) . . . The skies are grey (*tiddle-om*) . . . since my sweetie (*pom*) . . . went away,' sang Orlo Vosper, and Gloria Salt, in her bedroom above, clenched her hands as the words came floating in through the open window and stared before her with unseeing eyes.

Youth, according to most authorities, is the season for gaiety and happiness, but one glance at this girl would have been enough to show that nobody was likely to sell that idea to her. Her lovely face was twisted with pain, her dark eyes dull with anguish. If she had appeared, looking as she was looking now, in one of the old silent films, there would have been flashed on the screen some such caption as:

BUT CAME A DAY WHEN REMORSE GNAWED GLORIA SALT. THINKING OF WHAT MIGHT HAVE BEEN HER PROUD HEART ACHES.

And such a caption would have been roughly correct.

To Gloria Salt, as well as to Lord Vosper, the past few days had been days of severe strain, filling her with emotions so violent that she had become more like a volcano than a girl with a handicap of six at St Andrews. Arriving at Blandings Castle and finding herself confronted first crack out of the box by a man whom in that very instant she realized that she loved more passionately than ever, she had received a severe shock. Nor was the turmoil in her soul in any way lessened by the discovery that, since last heard of, he had gone and got engaged to that saffron-haired midget one saw bobbing about the place, answering, she understood, to the name of Penelope Donaldson.

Forced, this afternoon, to play mixed doubles with Jerry Vail against her lost lover, partnered by the midget, she had drained the bitter cup, the ordeal being rendered still more testing by the fact that the midget, displaying unexpected form at the net, had kept killing her warmest returns. And to-night she had been listening to Orlo Vosper's singing.

It was, in short, the last moment when a man with as many chins as Sir Gregory Parsloe should have thrust himself on her notice. And this he now unfortunately did. We have said that Gloria Salt's eyes, as she stared before her, were unseeing, but at this juncture the mists cleared and they began to focus. And the first thing they saw was the photograph of Sir Gregory on the dressing-table.

Strolling through the jungles of Brazil, the traveller sometimes sees a barefoot native halt with a look of horror, his body rigid except for a faint vibration of the toes. He has seen a scorpion in his path. It was with just such a look of horror that Gloria gazed at the photograph of Sir Gregory Parsloe. Very imprudently, he had had himself taken side face and, eyeing those chins, she winced and caught her breath sharply. She took another look, and her mind was made up. She had thought it could be done, but she saw now that it could not be done. There are shots which are on the board, and shots which are not. It might be that some day some girl, veiled in white, would stand at the altar rails beside this vast expanse of Baronet while the organ played 'The Voice That Breathed O'er Eden', but that girl would not be G. Salt.

With a sudden, impulsive movement she snatched the photograph from its frame and with a quick flick of the wrist sent it skimming through the open window. Then, hurrying to the desk, she took pen and paper and began to write.

Half an hour later Sebastian Beach, crossing the hall, heard his name spoken and, turning, saw that what had come into his life was a sinuous form clad in some clinging material which accentuated rather than hid its graceful outlines.

'Miss?' he said.

This, he knew, was the fiancée of the Professor Moriarty of Matchingham Hall and as such to be viewed with concern and apprehension, but twenty years of buttling had trained him to wear the mask, and there was nothing in his manner to suggest that he was feeling like a nervous character in a Gerald Vail story trapped in a ruined mill by one-eyed Chinamen.

'I want this note taken to Sir Gregory Parsloe,' said Gloria. 'Could someone go over with it in the morning?'

Sinister, felt Beach, very sinister. Dispatches, probably in code. But he replied with his customary courtesy.

'The communication can be delivered to-night, miss. Sir Gregory's pig man is at this moment in my pantry. I will entrust it to his care.'

'Thank you, Beach.'

'Not at all, miss. The individual will be leaving shortly on his bicycle.'

If, thought Beach, he is able to ride a bicycle with all that stuff in him. He moved ponderously off. He was on his way to the cellar for a bottle of Bollinger. Mr Galahad's instructions had been that in the matter of entertaining their guest the sky was to be regarded as the limit, and George Cyril Wellbeloved had expressed a desire for that beverage. He had heard it mentioned, he said, by Sir Gregory's butler, his friend Herbert Binstead, and had often wondered what it was and wished he could have a pop at it.

4

The process of going to have a look at the Empress was always, when you did it in Lord Emsworth's company, a lengthy one, and nearly forty minutes elapsed before Maudie and her host returned to the terrace.

Lord Emsworth had employed these forty minutes shrewdly and well. Playing on his companion's womanly sympathy by telling her of the agonies he was enduring, having to make this dashed speech to these dashed Shropshire, Herefordshire, and South Wales Pig-Breeder chaps, he had won from her a promise that she would accompany him next day and see him through his ordeal. It made such a difference to someone, he explained, if someone had someone someone could sort of lean on at times like this, and Maudie said she quite understood. They would have to make a pretty early start, he warned her, because Shropshire, Herefordshire, and South Wales Pig-Breeders were assembling in Wolverhampton of all ghastly places, and Maudie said she liked early starts and spoke of seeing Wolverhampton as if it had been a lifelong dream of hers. In short, by the time they reached the terrace, their relations were practically those of Tristan and Isolde.

They found the terrace empty, for Penny had accepted Gally's invitation to go off with him in the car. She might be heartbroken, but she was not so heartbroken as to hold herself aloof from an enterprise which involved stealing pigs. Except for the winged creatures of the night which haunt English country house terraces when the shadows have fallen, nothing was to be seen except a small oblong object lying in the fairway. It looked like a photograph, and Lord Emsworth, picking it up, found that it was a photograph.

'God bless my soul!' he said. 'How very peculiar.'

'What is it?' asked Maudie.

'It is a photograph of a neighbour of mine, a Sir Gregory Parsloe. Lives out Matchingham way. Somebody must have dropped it out of the window. Though what anyone would want with a photograph of Sir Gregory Parsloe I cannot understand,' said Lord Emsworth, marvelling at the eccentric tastes of his fellow men.

Maudie took it from him, and gazed at it in silence. And as her eyes fell, for the first time in ten years, upon those once familiar features, her bosom seethed with feelings too deep for utterance. Like Gloria Salt, she had become a volcano.

Her one coherent thought, apart from the reflexion that this old love of hers had put on a bit of weight since she had seen him last, was that, even if it meant a three mile walk there and a three mile walk back, she intended to go to Matchingham Hall at the earliest opportunity and tell Tubby Parsloe what she thought of him.

5

Beach need have had no anxiety as to his guest's ability to negotiate without disaster the three miles that separated him from home. George Cyril Wellbeloved, even when as brilliantly illuminated as he was when he started his journey, did not fall off bicycles. He might swoop from side to side of the road like a swallow in pursuit of mayfly, but the old skill was all there and he remained in the saddle. In due season he arrived at the back door of Matchingham Hall, singing 'When Irish Eyes Are Smiling' in a pleasant light baritone, and proceeded to Sir Gregory's study to deliver Gloria Salt's note. It would have been far more fitting, of course, for him to have given it to Binstead, to be taken to the presence on a silver salver, but he was in merry mood and welcomed this opportunity of a chat with his employer.

The latter was reading a cookery book as he entered. Some hold the view that a sorrow's crown of sorrow is remembering happier things, but Sir Gregory found that it gave him a melancholy pleasure to be wafted back into the golden past by perusing the details of the sort of dishes where you start off with a dozen eggs and use plenty of suet for the pastry. At the moment he was deep in the chapter about Chocolate Soufflé. And he had just got to the part where the heroine takes two tablespoonfuls of butter and three ounces of Sunshine Sauce and was wondering how it all came out in the end, when he had a feeling that the air in the room had become a little close and, looking up, saw that he had a visitor.

'What the devil are you doing here?' was his kindly greeting, and George Cyril Wellbeloved, smiling a pebble-beached smile of indescribable suavity, replied that he had come to bring him a note. By a hair's breadth he avoided calling Sir Gregory 'cocky', but only by a hair's breadth, and the other gave him one of those keen looks of his.

'You've been drinking!' said Sir Gregory, an able diagnostician.

George Cyril Wellbeloved was amazed.

'Drinking, sir? Me, sir? No, sir. Where would I get a drink, sir?'

'You're as tight as an owl.'

This was a wholly unjustified slur on a most respectable breed of bird, for owls are as abstemious as the most bigoted temperance advocate could wish, and at another time

George Cyril Wellbeloved might have been tempted to take up the cudgels on their behalf. But his employer's charge had cut him to the quick, and he sank into a chair and brushed a tear from his eye.

'Sir,' he said, 'you will regret those words, regret 'em on your dying bed you will. On that last awful day, when we are all called to render account before the judgement seat, you'll be sorry you spoke so harsh. I'm not angry – just terribly, terribly hurt . . .'

'Stop drivelling. What's all this about a note? Who from?'

'That I am unable to tell you, sir, not knowing. It was entrusted to me by Butsch the beetler at Blandings Castle. Or, rather,' said George Cyril Wellbeloved, for he liked to get these things right, 'by Beet the bushler—'

'And might I ask what you were doing at Blandings Castle?'

George Cyril, though intoxicated, was able to dodge that one.

'I was revisiting the scenes of the past, sir. Nos-something, they call it. I spent many a happy year at Blandings Castle, and I wanted to see what the old place looked like. I don't know if you are familiar with the poem that begins "How dear to this heart are the scenes of my childhood, when fond recollection presents them to view." I learned it at Sunday school. It goes on about an old oaken bucket.'

There was something in the manner in which Sir Gregory damned and blasted not only his companion but the latter's Sunday school and the poems he had learned there that wounded the sensitive pig man afresh. He relapsed into a hurt silence, and Sir Gregory took the letter. He opened it, and the next moment a startled cry was echoing through the room.

'Bad news, old man?' asked George Cyril sympathetically, rising and leaning negligently on the arm of his host's chair.

Sir Gregory had sprung to the telephone and was busy getting the number of Blandings Castle.

'Beach? ... This is Sir Gregory Parsloe ... Never mind whether it's a good evening or not. I want to speak to Miss Salt ... Eh? ... I don't care if she has retired to her room. Go and fetch her. Tell her I want to speak to her about her letter—'

'Let *me* see that letter,' said George Cyril Wellbeloved, curtly.

He twitched it out of Sir Gregory's hand and with a little difficulty, for his eyes for some reason were not at their best to-night, spelled his way through it with now a 'Humph' and anon a 'Tut, tut', while Sir Gregory at the telephone continued his unsuccessful efforts to establish communication with Miss Salt.

'I tell you ... Oh, hell!' shouted Sir Gregory, and replaced the receiver with a bang.

George Cyril Wellbeloved laid down the letter.

'And now,' he said, 'I suppose you're waiting to hear what *I* think of all this.'

Sir Gregory, aware for the first time that his private correspondence had been read by a pig man, and a smelly pig man at that, was able for the moment merely to stare with bulging eyes, and George Cyril proceeded.

'Well, I'll tell you. It's the bird all right. What you've been doing to bruise that gentle heart, I don't know. That is a matter between you and your own conscience. But there's no two questions about it, she's given you the raspberry. If you've ordered your trousseau, cocky, cancel it.'

An animal howl burst from Sir Gregory Parsloe.

'What the devil do you mean by reading my letters? Get out! You're sacked!'

George Cyril's eyebrows rose.

'Did I hear you employ the word "sacked"?'

'Yes, you did. Get out of here, you foul blot, and be off the place first thing to-morrow.'

It is at moments like this that you catch a pig man at his best. Nothing could have been more impressive in its quiet dignity than George Cyril Wellbeloved's manner as he spoke.

'Very good,' he said. 'Have it your own way.' He paused on the verge of trying to say 'It's wholly immaterial to me,' but wiser counsels prevailed and he substituted the more prudent 'Okey doke'. 'The Alligultural Show'll be along at any minute now, and if you want to dispense with my services and see your ruddy pig fobbed off with an hon. mention, do so. But drop the pilot now, Sir Gregory Parsloe, and Queener Mash'n hasn't a hope. Not a nope,' said George Cyril Wellbeloved, and rested his case.

In these days when changes in the public taste have led to the passing from the theatre of the old-fashioned melodrama, it is not often that one sees a baffled Baronet. But anyone who had chanced to glance in at the window of Sir Gregory Parsloe's study now would have been able to enjoy that spectacle. In the old melodramas the baffled Baronet used to grab at his moustache and twirl it. Sir Gregory, having no moustache, was unable to do this, but in every other respect he followed tradition.

He recognized the truth of this man's words. Pigs are temperamental. With them, things have to be just so. Remove the custodian to whose society they have become accustomed and substitute a stranger, and they refuse their meals and pine away. Incredible as it seemed to Sir Gregory that a level-headed pig could detect charm in George Cyril Wellbeloved, he knew that it was so, and when he took out his handkerchief and blew his nose, that fluttering handkerchief was the white flag.

'We'll talk about it to-morrow,' he said. 'Go away and sleep it off,' he added, a little offensively, and George Cyril

Wellbeloved zigzagged to the door and left him to his thoughts.

Whether it was the gipsy in him, calling him out into the great open spaces, or merely a desire to cool a head heated almost to bursting point by his recent excesses, one cannot say. But now, zigzagging from the study and zigzagging to the front door, George Cyril Wellbeloved zigzagged out into the grounds of Matchingham Hall and presently found himself at Queen of Matchingham's sty.

Grasping the rail, he chirruped. After that unpleasant scene with his employer, a few words with a personal friend like Queen of Matchingham were just what he needed to restore his composure.

Usually he had but to stand here and start chirruping, and the first chirrup brought the noble animal out at a gallop, all eagerness for the feast of reason and flow of soul. But now all was silence. Not a movement could be heard from within the shed where the Queen retired for the night. He chirruped again. No response. A little annoyed at this absence of the get-together spirit, he climbed the rail, not without difficulty, and peered in at the entrance of the shed. The next moment he had uttered a wordless gasp. If that gasp had had words, those words would have been 'Gone! Gone without a cry!' For the outstanding feature of the interior of that shed was its complete freedom from pigs of any description.

Nothing is more sobering than a sudden, severe shock. An instant before, George Cyril Wellbeloved had been a jovial roisterer, Bollinger swishing about inside him and the vine leaves in his hair. An instant later, it was as though he had spent the evening drinking the lime juice they had tried to push off on him at the Beetle and Wedge or the milk with which he had been insulted at the Jolly Cricketers.

Bravely and forcefully though George Cyril had spoken to Sir Gregory Parsloe in their recent interview when the subject of the sack had come up, his words had been dictated by the beer, whisky, gin, and champagne surging in his interior. Now that they had withdrawn their support, he quailed as he thought of what must befall when Sir Gregory discovered that he was a pig short. The last thing he desired was to lose his excellent position.

How long he stood there, leaning against the empty sty, he would not have been able to say. But after an extended period of limp stupefaction life slowly returned to his drooping limbs. His face pale and drawn, he tottered to the house and made for the butler's pantry. There are moments when a fellow needs a friend, and his best friend on the premises of Matchingham Hall was Herbert Binstead.

6

When a man has gone about Market Blandings offering five to one on his employer's pig and, having booked a number of bets at those odds with the younger sporting set, learns that the pig has vanished like a Cheshire cat, it is excusable for him to show a little emotion. Binstead, who was reading the morning paper when George Cyril arrived with the bad news, tore it in half with a convulsive jerk and leaped from his chair as if a red-hot skewer had come through its seat.

'Pinched?' he gasped.

'R.,' said George Cyril, and added, prefacing the latter's name with some rather regrettable adjectives, that this was the work of the Hon. Galahad Threepwood. He mentioned some of the things, mostly of a crudely surgical nature, which, if given a free hand, he would have liked to do to that ingenious old gentleman.

Having said all he could think of on the spur of the moment with reference to Gally, he paused and looked at Herbert Binstead, not exactly confidently but with a faint touch of hope. It might be, he felt, that the other would have something to suggest. Binstead was one of those fox-faced, quick-witted young men who generally have something to suggest.

His trust had not been misplaced. A considerable time elapsed before his companion was able to point the way, but eventually a sudden gleam in his eye showed that he had received the necessary inspiration.

'Look,' said Binstead. 'Do you know where this pig of old Emsworth's is?'

George Cyril said the Empress was at Blandings Castle, and Binstead clicked his tongue impatiently.

'Whereabouts at Blandings Castle?'

'Down by the kitchen garden.'

'And she knows you?'

'Of course she knows me. I looked after her for a year or more.'

'So if you went and snitched her, she wouldn't make a fuss about it?'

'Coo!' said George Cyril, stunned as the brilliancy of the idea hit him. He had known all along, he told himself, that good old Herb would be equal to the emergency.

'She would let you take her?'

'Like a lamb,' said George Cyril. 'Without so much as a grunt.'

Binstead was now the big executive, the man who gets things done.

'Then come along,' he said. 'We can sneak the car from the garage. We'll load her in at the back.'

George Cyril Wellbeloved expelled a deep breath. The outlook was still a little dark, but one major point had been established. When on the morrow Sir Gregory Parsloe came to the sty for his morning visit of inspection, he was going to find a pig in it.

CHAPTER SIX

THE following day dawned bright and clear. The skies were blue, the birds twittered, all Nature smiled. But Nature's example was not followed by Lord Emsworth. Apart from the galling necessity of having to put on a stiff collar and a top hat and make the early start of which he had spoken, he had caught a cold. Sneezes and snuffles punctuated the unmanly complaints with which he damped all spirits at the breakfast table. Even the thought of having Maudie at his side seemed to do little to alleviate his gloom.

They got him off eventually, though Lady Constance had to exercise the full force of her personality to stop him going down to take a last farewell of the Empress, and Gally was restoring himself with a cigar on the terrace, when he observed Lord Vosper approaching. It seemed to be Lord Vosper's wish to have speech with him.

And this was odd, for their relations had never been intimate. There was little in the characters of the two that could serve as a common meeting-ground. Orlo Vosper, who was an earnest young man with political ambitions, given, when not slamming them back over the net, to reading white papers and studying social conditions, thought Gally frivolous; and Gally thought Orlo Vosper, as he thought most of his juniors in these degenerate days, a bit of a poop and not at all the sort of fellow he would have cared to take into the old Pelican Club.

But though a man one would have hesitated to introduce to Fruity Biffen, Plug Basham and the rest of the boys at the Pelican, Orlo Vosper belonged to the human race, and all members of the human race were to Gally a potential audience for his stories. It was possible, he felt, that the young man had not heard the one about the duke, the bottle of champagne and the female contortionist, so he welcomed him now with a cordial wave of his cigar.

'Nice day,' he said. 'Going to be hotter than ever. Well, we got old Clarence off.'

'That's right.'

'Never an easy task. Launching Clarence on one of these expeditions is like launching a battleship. I sometimes feel we ought to break a bottle of champagne over his head. Arising from that, have you heard the one about the duke, the bottle of champagne and the female contortionist?'

'No,' said Lord Vosper. 'Have you any smelling salts on you?'

Gally blinked. He found himself unable to follow the other's train of thought.

'Smelling salts?'

'That's right.'

'I'm sorry,' said Gally. 'I seem to have come out without mine this morning. Careless. What do you want smelling salts for?'

'I understand one uses them when women have hysterics.'

'Hysterics?'

'That's right.'

'Who's having hysterics?'

'That large girl in the trousers. Looks after the pigs.'

'Simmons?'

'Is that the name?'

'Monica Simmons, the pride of Roedean. Is she having hysterics?'

'That's right.'

'Why is she having hysterics?'

Lord Vosper seemed glad that his companion had put that question.

'Ah,' he said, 'that's what I asked myself. And, what's more, I asked her. I happened to be down in the vicinity of the pig bin just now and found her there, and it seemed to me rather peculiar that she should be laughing and crying and wringing her hands and all that, so I put it to her straight. "Is something the matter?" I said.'

'Came right to the point, didn't you? And was there?'

'Yes, as I had suspected from the outset, there was. She was a bit incoherent at first, gasping and gurgling and calling on the name of her Maker and so forth, but the gist gradually emerged. She had had a bereavement. It appears that that pig of Lord Emsworth's, the one they call the Empress, is missing.'

At any other moment Gally would have said 'On how many cylinders?', for he liked his joke of a morning, but these devastating words put whimsical comedy out of the question. It was as though he had been hit over the head with a blunt instrument. He stood yammering speechlessly, and Lord Vosper thought his emotion did him credit.

'Bad show, what?' he said. 'One needs smelling salts.'

Gally spoke in a low, grating voice.

'You mean the Empress isn't there? She's gone?'

'That's right. Gone with the wind. Or so this Simmons tells me. According to the Simmons, her room was empty and her bed had not been slept in. The pig's bed, I mean, not the Simmons's. I know nothing of the Simmons's bed. For all I've heard to the contrary, it was slept in like billy-o. The point I am making –'

He would have proceeded to elucidate the matter further, rendering it clear to the meanest intelligence, but it would have meant soliloquizing, for Gally had left him. His dapper form was flashing along the terrace, and now it disappeared from view, moving rapidly.

'Odd,' thought Lord Vosper. 'Most extraordinary.'

He went off to see if Lady Constance had smelling salts. He was convinced that in some way smelling salts ought to enter into the thing.

Over at Matchingham Hall, Sir Gregory Parsloe was in his study doing *The Times* crossword puzzle, his brow wrinkled as he tried to think what a word in three letters, beginning with E and signifying a large Australian bird, could possibly be. He liked crossword puzzles, but was not very expert at them. Anything more abstruse than the Sun God Ra generally had him baffled.

To those who recall his overnight anguish, it may seem odd that this jilted lover should have been occupying himself with large Australian birds on the morning after the shattering of his romance. But British Baronets, like British pig men, are resilient. They rise on stepping stones of their dead selves to higher things and are quick to discern the silver lining in the clouds. A night's sleep had done wonders for the Squire of Matchingham. We left him a broken man. We find him now mended, in fact practically as good as new.

When a man of Sir Gregory's age and temperament is informed by his prospective bride shortly before the date fixed for their union that she has made other plans and that there will be no wedding bells for him, he is naturally annoyed, but his chagrin is never so deep or so enduring as would be that of someone like Romeo in similar circumstances. Passion, as it is understood by the Romeos, seldom touches the Sir Gregory Parsloes of this world. What passes for love with them is really not much more than a tepid preference. The poet Berlin, seeking material for another 'What'll I Do?' would have had to go elsewhere for inspiration, if he had come looking for it from Sir Gregory Parsloe.

Sir Gregory was mildly fond of Gloria Salt, and had been on the whole rather attracted by the idea of marrying her, but it had not taken him long to see that there was a lot to be said in favour of the celibate life. What was enabling him to bear his loss with such fortitude was the realization that, now that she had gone and broken off the dashed engagement, there was no longer any need for all that bally dieting and exercising nonsense. Once more he was the master of his fate, the captain of his soul, and if he felt like widening his waistline, could jolly well widen it, and no kick coming from any quarter. For days he had been yearning for beer with an almost Wellbelovedian intensity, and he was now in a position to yield to the craving. A tankard stood beside him at this very moment, and in the manner in which he raised it to his lips there was something gay and swashbuckling. A woman is only a woman, he seemed to be saying, but a frothing pint is a drink.

And so, even more so, are two frothing pints. He pressed the bell, and Binstead appeared.

'Hey!' said Sir Gregory. 'Another of those.'

'Very good, sir.'

'Hey!' said Sir Gregory, when a few minutes later the butler returned with the life-giving fluid. He had just remembered something. 'Where did you put that Slimmo stuff?' he asked.

'I placed it in the store-room cupboard, sir. Should I fetch a bottle, sir?'

'No. I don't want ... I've heard from my distant connexion, and he doesn't want the stuff. Pour it down the sink.'

'Or should I return it to the chemist, sir? He would possibly be willing to refund the money.'

'All right. Do that, if you like. If you can get anything out of him, you can keep it.'

'Thank you very much, sir,' said Binstead. There might not be much in the transaction, but there ought to be something. And every little bit added to what you've got makes just a little bit more.

It was now approaching the hour when it was Sir

Gregory's custom to go and pay his respects to Queen of Matchingham, and as he had finished his beer and saw no prospect of ever solving the mystery of that large Australian bird, he rose, lit a fresh cigar with a debonair flourish and made his way to the sty.

The first thing he beheld on arrival was George Cyril Wellbeloved propped up against a tree, obviously in the grip of one of those hangovers that mark epochs, the sort of hangover you tell your grandchildren about when they come clustering round your knee. He looked like the things you find in dust-bins, which are passed over with a disdainful jerk of the head by the discriminating alley cat, and so repellent was his aspect that after a brief 'Good morning' – and even that caused the pig man to quiver like a smitten blancmange – Sir Gregory averted his gaze and transferred it to the occupant of the sty.

And as he did so, he suddenly stiffened, blinked, gasped, dropped his cigar and stood staring.

'What?' he stammered. 'What? What? What?'

The next moment, it seemed to George Cyril Wellbeloved that the end of the world had come and Judgement Day set in with unusual severity. Actually, it was only his employer shouting his name, but that was the illusion it created.

'Sir?' he whispered feebly, clutching his temples, through which some practical joker was driving white-hot spikes.

'Come here!' bellowed Sir Gregory.

George Cyril obeyed his master's voice, but reluctantly. Sir Gregory, he had not failed to observe, in addition to being yellow in colour and flickering at the edges, was looking like a touchy tribal god who, dissatisfied with the day's human sacrifice, is preparing to say it with thunderbolts. He feared the shape of things to come.

'What's all this?' the employer roared.

'Sir?'

'What's been going on here?'

'Sir?'

'Don't stand there bleating like a sheep, you loathsome excrescence. You know perfectly well what I mean, blister your insides. Where's my pig? This isn't my pig. What's become of Queen of Matchingham, and what's this damned animal doing here? You've removed my pig and substituted a blasted changeling.'

Except for Lord Emsworth, on whose capabilities in that direction we have already touched, there was not in all Shropshire – and probably not in Herefordshire and South Wales – a more gifted exponent of stout denial than George Cyril Wellbeloved, and in this moment of peril a special effort might have been expected from him. But, in order to deny with the adequate measure of stoutness, a man has to be feeling at the top of his form, and we have been strangely remiss if we have left our public with the impression that George Cyril was at the top of his. He was but a shadow of his former self, his once alert brain a mere mass of inert porridge.

'WELL?'

George Cyril Wellbeloved cracked beneath the strain. One last futile attempt to find an explanation that would cover the facts, at the same time leaving him with an unsullied reputation, and he was telling all, omitting no detail however slight.

It went considerably better than he had anticipated. True, his audience punctuated the narrative by calling him a number of derogatory names, but he was not torn limb from limb, as at one point had seemed likely. Encouraged, he became fluent, and the story went better than ever. As he told of his journey to Blandings Castle and the theft of the Empress, something like a faint smile of approval seemed to flicker across his employer's face.

And, indeed, Sir Gregory was not ill pleased. He began to see daylight. It seemed to him that the position of affairs was somewhat similar to that which would have prevailed in the Malemute saloon if Dangerous Dan McGrew and one of his friends had got the drop on each other simultaneously. And on such occasions compromise and bargaining become possible. Moreover, if he now dispatched this pig man of his to scout around in the grounds of Blandings Castle, it might be possible to ascertain where the hellhounds of the opposition had hidden the Queen. That knowledge acquired, what simpler than to send an expeditionary force to the rescue?

A few minutes later, accordingly, George Cyril Wellbeloved, relieved to find himself still in one piece, was bicycling once more along the old familiar road, while Sir Gregory went to the garage to get out his car. It was his intention to beard Lord Emsworth and that old image, his brother Galahad, in their lair, and tell them one or two things about the facts of life.

'Lord Emsworth in?' he asked, having reached journey's end.

Beach was courtly, but distant.

'His lordship has gone to Wolverhampton, sir.'

'Where's Mr Threepwood?'

'Mr Galahad is also absent.'

'H'm,' said Sir Gregory, wondering what to do for the best, and as he spoke Lady Constance came through the hall.

'Why, good morning, Sir Gregory,' said Lady Constance. 'Have you come to see Clarence?'

'Eh? Oh, good morning. Yes. Wanted to speak to him about something.'

'He won't be back till to-night, I'm afraid. He has gone to Wolverhampton.'

'So Beach was saying.'

'He is making a speech there to some sort of pig-breeding society. But you will stay to lunch, won't you?'

Sir Gregory considered. Lunch? Not a bad idea. He had a solid respect for the artistry of the castle cook, and now

that Gloria Salt had given him the old heave-ho, there was
no obstacle to his enjoyment of it.

'Kind of you,' he said. 'Delighted.'

He looked forward to filling himself to the brim under
Gloria's eyes, defiantly sailing into the potatoes and generally raising hell with the calories. That, in his opinion,
would show her she wasn't everybody.

3

When Gally had left Lord Vosper so abruptly in the middle
of their conversation on the terrace, it was with the intention
of hastening to Matchingham Hall and confronting its proprietor, and such was his agitation of spirit that he was half
way there before he realized that a sensible man would have
taken the car instead of walking. It being too late to turn
back now, he completed the journey on foot, using the short
cut across the fields, and reached his destination in a state of
considerable warmth.

Binstead's manner, as he imparted the information that
Sir Gregory was not at home, should have cooled him, for it
was frigid in the extreme. It was impossible for so young a
butler to be as glacial as Beach would have been in similar
circumstances, but he was as glacial as he knew how to be,
and it disappointed him that this visiting pig stealer appeared quite oblivious to his chilliness. Gally was much too
exhausted by his hike to make a close study of butlers and
notice whether they were hot or cold.

'I'll come in and wait,' he said, and Binstead, though in
inward revolt against the suggestion, did not see what he
could do to prevent the intrusion. Reluctantly he conducted Gally to the study, and Gally, making for the sofa,
put his feet up with a contented sigh. He then outraged
Binstead's feelings still further by asking for a whisky and
soda.

'A good strong one,' said Gally, and such was the magic of his personality that the butler, who had stiffened from head to foot, relaxed with a meek 'Yes, sir'.

When he returned with the restorative, Gally had settled down to *The Times* crossword puzzle.

'Thanks,' he said. 'You don't know what a large Australian bird in three letters beginning with E is, do you?'

'I do not, sir,' said Binstead icily, and withdrew.

For some minutes after he was alone, Gally gave himself up to the crossword puzzle, concentrating tensely. But crossword puzzles are only a palliative. They do not really cure the aching heart. Soon his mind was straying back to the burden that weighed on it, and he put the paper down with a weary sigh and gave himself up to thought.

It might have been supposed that a man who had himself purloined a pig on the previous night would have looked with an indulgent eye on the pig-stealing activities of others, on the principle that a fellow-feeling makes one wondrous kind. But there was nothing resembling tolerant sympathy in Gally's mind as he sat there brooding on Sir Gregory Parsloe. The blackness of the other's villainy appalled him. He could see no excuse for the fellow. Still, there it was and no use thinking about it. He tried to envisage the outcome, were the man to stick to his guns and refuse to restore the Empress.

A superficial thinker would have said in his haste that the thing was a stand-off. If Empress of Blandings had been removed from circulation, he would have reasoned, so had Queen of Matchingham. Here, in other words, were two pigs, both missing, and these two pigs cancelled each other out.

But Gally saw more deeply into the matter, and shuddered at what he saw. What the superficial thinker was overlooking was the fact that while the Empress was the solitary jewel in Lord Emsworth's crown, the man Parsloe had another pig up his sleeve which he could thrust into the arena at a moment's notice. In the whirl of recent events, Pride of Matchingham, the original Parsloe entry, had rather receded into the background, but it was still there, a unit in the Parsloe stable, and if necessary it could do its stuff.

And with what hideous effectiveness! For two years Pride of Matchingham had been runner-up in the contest, and in the absence of the Empress its triumph was assured. In other words, all the man Parsloe had to do was to hang on to the Empress, and he would flourish like a green bay tree. If there was a bitterer thought than that, Gally would have been interested to learn what it was. It was the sudden realization of this angle that had caused Sir Gregory to perk up so noticeably towards the end of his interview with George Cyril Wellbeloved.

After a three mile walk on a hot summer morning, followed by a stiffish whisky-and-soda in a comfortable arm chair, a man who is getting on in years tends to become drowsy, and at this point in his meditations Gally's head began to nod.

For a long time the study remained hushed and still except for an occasional gurgle, like that of a leaky radiator. Then the telephone bell rang, and Gally sat up with a jerk.

He lifted the receiver. Somebody at the other end of the wire was saying 'Sir' – huskily, like a voice speaking from the tomb.

'Who's that?'

'Wellbeloved, Sir Gregory.'

The last mists of sleep cleared from Gally's mind. He became keen and alert. He was a man of the world, and he knew that pig men do not call their employers on the telephone unless they have something urgent to say. Plainly this Wellbeloved was about to plot, and he was consequently in the position of a Private Eye who is listening in on the intimate agenda of the Secret Nine.

'Where are you?'

'I'm phoning from the Beetle and Wedge, Sir Gregory. And I was wondering, Sir Gregory,' proceeded George Cyril Wellbeloved, a pleading note creeping into his voice, 'if under the circs, it being such a warm day and me all worn out from toiling in your interests, I might have a glass of beer.'

'Certainly, certainly,' said Gally heartily. 'Have all you want and tell them to charge it to me.'

There was a silence. It seemed for a moment that the pig man had swooned. When he resumed, it was plain from the new animation with which he spoke that he was feeling that there had been a great improvement in his employer since they had last met. This, he seemed to be saying to himself, was something like sweetness and light.

'Well, sir,' he said, sunnily, 'I've found her.'

'Eh?'

'The Queen, sir.'

Gally reeled. The words had been like a blow between his eyes. He had been so sure that his secret was safe from the world, and here he was, unmasked by a pig man. For a long instant he stood speechless. Then he managed to utter.

'Good God!'

'Yes, sir, it took a bit of doing, but I did it, and I came along here to the Beetle and Wedge to apprise you of her whereabouts. Following your instructions, sir, I proceeded to Blandings Castle ... About that beer,' said George Cyril Wellbeloved, digressing for a moment. 'Would it run to a spot of gin in it, sir?'

'Yes, yes, yes.'

'Thank you, sir. I find it improves the flavour. Well, sir, as I was saying, I proceeded to Blandings Castle and proceeded to lurk unseen. What had occurred to me, thinking it over, was that if the Queen was being held in durance vile – that's an expression they use, sir, I don't know if it's familiar to you – somebody would have to be feeding her pretty soon, and this, I presumed, would be done by an underling, if you understand the word, effecting an egress through the back door. So I lurked near the back door, and sure enough out came Mr Beach, the butler, carrying in his hand a substantial pail and glancing very nervous from side to side as much as to say "Am I observed?" Well, sir, to cut a long story short, he proceeded to proceed to what is known as the west wood – which is a wood lying in a westerly direction – and there fetched up at an edifice which I assumed to have been at one time the residence of one of the gamekeepers. He went in. He effected an entrance,' said George Cyril Wellbeloved, correcting himself, 'and I crope up secretly and looked in through the window, and there was the Queen, sir, as large as life. And then I took my departure and proceeded here and rang you up on the telephone so as to apprise you of what had transpired and leave it to you to take what steps you may consider germane to the issue, trusting I have given satisfaction as is my constant endeavour. And, now, sir, with your permission, I will be ringing off and going and securing the beer you have so kindly donated. Thank you, sir.'

'Hey!' shouted Gally.

'Sir?'

'Where's the Empress?'

'Why, just where we left her, sir,' said George Cyril Wellbeloved, surprised, and hung up.

Gally replaced the receiver, and stood dazed and numb. He was thinking hard thoughts of George Cyril Wellbeloved and wondering a little that such men were permitted to roam at large in a civilized country. If at that moment he had learned that George Cyril Wellbeloved had tripped over a hole in the Beetle and Wedge's linoleum and broken his neck, he would, like Pollyanna, have been glad, glad, glad.

But men of the stamp of the Hon. Galahad Threepwood do not remain dazed and numb for long. Another moment, and he was lifting the receiver and asking for the number of Blandings Castle. And presently Beach's voice came over the wire.

'Hullo? Lord Emsworth's residence. Beach, the butler, speaking.'

'Beach,' said Gally, wasting no time in courteous preliminaries, 'pick up those flat feet of yours and race like a mustang to the west wood and remove that pig. That blasted Wellbeloved was tailing you up when you went to feed the animal, and has just been making his report to me, thinking that I was the man Parsloe. We've got to find another resting place for it before he realizes his error, and most fortunately I know of one that will be ideal. Do you remember Fruity Biffen? Don't be an ass, Beach, of course you remember Fruity Biffen. My friend Admiral Biffen. Until a few days ago he was living in a house on the Shrewsbury road. You can't mistake it. It's got a red roof, and it's called Sunnybrae. Take this pig there and deposit it in the kitchen. What do you mean, what will Admiral Biffen say? He isn't there. He went back to London, leaving the place empty. So put the pig ... What's that? *How*? Use a wheelbarrow, man, use a wheelbarrow.'

4

In his office in Long Island City, N.Y., Mr Donaldson of Donaldson's Dog Joy was dictating a cable to his secretary.

'Lady Constance Keeble, Blandings Castle, Shropshire, England. Got that?'

'Yes, Mr Donaldson.'

Mr Donaldson thought for a moment. The divine afflatus descended on him, and he spoke rapidly.

'"Cannot understand your letter just received saying you find my old friend Mrs Bunbury so charming. Stop. Where do you get that old friend Mrs Bunbury stuff. Query mark. I never had an old friend Mrs Bunbury. Stop. If person calling self Mrs Bunbury has insinuated self into Blandings Castle claiming to be old friend of mine, comma, she is a goshdarned impostor and strongly advocate throwing her out on her . . ." What's the word, Miss Horwitt?'

'Keister, Mr Donaldson.'

'Thank you, Miss Horwitt. "Strongly advocate throwing her out on her keister or calling police reserves. Stop. Old friend of mine forsooth. Stop. The idea. Stop. Never heard of such a thing. Stop."'

'Shall I add "Hoity-toity", Mr Donaldson?'

'No. Just kindest regards.'

'Yes, Mr Donaldson.'

'Right. Send it direct.'

CHAPTER SEVEN

THE annual binge or jamboree of the Shropshire, Herefordshire and South Wales Pig Breeders' Association is always rather a long time breaking up. Pig breeders are of an affectionate nature and hate to tear themselves away from other pig breeders. The proceedings concluded, they like to linger and light pipes and stand around asking the boys if they know the one about the young man of Calcutta. It was consequently not till late in the afternoon that the car which had taken Lord Emsworth and Maudie to Wolverhampton – Alfred Voules, chauffeur, at the wheel – began its return journey.

Stress was laid earlier in this narrative on the fact that the conscientious historian, when recording any given series of events, is not at liberty to wander off down byways, however attractive, but is compelled to keep plodding steadily along the dusty high road of his story, and this must now be emphasized again to explain why the chronicler does not at this point diverge from his tale to give a word for word transcript of Lord Emsworth's speech. It would have been a congenial task, calling out all the best in him, but it cannot be done. Fortunately the loss to Literature is not irreparable. A full report will be found in the *Bridgnorth, Shifnal and Albrighton Argus* (with which is incorporated the *Wheat Growers' Intelligencer and Stock Breeders' Gazetteer*), which is in every home.

Nor is he able to reveal the details of the conversation in the car, because there was no conversation in the car. It was Lord Emsworth's custom, when travelling, to fall asleep at the start of the journey and remain asleep throughout. Possibly on a special occasion like this a strong man's passion might have kept him awake, at least for the first mile or two, but the cold from which he was suffering lowered his resistance and he had had a tiring day trying to keep his top hat balanced on his head. So Nature took its toll, and Maudie, watching him, was well pleased, for his insensibility fitted in neatly with her plans. She was contemplating a course of action which she would have found difficult to carry out with a wakeful host prattling at her side.

As the car neared the home stretch and his thoughts, like drifting thistledown, had begun to turn to supper and beer, Alfred Voules heard the glass panel slide back behind him and a hushed voice say 'Hey!'

'Listen,' whispered Maudie. 'Do you know a place called Matchingham Hall? And don't yell, or you'll wake Lord Emsworth.'

Alfred Voules knew Matchingham Hall well. He replied in a hoarse undertone that it was just round the next bend in the road and they would be coming to it in a couple of ticks.

'Stop there, will you. I want to see Sir Gregory Parsloe about something.'

'Shall I wait, ma'am?'

'No, don't wait. I don't know how long I shall be,' said Maudie, feeling that hours – nay days – might well elapse before she had finished saying to Tubby Parsloe all the good things which had been accumulating inside her through the years. Hell hath no fury like a woman scorned, and when a woman scorned starts talking, she likes to take plenty of time. She does not want to have to be watching the clock all the while.

The car slowed down and slid to a halt outside massive iron gates flanked by stone posts with heraldic animals on top of them. Beyond the gates were opulent-looking grounds and at the end of the long driveway a home of England so stately that Maudie drew her breath in with a quick

'Coo!' of awe. Tubby, it was plain, had struck it rich and come a long way since the old Criterion days when he used to plead with her to chalk the price of his modest refreshment up on the slate, explaining that credit was the life-blood of Commerce, without which the marts of trade could have no elasticity.

'This'll do,' she said. 'Drop me here.'

2

Sir Gregory Parsloe had just sat down at the dinner table when the door bell rang. He had had three excellent cocktails and was looking forward with bright anticipation to a meal of the sort that sticks to the ribs and brings beads of perspiration to the forehead. He had ordered it specially that morning, taking no little trouble over his selections. Some men, when jilted, take to drink. Sir Gregory was taking to food. Freed from the thrall of Gloria Salt, he intended to make up for past privations.

Le Diner
Smoked Salmon
Mushroom Soup
Filet of Sole
Hungarian Goulash
Mashed Potatoes
Buttered Beets
Buttered Beans
Asparagus with Mayonnaise
Ambrosia Chiffon Pie
Cheese
Fruit
Petits Fours

Ambrosia Chiffon Pie is the stuff you make with whipped cream, white of egg, powdered sugar, seeded grapes, sponge cake, shredded coconut and orange gelatin, and it had been planned by the backsliding Baronet as the final supreme

146

gesture of independence. A man who has been ordered by his fiancée to diet and defiantly tucks into Ambrosia Chiffon Pie has formally cast off the shackles.

He had unfastened the lower buttons of his waistcoat and was in the act of squeezing lemon juice over his smoked salmon, when the hubbub at the front door broke out. It was caused by Maudie demanding to see Sir Gregory Parsloe immediately and Binstead explaining – politely at first, then, as the argument grew more heated, in a loud and hostile voice – that Sir Gregory was at dinner and could not be disturbed. And the latter was about to intervene in the debate with a stentorian 'What the devil's all that noise going on out there?' when the door flew open and Maudie burst in, with Binstead fluttering in her wake.

The butler had given up the unequal struggle. He knew when he was licked.

'Mrs Stubbs,' he announced aloofly, and went off, washing his hands of the whole unpleasant affair and leaving his employer to deal with the situation as he thought best.

Sir Gregory stood staring, the smoked salmon frozen on its fork. It is always disconcerting when an unexpected guest arrives at dinner time, and particularly so when such a guest is a spectre from the dead past. The historic instance, of course, of this sort of thing is the occasion when the ghost of Banquo dropped in to take pot luck with Macbeth. It gave Macbeth a start, and it was plain from Sir Gregory's demeanour that he also had had one.

'What? What? What? What? What?' he gasped, for he was a confirmed what-whatter in times of emotion.

Maudie's blue eyes were burning with a dangerous light.

'So there you are!' she said, having given her teeth a little click. 'I wonder you can look me in the face, Tubby Parsloe.'

Sir Gregory blinked.

'Me?'

'Yes, you.'

It occurred to Sir Gregory that another go at the smoked salmon might do something to fortify a brain which was feeling as if a charge of trinitrotoluol had been touched off under it. Fish, he had heard or read somewhere, was good for the brain. He took a fork-full, hoping for the best, but nothing happened. His mind still whirled. Probably smoked salmon was not the right sort of fish.

Maudie, having achieved the meeting for which she had been waiting for ten years, wasted no time beating about the bush. She got down to the *res* without preamble.

'A nice thing that was you did to me, Tubby Parsloe,' she said, speaking like the voice of conscience.

'Eh?'

'Leaving me waiting at the church like that!'

Once more Sir Gregory had to fight down a suspicion that his mind was darkening.

'*I* left *you* waiting at the church? I don't know what you're talking about.'

'Don't try that stuff on me. Did you or did you not write me a letter ten years ago telling me to come and get married at St Saviour's, Pimlico, at two o'clock sharp on June the seventh?'

'June the what?'

'You heard.'

'I did nothing of the sort. You're crazy.'

Maudie laughed a hard, bitter laugh. She had been expecting some such attitude as this. Trust Tubby Parsloe to try to wriggle out of it. Fortunately she had come armed to the teeth with indisputable evidence, and she now produced it from her bag.

'You didn't, eh? Well, here's the letter. I kept it all these years in case I ever ran into you. Here you are. Look for yourself.'

Sir Gregory studied the document dazedly.

'Is that your handwriting?'

'Yes, that's my handwriting.'

'Well, read what it says.'

'"Darling Maudie –"'

'Not that Over the page.'

Sir Gregory turned the page.

'There you are. "Two o'clock sharp, June seven".'

Sir Gregory uttered a cry.

'You're cockeyed, old girl.'

'How do you mean, I'm cockeyed?'

'That's not a seven.'

'What's not a seven?'

'That thing there.'

'Why isn't it a seven?'

'Because it's a four. June 4, as plain as a pikestaff. Anyone who could take it for a . . . Lord love a duck! You don't mean you went to that church on June the seventh?'

'Certainly I went to that church on June the seventh.'

With a hollow groan Sir Gregory took another fork-full of smoked salmon. A blinding light had shone upon him, and he realized how unjustified had been those hard thoughts he had been thinking about this woman all these years. He had supposed that she had betrayed him with a cold, mocking callousness which had shaken his faith in the female sex to its foundations. He saw now that what had happened had been one of those unfortunate misunderstandings which are so apt to sunder hearts, the sort of thing Thomas Hardy used to write about.

'I was there on June the fourth,' he said.

'What!'

Sir Gregory nodded sombrely. He was not a man of great sensibility, but he could appreciate the terrific drama of the thing.

'In a top hat,' he went on, his voice trembling, 'and, what's more, a top hat which I had had pressed or blocked or whatever they call it and in addition had rubbed with stout to make it glossy. And when you didn't show up and after about a couple of hours it suddenly struck me that you weren't going to show up, I took that hat off and jumped on it. I was dashed annoyed about the whole business. I mean to say, when a man tells a girl to meet a fellow at two o'clock sharp on June the fourth at St Saviour's, Pimlico, and marry him and so on, and he gets there and there isn't a sign of her, can a chap be blamed for feeling a bit upset? Well, as I was saying, I jumped on the hat, reducing it to a mere wreck of its former self, and went off to Paris on one of the tickets I'd bought for the honeymoon. I was luckily able to get a refund on the other. I had quite a good time in Paris, I remember. Missed you, of course,' said Sir Gregory gallantly.

Maudie was staring, round-eyed, the tip of her nose wiggling.

'Is that true?'

'Of course it's true. Dash it all, you don't suppose I could make up a story like that on the spur of the moment? You don't think I'm a ruddy novelist or something, do you?'

This was so reasonable that Maudie's last doubts were resolved. She gulped, her eyes wet with unshed tears, and when he offered her a piece of smoked salmon, waved it away with a broken cry.

'Oh, Tubby! How awful!'

'Yes. Unfortunate, the whole thing.'

'I thought you had blown in the honeymoon money at the races.'

'Well, I did venture a portion of it at Sandown Park, as a matter of fact, now you mention it, but by great good luck I picked a winner. Bounding Bertie in the two-thirty at twenty to one. What a beauty! I won a hundred quid.

That is what enabled me to buy that hat. The money came in handy in Paris, too. Very expensive city, Paris. Never believe anyone who tells you living's cheap there. They soak you at every turn. Though, mark you, the food's worth it, the way they cook it over there.'

There was a silence. Maudie, like Gloria Salt, was thinking of what might have been, and Sir Gregory, his mind back in the days of his solitary honeymoon, was trying to remember the name of that little restaurant behind the Madeleine, where he had had the most amazingly good dinner one night. The first time, he recalled, that he had ever tasted bouillabaisse.

Binstead, who had spent the last ten minutes panting feebly in his pantry, for Acts of God like Maudie had never before come bursting into his placid life and he was feeling somewhat unnerved, had at last succeeded in restoring his aplomb sufficiently to enable him to resume his butlerine duties. He now entered, bearing a tureen, and Sir Gregory was recalled with a start to a sense of his obligations as a host.

'What ho, the soup!' he said, welcoming it with a bright smile. 'I say, now you're here, you'll stay and have a bite of dinner, old girl, what? Eh? Got to be getting along? Don't be silly. You can't turn up after all these years and just say "Hullo, there" and dash off like a ruddy jack rabbit. We've got to have a long talk about all sorts of things. My chauffeur can take you back to wherever you're staying. Where are you staying, by the way, and how on earth do you happen to be in these parts? You could have knocked me down with a toothpick when you suddenly popped up out of a clear sky like that. Mrs Stubbs and I are old friends, Binstead.'

'Indeed, Sir Gregory?'

'Knew each other years and years ago.'

'Is that so, Sir Gregory?'

'You didn't tell me where you were hanging out, Maudie.'

'I'm at Blandings Castle.'

'How the devil did you get there?'

'Gally Threepwood invited me.'

Sir Gregory puffed his cheeks out austerely.

'That gumboil!'

'Why, Tubby, he's nice.'

'Nice, my foot! He's a louse in human shape. Well, come along and sit down,' said Sir Gregory, abandoning the distasteful subject. 'There's a Hungarian goulash due at any moment which I think you'll appreciate, and I stake my all on the Ambrosia Chiffon Pie. It's made of whipped cream, white of egg, powdered sugar, seeded grapes, sponge cake, shredded coconut, and orange gelatin, and I shall be vastly surprised if it doesn't melt in the mouth.'

The presence of Binstead, hovering in the background with his large ears pricked up, obviously hoping to hear something worth including in his Memoirs, prevented anything in the nature of intimate exchanges during the meal. But when he had served the coffee and retired, Sir Gregory, heaving a sentimental sigh, struck the tender note.

'Dashed good, that goulash,' he said. 'It isn't every cook in this country who knows how to prepare it. The paprika has to be judged to a nicety, and there are other subtleties into which I need not go at the moment. Which reminds me. I wonder, old girl, if you remember me standing you dinner one evening years ago – or, rather, you standing me, as it turned out, because I was compelled to stick you with the bill – at a little place in Soho where they dished up a perfectly astounding Hungarian goulash?'

'I remember. It was in the spring.'

'Yes. A lovely spring evening, with a gentle breeze blowing from the west, the twilight falling, and a new moon glimmering in the sky. And we went to this restaurant and there was the goulash.'

'You had three helpings.'

'And you the same, if memory serves me aright. With a jam omelette to follow. That's what I always admired about you, Maudie, you never went in for this dieting nonsense. You enjoyed your food, and when you had had it, you reached out for more, and to hell with what it did to your hips. Too many girls nowadays are mad about athletics and keeping themselves fit and all that, and if you ask me, they're a worse menace to the peaceful life of the country-side than botts, glanders, and foot-and-mouth disease. An example of this type of feminine pestilence that springs to the mind is my late fiancée, Gloria Salt. Physical fitness was her gospel, and she spread disaster and desolation on every side like a sower going forth sowing.'

'Aren't you still engaged to Miss Salt?'

'Not any more. She sent me round a note last night telling me to go and boil my head. And a very good thing, too. I should never have asked her to marry me. A rash act. One does these foolish things.'

'Didn't you love her?'

'Don't be silly. Of course I didn't love her. There was some slight feeling of attraction, possibly, due to her lissom figure, but you couldn't call it love, not by a jugful. I've never loved anyone but you, Maudie.'

'Oh, Tubby!'

'You ought to know that. I told you often enough.'

'But that was years ago.'

'Years don't make any difference when a fellow really bestows his bally heart. Yes, dash it, I love you, old girl. I fought against it, mark you. Thinking you had let me down, I tried to blot your image from my mind, if you follow what I mean. But when you came in at that door, looking as beautiful as ever, I knew it was no good strug-gling any longer. My goose was cooked. It was just as though I had been taken back to the old days and was

153

leaning against your bar, gazing into your eyes, while you poured the whisky and uncorked the small soda.'

'Oh, Tubby!'

'And later, when I watched you wading into that Ambrosia Chiffon Pie, obviously enjoying it, I mean to say *understanding* it, not pecking at it the way most of these dashed women would have done but plainly getting its inner meaning and all that, I said to myself "My mate!" I realized that we were twin souls and that was all there was about it.'

'Oh, Tubby!'

Sir Gregory took a moody salted almond, frowning as he ate it.

'You keep saying, "Oh, Tubby!" but a fat lot of use that is. I said we were twin souls, and we are twin souls, but under prevailing conditions what's the *good* of our being twin souls? Where do we go from there? I mean, you can't get away from the fundamental fact that you're married.'

'No, I'm not.'

'Pardon me. You must have forgotten. I distinctly heard Binstead announce you as "Mrs Stubbs".'

'But Cedric's dead.'

'I'm sorry to hear that,' said Sir Gregory politely. 'Here to-day and gone to-morrow, what? Who is Cedric?'

'My husband.'

Sir Gregory, who had taken another salted almond, held it poised in air. He looked at her with a wild surmise.

'Your husband?'

'Yes.'

'He's *dead*?'

'He died five years ago.'

Sir Gregory was so moved that he returned the salted almond to its dish untasted.

'Let's get this straight,' he said, his voice and chins

shaking a little. 'Let's keep our heads and thresh this thing out calmly and coolly. You say your husband is no longer with us? He has handed in his dinner pail? Then, as I see it, this means that you're at a loose end, like me.'

'Yes.'

'Nothing in the world to stop us getting married any dashed moment we care to.'

'No.'

Sir Gregory reached out for her hand as if it had been a portion of Ambrosia Chiffon Pie.

'Then how about it, old girl?'

'Oh, Tubby!' said Maudie.

3

Most men, having started out in a car with a lady friend and discovered at journey's end that she was no longer there, would have felt a certain surprise at this shortage and probably asked a lot of tedious questions. To Lord Emsworth, woken with a respectful prod in the ribs by Alfred Voules at the door of Blandings Castle and finding himself alone, it never occurred to wonder what had become of Maudie en route. He seldom worried about things like that. If women vanished out of cars, they vanished. There was nothing you could do about it, and no doubt all would be explained in God's good time. So he merely blinked, said 'Eh? What? We're there, are we? Quite. Capital,' and tottered in, sneezing. And Gally, who was passing through the hall with Jerry, stared at him, concerned.

'That's a nasty cold you've got, Clarence,' he said, and Jerry thought so, too.

'That *is* a nasty cold you've got, Lord Emsworth,' said Jerry.

Beach appeared, took one look at his employer and formed a swift diagnosis.

'Your lordship has a nasty cold,' he said.

Lord Emsworth, who had subsided into a chair, sniffed without speaking, and the three men looked at one another.

'There's only one thing to do for a cold,' said Gally. 'Boil the feet and slap on an onion poultice.'

'I should have said vinegar tea and a lump of sugar soaked in kerosene,' said Jerry.

'If I might offer a suggestion, Mr Galahad,' said Beach, 'I was reading in the paper this morning of a new American cereal called Cute Crispies. It contains sixty-two per cent of nutro-glutene, and one tablespoonful, I understand, provides nourishment equal to that of a pound and a half of steak. Such a preparation might prove efficacious.'

'I'll tell you what,' said Jerry. 'Suppose I dash off to Market Blandings and collect a few things at that chemist's in the High Street?'

'An excellent idea. Bulstrode's, you mean. It'll be shut, but the blighter lives over the shop, so hammer at the door till he comes down and place your order. What do you think you're doing, Clarence?' asked Gally sternly, for the sufferer had risen and seemed about to accompany Jerry into the great open spaces.

'I was going down to have a look at the Empress.'

Gally and Beach exchanged glances. 'Secrecy and silence!' said Gally's. 'Yes, sir. Precisely, sir,' said that of Beach.

'You're crazy,' said Gally. Do you want to get pneumonia? Bed's the place for you. Beach will bring your dinner on a tray. Won't you, Beach?'

'Certainly, Mr Galahad.'

'And not a word to Lady Constance. We don't want her coming fussing over the poor devil and driving him off his rocker. The one thing a man with a cold in the head must avoid is the woman's touch.'

'Her ladyship is not at home, sir. She has gone to attend

the weekly meeting of the Literary Society at the Vicarage.'

'That's good. It removes a grave threat. Upsydaisy, Clarence.'

'But, Galahad, the Empress.'

'What about her?'

'I want to see how she is.'

Once more that significant glance passed between Gally and Beach.

'Don't you worry about the Empress. I was down taking a look at her only just now, and she's fine. Sparkling eyes. Rosy cheeks. You come along to bed, my dear chap,' said Gally, and a short while later Lord Emsworth was between the sheets, a hot water bottle at his toes, a dinner tray on his lap, and at his side a couple of Edgar Wallaces, donated by Beach in case he felt like reading. On his departure for America, Lord Emsworth's younger son, Freddie Threepwood, had bequeathed to Beach his library of who-dun-its, generally supposed to be the most complete in Shropshire, and he was always glad to give of his plenty.

But Lord Emsworth was in no mood for Faceless Fiends and Things In The Night. A glance at the first of the two volumes had told him that there was a gorilla in it which went climbing up waterpipes, snatching girls with grey eyes and hair the colour of ripe wheat out of their beds in the small hours, but he was a man who could take gorillas or leave them alone. He closed the book and lay there sneezing softly and thinking of Maudie. It saddened him to look back and reflect that by going to sleep in the car he had missed an opportunity which might not occur again of pouring burning words of love into her alabaster ear.

In the matter of pouring burning words of love into people's alabaster ears, Lord Emsworth was handicapped. Blandings Castle was full to bursting point of Nosey Parkers who seemed to have nothing to do except interrupt private conversations, and this rendered it difficult ever to get the desired object alone. Every time you had the stage set for an intimate exchange of ideas, along came somebody breaking it up, and all the weary work to do over again.

It was at this point in his meditations that his eye fell on the desk across the room, and it suddenly struck him that modern civilization has provided other methods of communication between person and person than the spoken word. In the pigeon-holes of that desk were single sheets of notepaper, double sheets of notepaper, postcards, envelopes, telegraph forms, and some of those little pads which enable you to jot down bright thoughts on life in general, while on the desk itself were pens, ink, indiarubber, sealing wax, and what looked like an instrument for taking stones out of horses' hooves. Rising from his sick bed, and ignoring the indiarubber, the sealing wax, and the horses' hooves instrument, Lord Emsworth took pen and paper and began to compose a letter.

It came out splendidly. He was not a very ready letter-writer as a rule, but after a couple of false starts the impassioned prose began gushing up like a geyser. When he had finished, he read the thing over and was stunned by his virtuosity. Just the right note of respectful fervour, he considered, and felt that that drowsiness in the car had been all for the best, for he could never have hoped to speak half as fluently as he had written. What he had got down on four sides of a double sheet of notepaper was the sort of thing that would have earned him a brotherly pat on the back from the author of the Song of Solomon.

As he was licking the envelope, Jerry came in, laden with parcels like a pack mule.

'I've brought you cinnamon, aspirin, vapex, glycerine of thymol, black currant tea, camphorated oil, a linseed poultice, and some thermogene wool,' said Jerry. 'A wide

158

selection is always best, don't you think? And old Pop Bulstrode says you ought to drink hot milk and wear flannel next your skin.'

Lord Emsworth agreed that this sounded like an interesting and even amusing way of passing the time, but his mind was on his letter.

'Er,' he said.

'Yes?' said Jerry eagerly, in pursuance of his policy of hanging on his employer's lightest word.

'I wonder,' said Lord Emsworth, 'if you would do something for me, my dear fellow.'

'Anything, anything,' said Jerry heartily. 'Give it a name.'

'I have written a letter ... a letter ... in short, a letter – '

'I see,' said Jerry, following him so far. 'You mean a letter.'

'Exactly. A letter. A letter to Mrs – ah – Bunbury. I want it delivered as soon as possible, and I thought you might convey it to her.'

'Of course, of course. What a splendid idea! Nothing simpler. I'll slip it to her the moment I see her.'

'No, don't do that. There's sure to be someone hanging about watching your every move. You know how it is in this house. Put it in her room.'

'Pinned to the pincushion?'

'Precisely. Pinned to the pincushion. An excellent suggestion.'

'Which is her room?'

'The second on the right as you go along this corridor.'

'Consider it done,' said Jerry.

As simple a way of endearing himself to the boss, he felt, as could have been thought of. He trotted off, feeling that things were moving.

He was extremely curious to know what the dickens the

old boy was writing letters to Mrs Bunbury about, but he could hardly ask, and if the idea of steaming the thing open with a kettle presented itself to his mind, he dismissed it resolutely. Like Lord Vosper, he was an Old Harrovian.

CHAPTER EIGHT

LORD EMSWORTH lay back in bed. His letter on its way, he was wondering, like all authors who have sent their stuff off, if it could not have been polished a bit and given those last little touches which make all the difference. However, again like all authors, he knew that what he had written, even without a final brush-up, was simply terrific, and it was with a mind at rest that he took up his Edgar Wallace once more.

And he was just thinking that he personally would not have cared to be a gorilla in the employment of a master criminal . . . broken sleep, no regular hours, always having to be shinning up water pipes and what not . . . when a cheery 'Bring out your dead!' interrupted his meditations, and his brother Galahad came in.

'Hullo, Clarence,' said Gally. 'How are you feeling now? I've been thinking about that cold of yours, and I'll tell you the stuff to give it. You want to take a deep breath and hold it as long as you possibly can. This traps the germs in your interior, and not being able to get fresh air, they suffocate. When you finally exhale, the little sons of guns come out as dead as doornails and all you have to do is buy a black tie and attend the funeral. But what profits it to get rid of germs,' he went on, a grave note creeping into his voice, 'when at any moment you are going to have a super-bacillus like Connie at your throat?'

'Eh?'

'That's what I came to tell you. I think you will be receiving a visit from Connie shortly.'

'Oh, dash it!'

'I know just how you feel.'

'She's back, then?'

'With her hair in a braid. And they tell me she is considerably hotted up. I haven't seen her myself, but Beach, who had an extended interview with her, describes her as resembling a gorilla roaring and beating its chest and preparing to rip the stuffing out of the citizenry.'

Lord Emsworth was struck by a coincidence.

'I was reading a story about a gorilla when you came in. A curious animal.'

'What did it do?'

'Well, it seemed to spend most of its time climbing up water pipes and snatching girls from their beds.'

Gally was not impressed. He sneered scornfully.

'Sissy stuff. Obviously a mere amateur. Wait till you meet Connie.'

'But what is the matter with Connie?'

'Ah!' said Gally. 'I'm glad you asked me that. I'd have told you long ago, only you wouldn't let me get a word in edgeways.'

He sat down on the bed, adjusted his monocle and proceeded to tell a tale of strange happenings.

'Omitting birth, early education, and all that sort of thing, we start the Connie Story with her returning to the house at the conclusion of the weekly meeting of the Market Blandings Literary Society. It had been an interesting meeting, and she was in excellent spirits. She walked with a springy step. It wouldn't surprise me if she wasn't singing a snatch of song. In short, at that moment a child could have played with her, and she would probably have given it twopence to buy sweets with.'

Lord Emsworth, as nearly always when listening to a story, was a little fogged.

'I thought you said she was hotted up.'

'So she was . . . a couple of minutes later, and I'll tell you why. On the table in the hall was lying a telegram. Well, when I say telegram, it was actually a cable, shot off from

Long Island City in the United States of America by old man Donaldson, the dog biscuit despot. It was about Mrs Bunbury.'

'I believe they're old friends.'

'Donaldson doesn't. The gist of his cable was that he had never heard of her in his life.'

'Well, I'll be damned!'

'Exactly what Connie said, and she went off to find Mrs Bunbury and ask her for further particulars. She discovered her eventually in the passage near the stairs which lead to Beach's pantry. She was folded in Beach's arms, and he was kissing her fondly on both cheeks.'

Lord Emsworth sneezed.

'*Beach* was?'

'I appreciate your surprise. Strongly anti-traditional, you are feeling. Butlers, you say to yourself, don't kiss guests. Chauffeurs, perhaps. Gamekeepers, possibly. But butlers, never. In extenuation of his odd behaviour, however, I must mention that he is her uncle.'

'Her *uncle*?'

'Yes. Her Uncle Sebastian. I ought to have told you before, and I don't know how it happened to slip my mind, but Mrs Bunbury isn't Mrs Bunbury. She is the widow Stubbs. Her maiden name was, of course, Beach, though when I knew her in the old days as a barmaid at the Criterion, she called herself Maudie Montrose.'

Lord Emsworth looked as if he were about to pick at the coverlet.

'She is a *barmaid*?'

'She was a barmaid. Later, she married the proprietor of a private detective agency, now residing with the morning stars, and it was Beach's revelation of the fact that she was connected with the gumshoe industry that gave me the idea of getting her down here in order to keep an eye on young Parsloe and foil his machinations regarding the Empress.

It seemed to me that she would have the trained mind. She hasn't as a matter of fact, but she can't help that, poor soul, and it's been delightful having her here and swopping stories of the old days. A fascinating companion. But don't let me wander from the main issue. Resuming the run of the scenario, Connie, already sent rocking back on the heels of her short French vamps by that cable, was naturally stirred even further by the spectacle of butlers bounding about the place embracing people. Is this Blandings Castle, she asked herself, or is it the *Folies Bergère*? She reeled off to her boudoir, rang for Beach and started a probe or quiz.'

Gally waited courteously for Lord Emsworth to finish groaning, and resumed.

'It was during this chat that Beach was struck by her resemblance to a gorilla with stomach ulcers, and we can hardly blame him for cracking under the strain. No more loyal fellow than Sebastian Beach ever swigged port, but every man has his breaking-point. Connie, when she comes down like a wolf on the fold with her cohorts all gleaming with purple and gold, is pretty hot stuff, and I'm not surprised that after she had given him the treatment for about a couple of minutes he threw in his hand and spilled the beans. You spoke?'

Lord Emsworth shook his head. He had merely groaned once more.

'Now while Connie realizes, of course, that I was the spearhead of the movement, for I gather that Beach gave me away fairly completely, it is quite possible that she may be suspecting you of complicity in the affair. You know what Connie's like. She takes in a wide field. So I thought the friendly thing was to come and warn you to be prepared. Have your story all planned out. Get tough with her. Talk out of the side of your mouth. For heaven's sake, Clarence, don't keep groaning like that. She can't eat you.

And I don't suppose she'll want to,' said Gally, 'for anything more closely resembling a condemned food product I never saw in my life.' And with a final 'Tails up!' he went out, explaining that while he was not actually afraid of Connie there were moments when women are better avoided till they have come off the boil a bit. One did not, said Gally, want a vulgar brawl.

He left Lord Emsworth frozen where he lay, like a male Lot's wife turned into a pillar of salt.

But he was no longer sneezing. It is a remarkable fact, and one which will interest medical men, that of all the remedies for the common cold which had been suggested to him that night, the shock he had received from Gally's revelations was the only one that had done him any real good. Quite suddenly he had become a well man. It was as though after a course of vinegar tea and Cute Crispies he had taken a deep breath and asphyxiated every germ in his system, regardless of age or sex.

But though physically so greatly improved, spiritually he was in the poorest shape. It is a sad thing to have to record, but his love for Maudie had died as swiftly as if someone had taken it down a dark alley and hit it over the head with a blackjack. All he could think of now was what his sister Constance, always an outspoken woman, would say when she learned that he had written a letter proposing marriage to an ex-barmaid linked by ties of blood to the family butler.

No, not quite all. He was also thinking that after Connie had stopped talking – if she ever did – two alternatives would lie before him . . . one, to be sued for breach of promise; the other, to have to go through life calling Beach 'Uncle Sebastian'.

It was at this moment that Jerry entered, all of a glow. He had just met Penny in the corridor and received renewed assurance of her undying love. True, she was still betrothed to another, but she had flung herself into his arms and kissed him, and that was enough to make his evening. He beamed on Lord Emsworth.

'I deposited the letter,' he said, like a Boy Scout reporting his day's act of kindness.

Lord Emsworth came to life. From a pillar of salt he turned into a semaphore.

'Get it back!' he cried, waving his arms emotionally.

Jerry was perplexed. He could not follow his employer's thought processes.

'Get it back?'

'Yes.'

'You mean unpin it from the pincushion?'

'Yes, yes, yes. I cannot explain now, for every moment is precious, but hurry and bring it back to me.'

If Jerry had any comment to make on this strange attitude, he was unable to give it utterance, for the door had opened and Lady Constance was coming in to join the party.

He thought she eyed him rather frostily on seeing him there, as though any affection she might have been feeling for him had waned a good deal, but a man who has just been kissing dream girls in corridors pays little attention to frosty looks from prominent Society hostesses. He gave her a friendly smile, and said he would be going off and getting that paper.

'What paper?'

'Just a paper Lord Emsworth wanted me to bring him.'

'Why do you want Mr Vail to bring you papers, Clarence?'

'Dash it all,' said Lord Emsworth, panic lending him a weak belligerency. 'Why shouldn't he bring me papers? It's his job, isn't it? He's my secretary, isn't he?'

Lady Constance followed Jerry, as he left the room, with an eye that was bleaker than ever.

'He will not be your secretary long, if I have my way,' she said grimly.

Lord Emsworth was enchanted at this opportunity of steering the conversation away from butlers and their nieces.

'Why won't he be my secretary long, if you have your way?'

'Because I strongly suspect him of making love to Penelope Donaldson and trying to lure her away from Orlo Vosper.'

'Vosper? Vosper? Vosper? Ah, yes, Vosper,' said Lord Emsworth, just in time. A 'Who is Vosper?' might have had the worst results. 'What makes you think he's doing that?'

'I will tell you. When we were in London, a mysterious man rang up on the telephone, asking for Penelope. He gave his name as Gerald Vail and had apparently had a clandestine dinner engagement with her. Next day he arrives here as your secretary, obviously having followed her in accordance with a prearranged plan. And just now, as I was coming along the corridor, I saw them together. Close together,' said Lady Constance significantly.

'God bless my soul! What, *clinched* together?'

'When I saw them, they were not actually embracing, if that is what you mean by that peculiar expression,' said Lady Constance coldly. 'But Penelope's face was flushed, and I suspected the worst. If I can find the slightest excuse, I shall dismiss that young man. Really, with all these things happening, Blandings Castle has become a mad-house. Secretaries kissing girls entrusted to my care, butlers kissing – '

'Ah, yes,' said Lord Emsworth airily. 'Galahad was speaking to me about that. He was saying something, if I recollect rightly, about Mrs Bunbury not being Mrs Bunbury.'

'Her name is Stubbs, and she is Beach's niece.'

'Yes, I seem to recall him mentioning that. I remember

thinking at the time that it was curious that a woman should say she was Mrs Bunbury if she wasn't Mrs Bunbury. Seemed a silly thing to do. You don't happen to know what the thought at the back of that was, do you?'

Lady Constance eyed him narrowly.

'Do *you*?'

'Me?'

'Were you in this plot, Clarence?'

Lord Emsworth stiffened his sinews and summoned up the blood.

'What do you mean, was I in this plot? Which plot? What plot? I haven't been in any plots. Do you suppose a busy man like me has time to waste being in plots? Tchah! Bah! Preposterous!'

A lesser woman might have wilted beneath his stern wrath. Lady Constance bore it with fortitude.

'No, I don't think you were. I am sure it was Galahad who was responsible for the whole thing, aided and abetted by Penelope Donaldson, who told me this Mrs Bunbury was an old friend of her father's. I must say I am shocked at the way Penelope has behaved. I thought her such a nice girl, and she has turned out to be thoroughly sly and untrustworthy. If I had not had a cable from Mr Donaldson saying that he had never met a Mrs Bunbury in his life, I might never have discovered what was going on. Of course, my first impulse was to turn the woman out of the house.'

'She's leaving, is she?' said Lord Emsworth, feeling that all things were working together for good.

'No, she is not leaving. Impossible as the situation is, after what Beach told me I have no option but to allow her to remain. I can't offend Sir Gregory.'

'You mean Parsloe?'

'He is the only Sir Gregory we know, I believe.'

'But what's Parsloe got to do with it?'

Lady Constance's expression seemed to suggest that she was swallowing a bitter pill and not liking it.

'According to Beach, this woman and Sir Gregory became engaged to be married this evening.'

'What!'

'I don't wonder you're surprised.'

'I'm amazed. I'm astounded. Dash it, I'm stunned.'

'So was I when Beach told me. I could hardly believe my ears.'

'You mean Parsloe met her for the first time this evening and asked her to marry him?' said Lord Emsworth, with a mild man's respect for a quick worker.

'Of course he did not meet her for the first time this evening. They appear to have known each other in the days before Sir Gregory came into the title. I found Beach kissing her, and he explained that she had just told him the news and he was congratulating her and wishing her happiness. Obviously, if this Mrs Bunbury or Mrs Stubbs or whoever she is is going to marry Sir Gregory, I cannot insult him by turning her out of the house. Life in the country is impossible if you are not on good terms with your neighbours.'

A horrid thought struck Lord Emsworth.

'Are you going to sack Beach?'

'I don't know.'

'I do. I'm dashed if you're going to sack Beach, because ... because I'm dashed if you are,' said Lord Emsworth stoutly. Life without Beach was a thing he did not care to contemplate.

'No,' said Lady Constance, after a moment's thought. 'No, I shall not dismiss Beach. I take the view that he was led astray by Galahad. Galahad! I remember, when we were children,' said Lady Constance wistfully, 'seeing Galahad fall into that deep pond in the kitchen garden. And just as he was sinking for the last time, one of the gardeners came along and pulled him out,' she added, speaking with a sort of wild regret. It was plain that she was in agreement with the poet that of all sad words of tongue or pen the saddest are these 'It might have been'. She paused a moment, brooding on the thoughtless folly of that chuckle-headed gardener. 'Well,' she said, 'I am going to my room to bathe my temples with eau-de-Cologne. I don't know whether I am standing on my head or my heels.'

She went out, and Lord Emsworth, sinking back on his pillows, gave himself up to the first agreeable thoughts he had had for what seemed to him a lifetime.

Engaged to Parsloe, was she? Then at the eleventh hour he was saved and need no longer dread that breach of promise action or its even ghastlier alternative. What happier ending could there be to a good man's vicissitudes? Lord Emsworth had often speculated as to whether there were really such things as guardian angels, and this evening's happenings convinced him of their existence. Only a thoroughly efficient guardian angel who knew his job backwards could have snatched him from the soup with this amazing dexterity just when he had supposed himself to be getting down in it for the third time, like Galahad in his pond.

He regretted that there was presumably no way of getting in touch with his benefactor. It would have been a real pleasure to have sought him out and shaken him by the hand.

2

In houses of the size of Blandings Castle there are always plenty of nooks which might have been specially designed for the convenience of men desirous of avoiding angry women. The billiard-room was Gally's selection on leaving Lord Emsworth. Connie, he felt, whatever her faults, and they were numerous, was not likely to come poking her head into billiard-rooms.

The first thing he saw on entering was Lord Vosper practising cannons in a distrait sort of way, as if his mind were elsewhere. There was a preoccupied look on his handsome face, and the fact that he was bringing off some nice shots appeared to give him little pleasure. On seeing Gally, he brightened, like a shipwrecked mariner sighting a sail.

Lord Vosper, as has been said, considered Gally frivolous and found much to disapprove of in his attitude to life, but he had a solid respect for him as a man of the world who knew what was what, and it was a man of the world who knew what was what that he was in need of now. Problems had arisen in Orlo Vosper's life, and he felt unequal to coping with them alone.

'Oh, hullo,' he said. 'I say, Mr Threepwood, could I speak to you about something?'

'Touch on any topic that comes into your head, my boy, and you will find in me a ready listener,' said Gally cordially. 'What is on your mind? Are you worrying about the situation in the Far East?'

'Not so much the situation in the Far East,' said Lord Vosper, 'as the one right here in Blandings Castle. Some rather disturbing things have been happening and I should very much like your advice. If you have a moment?'

'My time is at your disposal.'

'It's a longish story.'

'Your stories can never be too long, my dear fellow,' said Gally courteously. 'Suppose we park ourselves on this settee and you get it off your chest.'

Seated on the settee with Gally at his side, his face registering sympathetic interest, Lord Vosper seemed to find a difficulty in beginning his story.

'Do you play tennis?' he said at length.

'I was wondering if you were going to ask me that,' said Gally. 'I suppose you're going to ask me next if I've read any good books lately?'

Lord Vosper blushed apologetically. He saw that he had selected the wrong opening for his narrative.

'I don't mean so much Do you play tennis as would you believe that a great romance could be wrecked on the tennis court?'

'Ah, now you're talking. Good heavens, yes. My old friend Buffy Struggles was at one time engaged to a girl who was a keen tennis player, and she returned the ring and letters because, when they were partnered in the mixed doubles one day, he insisted on charging into her half of the court and poaching her shots. And before he could effect a reconciliation, he was run over by a hansom cab in Piccadilly and killed instantaneously.'

'Great Scott!' Lord Vosper was staring, amazed. 'Why, that's exactly what happened to me.'

'Were you killed by a hansom cab?'

'No, but I was engaged to a girl, and she broke it off because I poached her shots.'

'Ah, I see. I misunderstood you. When did this happen?'

'About two months ago.'

'But you've only been engaged to Penny Donaldson two or three days.'

'I'm not talking about Penny Donaldson, I'm talking about Gloria Salt.'

'You mean you were engaged to Gloria Salt?'

'I still am.'

'But you're engaged to Penny Donaldson.'

'I know. That's the trouble. I'm engaged to both of them.'

Gally removed his monocle and polished it. He found his companion's story, though full of human interest, a little difficult to follow.

'Intricate,' he said.

'It is a bit,' agreed Lord Vosper. 'I'd better take you through it step by step. I was engaged to Gloria, and she gave me the push. You've got that?'

'I've got it.'

'I then became engaged to Penny. All straight so far?'

'Quite straight. By way of a defiant sort of gesture, I suppose?'

'Well, more or less by way of a defiant sort of gesture, no doubt, though of course I'm very fond of her. Nice girl.'

'Very.'

'I asked her to marry me in London, when I was giving her a bite of dinner at Mario's, and she seemed to like the idea, so that was the position when we got back here. And all might have been well, had not Gloria suddenly blown in.'

'I begin to understand. Seeing her once more, you found that the old love still lingered?'

'That's right. And it had lingered in her, too. Like the dickens, apparently. I didn't know it till to-night, but she also was racked with remorse because she felt that she had chucked away a life's happiness.'

'How did it happen to dawn on you to-night?'

'I was taking a stroll in the garden, and I came upon her weeping bitterly in the moonlight. Well, naturally that struck me as odd, so I said "Oh, hullo. Is anything up?" and she said "Oh, Orlo!" and it all came out. And then . . . well, one thing led to another, don't you know, and before we knew where we were, we were in each other's arms.'

'Murmuring brokenly?'

'That's right, and I don't mind telling you I hope you will have something to suggest, because at the moment you wouldn't be far out in describing me as nonplussed.'

Gally nodded.

'I see your difficulty. You are a man of honour, and you feel that you are bound to Penny?'

'That's right.'

'But your heart belongs to Daddy.'

'Eh?'

'I mean to Gloria. You love this Salt?'

'That's right.'

'Well, these things happen. Nobody is to blame. There's only one thing for you to do, as I see it. You will have to explain the situation to Penny.'

'I suppose so. I hope she won't mind.'

'I hope not. Still, she should be informed, I think.'

'So does Gloria. She told me to go and tell her.'

'Not a pleasant job having to give a warm-hearted young girl the push.'

'No.'

'Perhaps you would prefer that some kindly third party broke the news?'

Lord Vosper started.

'I say! Would you?'

'I was not thinking of myself. The man I had in mind was . . . Ah, here he is in person, right on cue,' said Gally, as the door opened and Jerry entered. 'Jerry, our friend Vosper here is in something of a dilemma, or quandary, as it is sometimes called. He has become betrothed to Gloria Salt, and, as you are aware, he is also betrothed to Penny Donaldson, and he is looking for a silver-tongued intermediary to take on the job of explaining to Penny that he will not be at liberty to go through with his commitments to her. I thought you might be just the man, you being a mutual friend of both parties. I will leave you to discuss it. If you want me, you will find me on the terrace.'

3

The moon, shining down on the terrace, illuminated a female figure seated in a deck chair, and Gally's heart, though a stout one, skipped a beat. Then he saw that it was not, as for a moment he had supposed, his sister Constance, but his young friend Penny Donaldson.

'Hullo there, Penny,' he said, taking the chair at her side. 'Well, we are living in stirring times these days. Did Beach tell you about that pig of Parsloe's?'

'Yes.'

'He got it away all right and put it in the house Fruity Biffen used to have.'

'Yes.'

'Extraordinary bit of luck Wellbeloved thinking I was Parsloe and pouring out his heart to me over the telephone.'

'Yes,' said Penny.

Gally gave her a quick look. Her voice had had a dull, metallic note, and eyeing her he saw that her brow was clouded and the corners of her mouth drawn down as though the soul were in pain.

'What's the matter?' he asked. 'You seem depressed.'

'I am.'

'Well, I've got some news for you that will cheer you up. I've just been talking to my Lord Vosper.'

'Oh?'

'And what do you think? He wants to call the whole thing off.'

'To do what?'

'Cancel the engagement, countermand the wedding cake. He's going to marry the Salt girl. It seems that they were like ham and eggs before you entered his life, but the frail bark of love came a stinker on the rocks. It has now been floated off and patched up and a marriage has been arranged and will shortly take place. He was a bit apologetic about it, and hoped you wouldn't mind, but he made it quite clear that that was how matters stood. So you are back in circulation and free to carry on with Jerry along the lines originally planned.'

'I see.'

Gally was hurt. He was feeling as the men who brought the good news from Aix to Ghent would have felt if the citizens of Ghent had received them at the end of their journey with a yawn and an 'Oh, yes?'

'Well, I'm dashed!' he said disapprovingly. 'I must say I expected a little more leaping about and clapping the hands in girlish glee. I might be telling you it's a nice evening.'

Penny heaved a sigh.

'It's the most loathsome evening there ever was. Do you know what's happened, Gally? Jerry's been fired.'

'Eh?'

'Given the gate. Driven into the snow. Lady Constance says if he isn't out of the place first thing to-morrow morning – '

'What?'

' – she'll set the dogs on him.'

Gally's monocle, leaping from the parent eye socket, flashed in the moonlight. He drew it in like an angler gaffing a fish, and having replaced it stared at her uncomprehendingly.

'What on earth are you talking about?'

'I'm telling you.'

'But it doesn't make sense. What's Connie got against Jerry?'

'She didn't like it when she found him in her closet.'

'In her *what*?'

'Well, cupboard, then, if you prefer it. The cupboard in her bedroom.'

'What the dickens was he doing in the cupboard in Connie's bedroom?'

'Hiding.'

Gally gaped.

'Hiding?'

'Yes.'

'In the cupboard?'

'Yes.'

'In Connie's bedroom?'

'Yes.'

A theory that would cover the facts came to Gally.

'This young man of yours isn't a little weak in the head, is he?'

'No, he isn't a little weak in the head. Lord Emsworth seems to be.'

'Quite,' said Gally, conceding this obvious truth. 'But how does Clarence come into it?'

Penny began to explain in a low, toneless voice. One cannot expect of a girl whose hopes and dreams have been shattered that her voice shall be resonant and bell-like.

'Jerry has been telling me about it. It started with Lord Emsworth writing a letter to your friend Maudie.'

'W –?' began Gally, and checked himself. Much as he would have liked to know what his brother had been writing letters to Maudie about, this was no time for interruptions.

'He gave it to Jerry and told him to put it in her room. Jerry asked which was her room, and he said the second on the right along the corridor. So Jerry put the letter there, and then Lord Emsworth told him to go and bring it back.'

Gally was obliged to interrupt.

'Why?'

'He didn't say why.'

'I see. Go on.'

'Well, Jerry went to get the letter, and he'd just got it when he heard someone outside the door. So of course he hid. Naturally he didn't want to be found there. He dived into the cupboard, and I suppose he must have made a noise, because the cupboard door was whipped open, and there was Lady Constance.'

'But what was Connie doing in Maudie's room?'

'It wasn't Maudie's room. It was Lady Constance's room. After he had finished talking to Lady Constance – or after she had finished talking to him – Jerry went back to Lord Emsworth, and Lord Emsworth, having heard the facts, smote his brow and said "Did I say the second door on the right? I meant second door on the left. That is how the mistake arose."'

Gally clicked his tongue.

'There you have Clarence in a nutshell,' he said. 'There is a school of thought that holds that he got that way from being dropped on his head when a baby. I maintain that when you have a baby like Clarence, you don't need to drop it on its head. You just let Nature take its course and it develops automatically into the sort of man who says "right" when he means "left". I suppose Jerry was annoyed?'

'A little. Not too well pleased. In fact, he called Lord Emsworth a muddleheaded old ass and said he ought to be in a padded cell. And if you're going to ask me if that annoyed Lord Emsworth, the answer is in the affirmative. They parted on distant terms. So Jerry's chances of ingratiating himself with the dear old man with a view to leading up to saying "Brother, can you spare two thousand pounds?" seem pretty dim, don't you feel? Well, I think I'll be strolling along to the lake.'

'What are you going to do there?'

'Just drown myself. It'll pass the time.'

Before Gally could ask her if this was the old Donaldson spirit – he had only got as far as a pained 'Tut, tut' – a figure came droopingly along the terrace.

'Ah, Jerry,' said Gally. 'Finished your chat? I've just been telling Penny about the Vosper-Salt situation, and she has been telling me about your misadventure. Too bad. What are you planning to do now?'

Jerry stared dully.

'I'm going back to London.'

'Ridiculous.'

'What else can I do?'

Gally snorted. It seemed to him that the younger generation was totally lacking in the will to win.

'Why, stick around, of course. You're not licked yet. Who knows what the morrow may bring forth? London, forsooth! You're going to take a room at the Emsworth Arms and wait to see what turns up.'

Jerry brightened a little.

'It's not a bad idea.'

'It's a splendid idea,' said Penny. 'You can come prowling about the grounds, and I'll meet you.'

'So I can.'

'The rose garden would be a good place.'

'None better. Expect me among the roses at an early date. You'll be there?'

'With bells on.'

'Darling!'

'Angel!'

'I was rather thinking that the conversation might work round to some such point before long,' said Gally. 'So there you are, my boy. It's always foolish to despair. You ought to know that. Penny has been giving me some of your stories to read, and a thing that struck me about them was that on every occasion, despite master criminals, pock-marked Mexicans, shots in the night, and cobras down the chimney, true love triumphed in the end. Do you remember a thing of yours called A Quick Bier For Barney? Well, the hero of that story got his girl through up against a bunch of thugs who would have considered my sister Constance very small-time stuff. And now, as the last thing you'll want at a moment like this is an old gargoyle like me hanging around, I'll say good night.'

He toddled off. He was feeling at the top of his form

again and thinking that now would be an admirable time to go and see Connie and put it across her properly. His prejudice against vulgar brawls had vanished. He felt just in the mood for a brawl, and the vulgarer it was, the better he would like it.

4

At nine o'clock on the following night Beach, seated in his pantry, was endeavouring with the aid of a glass of port to still the turmoil which recent events at Blandings Castle had engendered in his soul, and not making much of a go of it. Port, usually an unfailing specific, seemed for once to have lost its magic.

Beach was no weakling, but he had begun to feel that too much was being asked of one who, though always desirous of giving satisfaction, liked to draw the line somewhere. A butler who has been compelled to introduce his niece into his employer's home under a false name and on top of that to remove a stolen pig from a gamekeeper's cottage in a west wood and convey it across country to the detached villa Sunnybrae on the Shrewsbury road is a butler who feels that enough is sufficient. There were dark circles under Beach's eyes and he found himself starting at sudden noises. And it did not improve his state of mind that he had a tender heart and winced at the spectacle of all the sadness he saw around him.

A conversation he had had with Penny this evening had affected him deeply, and the sight of Lord Emsworth at dinner had plunged him still further in gloom. It had no longer been possible to withhold from Lord Emsworth the facts relating to Empress of Blandings, and it had been obvious to Beach, watching him at the meal, that the various courses were turning to ashes in his mouth.

Even Mr Galahad had seemed moody, and Maudie, who might have done something to relieve the funereal atmosphere, had been over at Matchingham Hall. The only bright spot was the non-appearance of Lady Constance, who had caught Lord Emsworth's cold and had taken her dinner in bed.

Beach helped himself to another glass of port, his third. It was pre-phylloxera, and should have had him dancing about the room, strewing roses from his hat, but it did not so much as bring a glow to his eye. For all the good it was doing him, it might have been sarsaparilla. And he was just wondering where he could turn for comfort, now that even port had failed him, when he saw that his solitude had been invaded. Gally was entering, and on his expressive face it seemed to Beach that there was a strange new light, as if hope had dawned.

Nor was he in error. Throughout the day and all through dinner Gally had been bringing a brain trained by years of mixing with the members of the Pelican Club to bear on the problems confronting his little group of serious thinkers. What Beach, watching him at the table, had mistaken for moodiness had in reality been deep thought. And now this deep thought had borne fruit.

'Port?' said Gally, eyeing the decanter. 'You can give me some of that, and speedily. My God!' he said, sipping. 'It's the old '78. You certainly do yourself well, Beach, and who has a better right to? If I've said once that there's nobody like you, I've said it a hundred times. Staunch and true are the adjectives I generally select when asked to draw a word-portrait of you. Beach, I tell people when they come inquiring about you, is a man who ... well, how shall I describe him? Ah yes, I say, he is a man who, if offered an opportunity of doing a friend a good turn, will leap to the task, even if it involves going through fire and water. He – '

It would be incorrect to say that Beach had paled. His was a complexion, ruddier than the cherry, which did not readily lose its vermilion hue. But his jaw had fallen, and he was looking at his visitor rather in the manner of the lamb mentioned by the philosopher Schopenhauer when closeted with the butcher.

'It ... It isn't anything else, is it, Mr Galahad?' he faltered.

'Eh?'

'There is nothing further you wish me to do for you, sir?'

Gally laughed genially.

'Good heavens, no. Not a thing. At least – '

'Sir?'

'It did, I admit, cross my mind that you might possibly care to kidnap George Cyril Wellbeloved and tie him up and force him to reveal where the Empress is hidden by sticking lighted matches between his toes. Would you?'

'No, sir.'

'Merely a suggestion. You could keep him in the coal cellar.'

'No, sir. I am sorry.'

'Quite all right, my dear fellow. It was just a random thought that occurred to me while reading one of those gangster stories in the library before dinner. I had an idea that it might have appealed to you, but no. Well, we all have our likes and dislikes. Then we must think of something else, and I believe I have it. It's true, is it, that Maudie is going to marry young Parsloe?'

'Yes, sir. I had the information from her personal lips.'

'And he loves her?'

'She inferred as much from his attitude, sir.'

'In that case, I should imagine that her lightest wish would be law to him.'

'One assumes so, Mr Galahad.'

'Then everything becomes quite simple. She must wheedle the blighter.'

'Sir?'

'You must take her aside, Beach, and persuade her to ask young Parsloe where the Empress is and use her feminine wiles till she has got the secret out of him. She can do it if she tries. Look at Samson and Delilah. Look at – '

Whatever further test cases Gally had been about to mention were wiped from his lips by the sudden ringing of the telephone, a strident instrument capable of silencing the stoutest talker. Beach, who had leaped in the air, returned to earth and took up the receiver.

'Blandings Castle. Lord Emsworth's butler spe ... Oh, good evening, sir ... Yes, sir ... Very good, sir ... Mr Vail, Mr Galahad,' said Beach, aside. 'He wishes me to inform Miss Donaldson that he has left the Emsworth Ar –'

It is not easy to break off in the middle of a single syllable word like 'Arms', but Beach had contrived to do so. Like a cloud across the moon, a look of horror and consternation was spreading itself over the acreage of his face.

Gally frowned.

'Left the Emsworth Arms?' he said sharply. A man who has taken the trouble to give the younger generation the benefit of his advice does not like to have that advice rejected. 'Let me talk to him.'

Slowly Beach replaced the receiver.

'The gentleman has rung off, sir.'

'Did he say where he was going?'

Beach tottered to the table, and reached out a feeble hand to his glass of port.

'Yes, Mr Galahad. He has taken a furnished house.'

'Eh? Where? What furnished house?'

Beach drained his glass. His eyes were round and bulging.

'Sunnybrae, sir,' he said in a low voice. 'On the Shrewsbury road.'

CHAPTER NINE

THE Pelican Club trains its sons well. After he has been affiliated to that organization for a number of years, taking part week by week in its informal Saturday night get-togethers, a man's moral fibre becomes toughened, and very little can happen to him that is capable of making him even raise his eyebrows. Gally, as he heard Beach utter those devastating words, did, it is true, give a slight start, but a member of the Athenaeum or the National Liberal would have shot six feet straight up in the air and bumped his head against the ceiling.

When he spoke, there was no suggestion of a quiver in his voice. The Club would have been proud of him.

'Are you trying to be funny, Beach?'

'No, sir, I assure you.'

'You really mean it? Sunnybrae?'

'Yes, sir.'

'What on earth does he want to go to Sunnybrae for?'

'I could not say, sir.'

'But he's on his way there?'

'Yes, sir.'

'And when he gets there . . .' Gally paused. He polished his monocle thoughtfully. 'Things look sticky, Beach.'

'Extremely glutinous, Mr Galahad. I fear the worst. The gentleman, on arriving at Sunnybrae, will find the pig in residence –'

'And what will the harvest be?'

'Precisely, sir.'

Gally nodded. He was a man who could face facts.

'Yes, sticky is the word. No good trying to conceal it from ourselves that a crisis has arisen. Jerry Vail is an author, and you know as well as I do what authors are.

Unbalanced. Unreliable. Fatheads, to a man. It was precisely because he was an author that I did not admit this Vail to our counsels in the matter of the Parsloe pig. Informed of the facts, he would have spread the story all over Shropshire. And he'll be spreading it all over Shropshire now, if we don't act like lightning. You agree?'

'Yes, indeed, sir.'

'Authors are like that. No reticence. No reserve. You or I, Beach, finding a pig in the kitchen of a furnished villa in which we had just hung up our hats, would keep calm and wait till the clouds rolled by. But not an author. The first thing this blighted Vail will do, unless nipped in the bud, will be to rush out and grab the nearest passer-by and say "Pardon me for addressing you, sir, but there appears to be a pig in my kitchen. Have you any suggestions?" And then what? I'll tell you what. Doom, desolation, and despair. In next to no time the news will have reached Parsloe, stirring him up like a dose of salts and bringing him round to Sunnybrae with a whoop and a holler. We must hurry, Beach. Not an instant to lose. We must get the car out immediately and fly like the wind to the centre of the vortex, trusting that we shall not be too late. Come on, man, come on. Don't just stand there. A second's delay may be fatal.'

'But I have to take the tray of beverages into the drawing-room at nine-thirty, Mr Galahad.'

'The what?'

'The tray of beverages, sir. For the ladies and gentlemen. Whisky and, for those who prefer it, barley-water.'

'Give it a miss. Let 'em eat cake. Good heavens, is this a time to be thinking of whisky and babbling of barley-water? I never heard such nonsense.'

Beach stiffened a little. In his long and honourable years of office at Blandings Castle, allowing deduction for an annual holiday by the sea, he had taken the tray of beverages into the drawing-room at nine-thirty a matter of six thousand six hundred and sixty-nine times, and to have the voice of the Tempter urging him to play hooky and not bring the total to six thousand six hundred and seventy was enough to make any butler stiffen.

'I fear I could not do that, Mr Galahad,' he said, coldly. 'Professional integrity constrains me to perform my allotted task. It is a matter of principle. I shall be happy to join you at Sunnybrae directly I am at liberty. I will borrow the chauffeur's bicycle.'

Gally wasted no time in fruitless argument. You cannot reason with a butler whose motto is Service.

'All right,' he said. 'Come on as soon as you can, for who knows what stern work may lie before us this night!'

And with a crisp 'You and your blasted trays of beverages!' he hurried out, heading for the garage.

2

Jerry Vail's sudden decision to move from the Emsworth Arms and start housekeeping for himself had been due to certain shortcomings in the general set-up of that in many respects admirable hostelry. The Emsworth Arms, like most inns in English country towns, specialized in beer, and when it came to providing its patrons with anything else was rather inclined to lose interest and let its attention wander.

Beds for instance. It did not worry much about beds. You could have one, if you wanted to, but Jerry, having inspected the specimen offered to him, shrank from the prospect of occupying it for an indefinite series of nights. If he had been an Indian fakir, accustomed from childhood to curling up on spikes, he could have wished for nothing better, but he was not an Indian fakir accustomed from childhood to curling up on spikes.

There was also the drawback that nowhere in the place was it possible for a man to write. The Emsworth Arms' idea of a writing-room was an almost pitch dark cubby-hole with no paper, no pens, and in the ink-pot only a curious sediment that looked like something imported from the Florida Everglades. And when he discovered that in addition to these defects the room was much infested by commercial travellers, talking in loud voices about orders and expense accounts, it is not difficult to understand why the quiet evenfall found him in the offices of Caine and Cooper, house agents, High Street, Market Blandings, inquiring about houses.

He was delighted when Mr Lancelot Cooper, the firm's junior partner, informed him that by a lucky chance there happened to be available a furnished villa ready for immediate occupancy, and he was still further pleased to learn that the residence in question had only recently been vacated by Admiral C. J. Biffen. Admiral Biffen, he told Mr Cooper, was a very old and valued friend of his, which would make any villa he had recently vacated seem like home, and the notorious tidiness of naval men gave assurance that everything would have been left in apple-pie order. Nice going, was his verdict, and Mr Cooper agreed with him.

'You intend to remain long in these parts?' he asked.

'Till the sands of the desert grow cold, if necessary,' said Jerry, thinking of Penny, and taking the keys he went off to the Emsworth Arms to pack and have a bite of dinner before settling in.

His new home, when he beheld it at about twenty minutes past nine, came at first glance as a disappointment. True, Mr Cooper had spoken of it throughout as a villa and the name Sunnybrae should have prepared him, but subconsciously Jerry had been picturing something with a thatched roof and honeysuckle and old Mister Moon climbing up over the trees, and it was disconcerting to find a red brick building which might have been transferred from the suburbs of London. Market Blandings itself was old and picturesque, but, as in other country towns, the speculative builder had had his way on the outskirts.

Still, it improved when you got inside. There was a cosy living-room, and in the corner of the living-room a good firm desk. And a good firm desk was what he particularly wanted, for in the intervals of sneaking up to Blandings Castle and meeting Penny among the rose bushes he planned to start composing what he was convinced was going to be his masterpiece.

The inspiration for it had hit him like a bullet the moment he had set eyes on Mr Lancelot Cooper. The junior partner of Caine and Cooper, though a man of blameless life, had one of those dark, saturnine faces which suggest a taste for the more sinister forms of crime, and on one cheek of that dark, saturnine face was a long scar. Actually it had been caused by the bursting of a gingerbeer bottle at a Y.M.C.A. picnic, but it gave the impression of being the outcome of battles with knives in the cellars of the underworld. And on top of all that he had been wearing lavender gloves.

It was those gloves that had set Jerry tingling. His trained mind saw them as the perfect box office touch. There is nothing so spine-chilling as a dressy assassin. All murderers make us shudder a bit, but when we encounter one who, when spilling human gore, spills it in lavender gloves, our backbone turns to ice. Mr Cooper, talking pleasantly of rent and clauses and deposits, had had no notion of it, but right from the start of their interview his client was seeing him as Lavender Joe, the man for whom the police had for years – vainly – been spreading a drag-net. Jerry had begun to jot down notes within two minutes of his departure from the Caine and Cooper offices, and he was still jotting down notes as he left the living-room and went upstairs to have a look at the bedroom.

The bedroom was all right. Quite a good bedroom, the bed springy to the touch. His spirits rose. A man, he felt, could be very happy and get through a lot of work in a place like this. He could see himself toiling far into the night, with nothing to disturb the flow.

Well, practically nothing. From the point of view of a writer who wanted peace and quiet so that he could concentrate on a goose-flesher about murderers in lavender gloves, Sunnybrae was nearly ideal. Its one small defect was that it appeared to be haunted.

From time to time, as he moved about his new home, Jerry had been aware of curious noises, evidently supernatural. If asked by the Committee of the Society of Psychical Research to describe these noises, he would have been rather at a loss. Well, sort of grunting noises, he would have told them.

Grunting?

Yes.

When you say grunting, do you mean *grunting*?

That's right. It doesn't go on all the time, of course. For a while there will be a kind of lull, as if the spectre were thinking things over and resting its vocal chords. Then, refreshed, off it goes again ... grunting, if you see what I mean.

Upon which, the Committee of the Society of Psychical Research would have said 'Well, Lord-love-a-duck!' grunting ghosts being new in their experience.

It was in the living-room that the sounds were most noticeable. Back there now, he was startled by a series of five or six almost at his elbow. The poltergeist, for such he assumed it to be, appeared to have holed up behind the door that led presumably to the kitchen, the only part of the house he had not yet inspected.

He opened the door.

It is not easy to state offhand what is the last thing a young man starting out in life would wish to find on the premises of the furnished villa ready for immediate occupancy which he had just begun to occupy. Bugs? Perhaps. Cockroaches? Possibly. Maybe defective drains. One cannot say. But a large black pig in the kitchen would unquestionably come quite high up on the list of undesirable objects, and Jerry, as he gazed at Queen of Matchingham, was conscious of that disagreeable sensation which comes to those who, pausing to tie a shoelace while crossing a railway line, find themselves struck in the small of the back by the Cornish express.

It was the unexpectedness of the thing that had unnerved him. It had caught him unprepared. If Lancelot Cooper, handing him the keys, had said 'Oh, by the way, when you get to Sunnybrae, you will find the kitchen rather full of pigs, I'm afraid,' he would have known where he was. But not a word had been spoken on the subject. The animal had come upon him as a complete surprise, and he sought in vain for an explanation of its presence. It was not as though it had been a corpse with a severed head. A corpse with a severed head in the kitchen of Sunnybrae he could have understood. As a writer of mystery thrillers, he knew that you are apt to find corpses with severed heads pretty well anywhere. But why a pig?

It was just after he had closed his eyes, counted twenty and opened them again, hoping to find that the apparition had melted into thin air, that the front door bell rang.

The moment was not one which Jerry would have chosen for entertaining a visitor, and the only thing that made him go and answer the bell was the thought that this caller might have something to suggest which would help to clarify the situation. Two heads, unless of course severed, are so often better than one. He opened the door, and found standing on the steps a large policeman, who gave him one of those keen, penetrating looks which make policemen so unpopular.

'Ho,' he said, in the sort of voice usually described as steely.

He was tough and formidable, like the policemen in Jerry's stories. Indeed, if Jerry had been capable at the moment of thinking of anything except pigs, he might have seen in his visitor an excellent model for Inspector Jarvis, the Scotland Yard man whom he was planning to set on the trail of Lavender Joe. He pictured Inspector Jarvis as a man who might have been carved out of some durable substance like granite, and that was the material which seemed to have been used in assembling this zealous officer.

'Ho!' said the policeman. 'Resident?'

'Eh?'

'Do you live in this house?'

'Yes, I've just moved in.'

'Where did you get the keys?'

'From Caine and Cooper in the High Street.'

'Ho.'

The policeman seemed to soften. His suspicions lulled, he relaxed. He tilted his helmet and passed a large hand over his forehead.

'Warm to-night,' he said, and it was plain that he was now regarding this as a social occasion. 'Thought at one time this afternoon we were in for a thunderstorm. Well, I must apologize for disturbing you, sir, but seeing a light in the window and knowing the house to be unoccupied, I thought it best to make inquiries. You never know. Strange occurrences have been happening recently in Market Blandings and district, and I don't like the look of things.'

This was so exactly what Jerry was feeling himself that he began to regard this policeman as a kindred soul, one to whose sympathetic ear he could confide his troubles and perplexities. And he was about to do so, when the other went on.

'Down at the station the boys think there's one of these crime waves starting. Two milk cans abstracted from doorsteps only last week, and now all this to-do up at Matchingham Hall. You'll have heard about Sir Gregory Parsloe's pig, no doubt, sir?'

Jerry leaped an inch or two.

'Pig?'

'His prize pig, Queen of Matchingham. Stolen,' said the policeman impressively. 'Snitched out of its sty and so far not a trace of the miscreant. But we'll apprehend him. Oh yes, we'll apprehend him all right, and then he'll regret his rash act. Very serious matter, pig stealing. I wouldn't care to be in the shoes of the fellow that's got that pig. He's laughing now,' said the policeman, quite incorrectly, 'but he won't be laughing long. Making an extended stay here, sir?'

'It may be some time.'

'Nice little house,' said the policeman tolerantly. 'Compact, you might call it. Mind you, you don't want to treat it *rough* . . . not go leaning against the walls or anything like that. I know the fellow that built this little lot. Six of them there are – Sunnybrae, Sunnybrow, Sunnywood, Sunnyfields, Sunnycot, and Sunnyhaven. I was having a beer with this chap one night – it was the day Sunnycot fell down – and he started talking about mortar. Mortar? I says. Why, I didn't know you ever used any. Made me laugh, that did. Well, I'll be getting along, sir. Got my round to do, and then I have to go and report progress to Sir Gregory. Not that there is any progress to report, see what I mean, but the gentleman likes us to confer with him. Shows zeal. Mortar!' said the policeman. 'Why, I didn't know you ever used any, I said. You should have seen his face.'

He passed into the night, guffawing heartily, and Jerry, tottering back to the living-room, sat down and put his head between his hands. This is the recognized posture for those who wish to think, and it was obvious that the problems that had arisen could do with all the thinking he was at liberty to give them. Fate, he perceived, had put him in a tight spot. At any moment he was liable to be caught with the goods and to become, as so many an innocent man has become, a victim of circumstantial evidence.

This sort of thing was no novelty to him, of course. He could recall at least three stories he had written in the past year or so in which the principal characters had found themselves in just such a position as he was in now, with the trifling difference that what they had discovered in their homes had been, respectively, a dead millionaire with his head battered in, a dead ambassador with his throat cut, and a dead dancer known as La Flamme with a dagger of Oriental design between her fourth and fifth ribs. Whenever the hero of a Vail story took a house, he was sure to discover something of that sort in it. It was pure routine.

But the fact that the situation was a familiar one brought no comfort to him. He continued agitated. *Vis-à-vis* with the corpses listed above, his heroes had never known what to do next, and he did not know what to do next. The only thing he was sure he was not going to do was answer the front door bell, which had just rung again.

The bell rang twice, then stopped. Jerry, who had raised his head, replaced it between his hands and gave himself up to thought once more. And he was wishing more earnestly than ever that something even remotely resembling a plan of action would suggest itself to him, when he seemed to sense a presence in the room. He had an uncanny feeling that he was not alone. Then there sounded from behind him a deferential cough, and turning he perceived that his privacy had been invaded by a long, lean, red-haired man with strabismus in his left eye, a mouth like a halibut's, a broken nose, and lots of mud all over him.

He stood gaping. Hearing that cough where no cough should have been, he had supposed for an instant that this time it really was the official Sunnybrae ghost reporting for duty, though what ghosts were doing, haunting a red-brick villa put up at the most five years ago by a speculative builder, he was at a loss to understand. Reason now told him that no spectre would be likely to be diffusing such a very strong aroma of pig, as was wafted from this long, lean, red-haired man, and his momentary spasm of panic passed, leaving behind it the righteous indignation of the house-holder who finds uninvited strangers in the house which he is holding.

'Who on earth are you?' he demanded, with a good deal of heat.

The intruder smirked respectfully.

'Wellbeloved is the name, sir. I am Sir Gregory Parsloe's pig man. Sir?'

Jerry had not spoken. The sound that had proceeded from him had been merely a sort of bubbling cry, like that of a strong swimmer in his agony. With one long, horrified stare, he reeled to a chair and sank into it, frozen from the soles of the feet upwards.

CHAPTER TEN

It was that light shining in the window that had brought George Cyril Wellbeloved to Sunnybrae, just as it had brought the recent officer of the Law. Happening to observe it as he passed along the road, he had halted spell-bound, his heart leaping up as that of the poet Wordsworth used to do when he saw rainbows. He felt like a camel which, wandering across a desert, comes suddenly upon a totally unexpected oasis.

The fact has not been mentioned, for, as we have explained, a historian cannot mention everything, but during the period of the former's tenancy of Sunnybrae relations of considerable cordiality had existed between Admiral G. J. Biffen and Sir Gregory Parsloe's pig man. They had met at the Emsworth Arms one night, and acquaintance had soon ripened into friendship. Admiral Biffen liked telling long stories about life on the China station in the old days, and no story could be too long for George Cyril Wellbeloved to listen to provided beer was supplied, as on these occasions it always was. The result was that many a pleasant evening had been passed in this living-room, with the gallant Admiral yarning away in a voice like a foghorn and George Cyril drinking beer and saying 'Coo!' and 'Lumme' and 'Well, fancy that!' at intervals. The reader will be able to picture the scene if he throws his mind back to descriptions he has read of the sort of thing that used to go on in those *salons* of the eighteenth century.

His host's abrupt departure had come as a stunning blow to George Cyril Wellbeloved. He would not readily forget the black despair which had gripped him that memorable night when, arriving at Sunnybrae in confident expectation of the usual, he had found the house in darkness and all the windows shuttered. It was as if a hart, panting for cooling streams when heated in the chase, had come to a cooling stream and found it dried up.

And then he had seen that light shining in the window, and had assumed from it that his benefactor had returned and that the golden age was about to set in anew.

All this he explained to Jerry as the latter sat congealed in his chair.

'Far be it from me to intrude on a gentleman's privacy,' said George Cyril Wellbeloved in his polished way. 'It is the last thing I would desire. But seeing a light in the window I thinks to myself "Coo! It's the Admiral come back," so I ring the bell, and then I ring it again, and then, when no reply transpires, I remember that the Admiral is a little hard of hearing, as is only natural in a gentleman of his advanced years, and I see the door on the jar as if someone had forgotten to close it, so I took the lib of barging in. I'm sorry to discover that it's not the Admiral come back, after all, though very glad to make your acquaintance, sir,' said George Cyril politely, 'and I'll tell you why I'm sorry. On a warm night like this, his kind heart melted by the thought that I'd been toiling all day at my numerous duties, Admiral Biffen would have given me a bottle of beer. And I don't mind telling you, sir,' said George Cyril, frankly laying his cards on the table, 'that what with it being a warm night and what with me all worn out from toiling at my numerous duties, a bottle of beer is what I'm fairly gasping for.'

He paused for a reply, but no reply came. Not, that is to say, from Jerry. But Queen of Matchingham, hearing that loved voice, had just uttered a cordial grunt of welcome. It seemed to Jerry's strained senses to ring through the room like the Last Trump, and he was surprised that his companion appeared not to have heard it.

'Admiral Biffen,' said George Cyril Wellbeloved,

throwing the information out casually, though with perhaps a certain undertone of significance, 'used to keep his bottles of beer in a bucket of cold water in the kitchen.'

And so saying, he moved a step towards the door, as if anxious to ascertain whether his present host pursued that same excellent policy.

For an instant, Jerry sat rigid, like a character in one of his stories hypnotized by a mad scientist. Then, leaping to his feet, he sprang across the room. In doing so, he overturned a small table on which were a bowl of wax fruit, a photograph in a pink frame of the speculative builder to whom Sunnybrae owed its existence, the one who never used mortar, and a china vase bearing the legend 'A Present From Llandudno'. It also contained the notebook in which he had been jotting down his notes for the story of Lavender Joe, and as his eye fell on it, inspiration came to him.

He looked at George Cyril Wellbeloved, and was encouraged by what he saw. He took another look, and was still more encouraged.

The world may be roughly divided into two classes – men who, when you tell them a story difficult to credit, will not believe you, and men who will. It was to this latter and far more likeable section of the community that, judging by his fatuous expression, George Cyril Wellbeloved belonged. He had the air, which Jerry found charming, of being a man who would accept without question whatever anybody cared to tell him. His whole aspect was that of one who believed everything he read in the Sunday papers.

'Listen,' said Jerry.

It was an unfortunate word to have used, for at this moment Queen of Matchingham uttered another grunt. But again the visitor appeared not to have noticed it. Like Admiral Biffen, he seemed to be hard of hearing.

'I suppose,' said Jerry, proceeding rapidly, 'you're wondering what I'm doing in this house?'

With an old-world gesture, George Cyril Wellbeloved disclaimed any such vulgar curiosity.

'I presume,' he said politely, 'that you live here, sir? Or, putting it another way, that this is your residence?'

Jerry shook his head.

'No. I live in London.'

'Sooner you than me,' said George Cyril Wellbeloved. 'Nasty noisy place.'

'And why do I live in London?'

'You like it, I suppose, sir. Some do, I'm told.'

'No. I live in London because I have to. To be handy for the Yard.'

'Sir?'

'Scotland Yard. I'm a Scotland Yard man.'

'Well, strike me pink,' said George Cyril Wellbeloved, properly impressed. 'Might I venture to enquire what you're doing here, sir?'

'I'm on duty. Working on a case. I was sent to watch out for a dangerous criminal known as Lavender Joe. So called because he always wears lavender gloves. From information received, we know that this man will be arriving to-night on the train from London that reaches Market Blandings at ten-fifteen, and we think that he will come to this house.'

George Cyril Wellbeloved asked what had put that idea into their heads, and Jerry said he was unable to tell him because of the Official Secrets Act, and George Cyril said 'Ah, there was always something, wasn't there.'

'But it is possible,' Jerry went on, 'that before coming to Sunnybrae he will go somewhere else, and it is essential that I know where. I ought to be at the station, watching his every move, but I have to remain here. You see my difficulty?'

George Cyril Wellbeloved thought for a moment.

'You can't be in two places at once,' he hazarded.

'Exactly. You've hit it. My God, you're shrewd. So I need your help. I want you to take my place at the station. Go there, meet the train that gets in at ten-fifteen and follow Lavender Joe wherever he goes. But mark this. It is quite possible that he will not come on the ten-fifteen train.'

'That'll be a bit of a mix-up. What they call an amparse. What do I do then?'

'You will have to meet all the other trains from London, even if it means staying there all night.'

'All night?'

'Yes.'

'Coo! Then I'd better have a bottle of beer first. Where d'you keep it?'

'I haven't any beer.'

George Cyril's jaw fell.

'No beer?'

'No. What do you think this place is? A pub? Come, come, man, we have no time to waste talking about beer. It's settled, then, that you go to the station and remain there as long as is necessary, and you ought to be starting right away. Thank you, Wellbeloved. You are a public-spirited citizen, and I'm proud of you. You're doing a fine job, and the Yard will not forget it. Your heroism will be brought to the notice of the men up top.'

George Cyril blinked.

'Heroism? How do you mean heroism?'

'Lavender Joe is a very dangerous man,' explained Jerry. 'He carries weapons, and never hesitates to use them. So you must be careful. I wouldn't like you to have your liver ripped out by a dagger of Oriental design.'

'I wouldn't like it myself.'

'Well, we'll hope it won't come to that,' said Jerry briskly. 'Any questions you want to ask before you go?'

'Yes,' said George Cyril, equally brisk, if not more so. 'What is there in it for me?'

Jerry stared.

'How do you mean, what is there in it for you? You'll be assisting Scotland Yard.'

'Well, I think Scotland Yard ought to assist me,' said George Cyril Wellbeloved.

A grunt from the kitchen seemed to suggest that Queen of Matchingham thoroughly approved of this business-like attitude, and Jerry, leaping as he heard it, felt it best not to argue.

'It might run to a quid,' he conceded.

'Ten quid,' corrected George Cyril Wellbeloved.

'Three quid.'

'Well, I'll tell you,' said George Cyril. 'I don't want to be hard on the Yard. Call it five.'

Jerry felt in his pocket.

'All I have on me is three pounds two and twopence.'

'Write a cheque.'

'I haven't a cheque book.'

'You could use a slip of paper and stick a stamp on.'

'I haven't a stamp.'

George Cyril Wellbeloved sighed. He seemed to be feeling that Jerry was armed at all points.

'All right. Three pounds two and tuppence.'

'Here you are.'

'Hoy!' cried George Cyril Wellbeloved. 'Where's the tuppence?'

A sordid scene, and one feels thankful that it is over. A minute later, Jerry was alone.

Five minutes later, the front door bell rang again.

2

It seemed to Jerry, whom recent events had left a little peevish, that he had been doing nothing since he was a small boy in a sailor suit but listen to the tinkling of the front door bell of this infernal villa ready for immediate occupancy. The moment one ringer left, another took his place. In all his experience he had never been associated with such a gregarious crowd as the residents of Market Blandings and district. Whenever time hung heavy on their hands, it was as though the cry went up 'Let's all go round to Vail's'.

The current pest, he felt morosely, was probably the Vicar, come to try to touch him for a subscription to his church's organ fund, and he had resolved to stay where he was and let the reverend gentleman go on ringing till his thumb wore out, when he abruptly changed his mind. A voice had called his name, and he recognized it as the voice of the Hon. Galahad Threepwood, the one person in the world he most desired to see. Gally might have his defects – his sister Constance, his sister Dora, his sister Julia, and all his other sisters could have named you hundreds – but he was sure to be a mine of information on what to do when you discovered a stolen pig in your kitchen one jump ahead of the police.

He opened the door and finding Gally on the top step, practically flung himself on his bosom.

'Mr Threepwood – '

'Mr Threepwood be blowed. Call me Gally. I'm not Mr Threepwood to a nephew of Plug Basham's. Is there something on your mind, my boy? You seem agitated. Or am I wrong?'

'No, you're not wrong. I'm on the verge of a nervous breakdown. There's a pig in the kitchen.'

'Ah, you've noticed that?'

Jerry started.

'You knew it was there?'

'It's what I've come about. This is no idle social call. Let us go inside and talk the whole thing over in a calm and detached spirit.'

He led the way to the living-room and settled himself comfortably in a chair.

'I can't understand why Fruity Biffen didn't like this place,' he said, gazing about him. 'Pretty snug, it looks to me. Wax fruit, presents from Llandudno ... I don't see what more a man could ask. But Fruity always was a peculiar chap. Odd. Temperamental. Did I ever tell you the story of Fruity and – '

Jerry broke in on the reminiscence. A host ought not, of course, to interrupt a visitor, but then, looking at it another way, a visitor ought not to put pigs in a host's kitchen. And a monstrous suspicion had begun to take root in Jerry's mind.

'Was it you who put that pig there?' he demanded, clothing it in words.

'Why, yes,' said Gally. 'That's right. Or, rather, Beach did, acting on my instructions. You see, a good deal of what you might call cut-and-thrust has been going on these last few days, and your pig – '

'I wish you wouldn't call it my pig.'

'The pig under advisement,' amended Gally, 'is one of the pawns in the game. To get a clear, over-all picture of the state of affairs, you must realize that my brother Clarence's porker, Empress of Blandings, and Parsloe's nominee, Queen of Matchingham, are running neck and neck for the Fat Pigs medal at the forthcoming Shropshire Agricultural Show, and Parsloe is a ruthless and unscrupulous man with a soul as black as the ace of spades who will resort to the lowest forms of crime to gain his ends. And so, knowing that it would be merely a question of time before he tried to pinch our pig, I thought it judicious to strike first by pinching his. Attack, as a thinker of my acquaintance pointed out not long ago, is the best form of defence. So we snitched the Queen while he on his side snitched the Empress. You always get a lot of this sort of

wholesome give and take on these occasions. We put the
Queen in a disused gamekeeper's cottage in the west wood,
but with fiendish cunning the opposition traced it there, so
we had to find another haven in a hurry. I fortunately
remembered that Sunnybrae was unoccupied.'

'Unoccupied!'

'Well, I thought it was.'

Jerry did not attempt to conceal his displeasure.

'You might have told me.'

'Yes, I suppose one should have done.'

'I would have been spared a very nasty shock. When I
opened that door and saw pigs in the kitchen as far as the
eye could reach,' said Jerry, with a shudder as he relived
that high spot in his career, 'I thought the top of my head
had come off.'

Gally murmured sympathetically.

'Quite a surprise it must have been, I should imagine.'

'It was.'

'Too bad. I can readily understand it tickling you up a
bit. Though it is a very moot point whether such shocks
aren't good for one. They stimulate the adrenal glands.'

'Well, I like my adrenal glands the way they are.'

'Quite, quite. Heaven forbid that I should try to dictate
to any man about his adrenal glands. Have them exactly
as you wish, my boy. This is Liberty Hall. But you appear
a little vexed with me, and I cannot see how I can be
blamed for what has occurred. How was I to know that
you would be coming to roost at Sunnybrae? Why did
you, by the way?'

'I didn't like the Emsworth Arms.'

'Bed not up to your specifications?'

'No. Hard lumps all over it.'

'You young fellows think too much of your comfort,'
said Gally reprovingly. 'Why, when I was your age, I
frequently slept on billiard tables. I remember on one

occasion Plug Basham, Puffy Benger, and I shared two chairs and an ironing board. It was when – '

Again Jerry interrupted, once more probably missing something good.

'Touching on this pig – '

'Ah, yes, the pig. I know the pig you mean. Go on, my boy.'

'It may interest you to learn that the police have been here, hot on its trail.'

'The police?'

'Well, a policeman. He saw the light in the window and came to make inquiries.'

'You didn't show him over the house, I hope?'

'No, we talked on the steps.'

'Good.'

'He was full of the stolen pig – '

'Courting dyspepsia.'

'Eh?'

'I merely meant it sounded rather indigestible. Go on. This policeman was full of the stolen pig, you were saying.'

'And he expects to make an early arrest.'

'One smiles.'

'I don't.'

'I do, and mockingly at that. I also laugh with a light tinkle in my voice. Have no anxiety about the local flatties, my boy. They couldn't find a bass drum in a telephone booth. What became of him?'

'He left. Shortly afterwards a man called Wellbeloved arrived.'

Gally gave a little jump.

'Wellbeloved?'

'He said he was Sir Gregory Parsloe's pig man. He, too, had seen the light in the window and thought it was Admiral Biffen come back. He and Admiral Biffen used to swig beer together, it seems.'

Gally nodded.

'That part about Fruity swigging beer rings true, but I should have thought he would have been more careful in his choice of friends. This Wellbeloved is a man of wrath, a deliberate and systematic viper if ever there was one. Did you talk to him on the steps?'

'No. He came in.'

'What on earth did you let him in for?'

'I didn't let him in. Apparently I had left the front door open. I was sitting wondering what to do for the best, and I sensed a presence and there he was.'

'What, in here? With only that door separating him from the pig?'

'He didn't see the pig.'

'But he has ears. Didn't the animal grunt?'

'Yes, several times. I was surprised he didn't hear it.'

Gally rose. His face was a little twisted, as a man's face so often is in the bitter hour of defeat.

'He heard it,' he said shortly. 'A good pig man can hear his personal pig grunt ten miles away in the middle of a thunderstorm and recognize its distinctive note even if a thousand other pigs are giving tongue simultaneously. He knew that pig was there, all right. I wonder he didn't denounce you on the spot. What did happen?'

'I got rid of him.'

'How?'

'I thought up a story to tell him.'

'What story?'

'Oh, just a story.'

Gally sniffed.

'Well, whatever it was, I'll bet he didn't swallow it.'

'He seemed to.'

'He would. Just humouring you, of course. He's probably squealing to Parsloe at this very moment. Ah, well, this is the end. I'll have to take the creature back to its sty. The secret of a happy and successful life is to know when things have got too hot and cut your losses. It's galling. One hates to admit defeat. Still, there it is.'

Jerry hesitated.

'You won't want me, will you?'

'To help with the pig? No, I can manage.'

'Good. I'm feeling a little unstrung.'

'You'd better wait here and entertain Beach. He will be arriving shortly.'

'Walking?'

'Bicycling,' said Gally. 'And it will be a lasting grief to me that I was not able to see him doing it. Well, bung-o.'

With a set face, he opened the door and strode into the kitchen.

It was about ten minutes after he had gone that there came from the great outdoors the unmistakable sound of a butler falling off a bicycle.

3

The years rob us of our boyish accomplishments. There had been a time, back in the distant past, when Sebastian Beach had yielded to none as a performer on the velocipede – once, indeed, actually emerging victorious in the choir boys' handicap at a village sports meeting, open to all whose voices had not broken before the second Sunday in Epiphany. But those days were gone for ever.

Only the feudal spirit, burning brightly within him, and the thought that Mr Galahad was relying on his co-operation had nerved him to borrow Alfred Voules's machine and set out on the road to Sunnybrae. Right from the start he had had misgivings, and they had proved to be well founded. It is a widely held belief that once you have learned to ride a bicycle, you never lose the knack. Beach had exploded this superstition. It was a bruised and shaken butler whom Jerry greeted at the front door and escorted to the living-room.

Having deposited him in a chair, Jerry found himself embarrassed. Excluded from Gally's little group of plotters, he had had no opportunity of seeing this man's more human side, and to him throughout his sojourn beneath Lord Emsworth's roof Beach had been an aloof, supercilious figure who had paralysed him with his majesty. He was paralysing him now. It is a very intrepid young man who can see an English butler steadily and see him whole without feeling a worm-like humility, and all Jerry's previous encounters with Beach – in corridors, in the hall, at lunch and at dinner – had left him with the impression that his feet were too large, his ears too red and his social status something in between that of a Dead End kid and a badly dressed leper. There were cats on the premises of Blandings Castle, and those gooseberry eyes had always made him feel that he might have been some unsavoury object dragged in by one of these cats, one of the less fastidious ones.

However, he was a host, and it was for him to set the conversation going.

'Have a nice ride?' he asked.

A shudder made the butler's body ripple like a field of wheat when a summer breeze passes over it.

'Not very enjoyable, sir,' he replied in a toneless voice. 'I have not cycled since I was a small lad, and I found it trying to the leg muscles.'

'It does catch you in the leg muscles, doesn't it?' said Jerry sympathetically.

'Yes, sir.'

'In the calves, principally.'

'Yes, sir.'

'You came a purler, didn't you?'

'Sir?'

'I thought I heard you falling off on arrival.'

'Yes, sir. I sustained several falls.'

'Unpleasant, falling off a bicycle. Shakes up the old liver.'

'Precisely, sir,' said Beach, closing his eyes.

Rightly feeling that this was about all his guest would wish to hear on the cycling theme, Jerry relapsed into silence, trying to think of some other topic which would interest, elevate and amuse.

'Mr Threepwood's taken that pig back,' he said at length.

He had struck the right note. The butler's eyes opened, and one could see hope dawning in them.

'Indeed, sir?'

'Yes, he deemed it best. Too many people were nosing round the place – policemen, pig men, and so on. He said the wisest move was to cut his losses before things got too hot. He left about a quarter of an hour ago, so the animal's probably in its sty now.'

Beach expelled a deep breath.

'I am extremely glad to hear that, sir. I was nervous.'

The news that a man like Beach could be nervous encouraged Jerry and put him at his ease. It was the first intimation he had had that human emotions lurked beneath that bulging waistcoat. Things were going with a swing, he felt, and he became chatty.

'Have you known Mr Threepwood long?' he asked.

'Nearly twenty years, sir.'

'As long as that? A weird old buster, don't you think?'

'Sir?'

'Well, I mean charging about the place, stealing pigs. Eccentric, wouldn't you say?'

'I fear you must excuse me from venturing an opinion, sir. It is scarcely fitting for me to discuss the members of my employer's household,' said Beach stiffly, and closed his eyes again.

The hot blush of shame mantled Jerry's cheek. He had never been snubbed by a butler before, and the novel experience made him feel as if he had been walking in the garden in the twilight and had stepped on a rake and had the handle jump up and hit him on the tip of the nose. It was difficult to know what to say next.

He ran through a few subjects in his mind.

The weather?

The crops?

The prospects at the next General Election?

Lord Emsworth, his treatment in sickness and in health?

Then he saw with profound relief that no further conversational efforts would be needed. A faint snore, followed by a series of louder ones, told him that his visitor was asleep. Worn out by his unaccustomed exertions in the saddle, Beach was knitting up the ravelled sleave of care.

Jerry rose noiselessly, and tiptoed out of the room. He was glad to go. He was a fair-minded young man and realized that he had probably not been seeing the other at his best and sunniest, but he preferred not to wait on the chance of improved relations in the future. What he wanted at the moment was a breath of fresh air.

The air was nice and fresh in the road outside Sunnybrae's little front garden, and he was drinking it in and gradually becoming restored to something like tranquillity, when the stillness of the summer night was broken by the sound of an approaching car, and Gally drove up. He was accompanied by a large pig.

It was difficult to be sure in the uncertain light of the moon, but Jerry had the impression that the animal gave him a friendly nod, and the civil thing to have done, of course, would have been to return it. But in moments of agitation we tend to forget the little courtesies of life. He stood staring, his lower jaw drooping on its hinge. Like Othello, he was perplexed in the extreme. That tranquillity to which we alluded a moment ago had been induced by the healing thought that, even if he had had to undergo the spiritual agony of being put in his place by a butler, he was at least free from pigs of every description. And here they were, back in his life again, bigger and better than ever.

He pointed a trembling finger.

'W – w – w . . . ?'

He had intended to say 'What?' but the word would not come. Gally cocked an enquiring monocle at him.

'W – w – w . . . ?'

'I had a dog that used to make a noise just like that when he was going to be sick,' said Gally. 'A dog named Towser. Parsloe once nobbled him with surreptitious steak and onions on the night when he was to have gone up against his dog Banjo in a rat contest. I must tell you all about it when we are more at leisure, for it will give you a rough idea of the lengths to which the man can go when he plants his footsteps on the deep and rides upon the storm. There isn't time now. It's a longish story, and we have to get the Empress indoors before the enemy discovers she's here and can do her a mischief. Her life would not be worth a moment's purchase if Parsloe knew where she was. He would have his goons out after her with sawn-off shot guns before she could wiggle her tail.'

Jerry was still dazed.

'I don't understand,' he said. 'Why do you say the Empress?'

'Why shouldn't I say the Empress? Oh, I see what you mean. I forgot to tell you, didn't I? I was just going to when you started making noises like my dog Towser about to give up all. It's quite simple. This is the Empress I've got here. When I got to Matchingham and had sneaked round to the sty, she was the first thing I saw in it. Parsloe, with a cunning for which one feels a reluctant admiration, was keeping her there, right on the premises where nobody would ever have dreamed of looking. Naturally I had been thinking in terms of lonely outhouses and underground cellars, never supposing for an instant that the man would put her practically out in the open. It was the same principle, of course, as Edgar Allan Poe's Purloined Letter and, as I say, one feels a grudging respect. So I picked her up and brought her along. But we mustn't waste time standing and talking. Is Beach here?'

'Yes, he's asleep in the living-room.'

'Then we won't disturb him,' said Gally considerately. 'Let the good man get his sleep. We'll take her in the back way.'

A few minutes later, though to Jerry it seemed longer, he stood rubbing his hands with a contented smile.

'And now,' he said, 'to notify Clarence of the happy ending. If you feel like coming to Blandings and having a word with Penny, I'll drive you there.'

4

Whatever a critic of aesthetic tastes might have found to say against Sunnybrae, and this was considerable, he would have been obliged to concede that it was a handy place from which to get to Blandings Castle. Only a mile or so of good road separated the two residences, and it was consequently not much more than a few minutes later that Gally's car drew up again at the Sunnybrae front door, this time with Lord Emsworth aboard.

Lord Emsworth, deeply stirred by Gally's news, had been twittering with excitement and ecstasy from the start of the journey. He was still twittering as they entered the living-room, and stopped twittering only when, thinking to see Beach, he observed Sir Gregory Parsloe. The Squire of Matchingham was seated in a chair, looking fixedly at the photograph of the speculative builder in the pink frame. He plainly did not think highly of the speculative builder. Indeed, if questioned, he would have said that he had never seen such a bally bounder in his life. And it must be admitted that, as speculative builders go, this one, considered from the angle of personal beauty, was not much of a speculative builder.

As Gally and Lord Emsworth entered, he transferred his gaze to them, and it was an unpleasant gaze, in quality and intentness not unlike the one the policeman had directed at Jerry in the opening stages of their conference on the front steps.

'Ha!' he said nastily. 'The Muster of the Vultures! I had an idea you would be coming along. If you're looking for that bloodstained butler of yours, you're too late.'

Lord Emsworth replaced his pince-nez, which, pursuing their invariable policy at moments when their proprietor was surprised and startled, had leaped from his nose like live creatures of the wild.

'Parsloe! What are you doing here?'

'Yes,' said Gally warmly. 'Who invited you to stroll in and make yourself at home? Of all the crust! I rather think this constitutes a trespass, and I shall advise young Vail that an action may lie.'

'Who's Vail?'

'The lessee of this house.'

'Oh, that chap? Action, did you say? He won't be bringing any actions. He'll be in prison, like Beach.'

'Beach?' Gally stared. 'Beach isn't in prison. You must be thinking of a couple of other fellows.'

'Constable Evans is probably locking him in his cell at this very moment,' said Sir Gregory with offensive gusto. 'He fortunately happened to be at my house when Well-beloved came with his news.'

'What news?'

Sir Gregory swelled, like a man who knows that he has a good story to tell.

'I was sitting in my study,' he began, 'enjoying a cigar and chatting with my fiancée, when Binstead, my butler, informed me that Wellbeloved wished to speak to me. I told him to tell him I would see him out on the drive, for I prefer to converse with Wellbeloved in the open air. I joined him there, and he had an amazing story to relate. He said he had been in this house, talking to this fellow Vail, who, I take it, is one of the minor cogs in your organization, and while they were talking, he suddenly heard Queen of Matchingham grunt.'

'But it isn't – '

'Wait, Clarence,' said Gally. 'I want to hear this. I can't make head or tail of it so far. Go on.'

Sir Gregory proceeded.

'Well, he thought for a moment, quite naturally, that he must have imagined it, but then the sound came again, and it was Queen of Matchingham all right. He recognized her grunt, and this time he was able to locate it. It had come from the kitchen. There was plainly a pig there.'

'But that's – '

'Clarence, please! Yes?'

'So he said to himself "Oho!"'

'O what?'

'Ho.'

'Right. Carry on.'

'He had noticed, he said, from the start of their conversation, that this fellow Vail seemed very nervous, and now he appeared to lose his head completely. He attempted to get rid of Wellbeloved with some absurd story about something or other which Wellbeloved says would not have deceived a child. I suppose these inexperienced crooks always do lose their heads in a crisis. No staying power. I don't know who this Vail is – '

'He's my secretary,' said Lord Emsworth.

'In your pay, is he? I thought so.'

'No, he isn't, now I come to think of it,' said Lord Emsworth. 'Connie sacked him.'

'Well, whether he's still your secretary or not is beside the dashed point,' said Sir Gregory impatiently. 'The thing that matters is that he's a minion whom you have bought with your gold. To go on with what I was saying, this bally Vail told Wellbeloved this bally story, straining every nerve to get him out of the house, and Wellbeloved very shrewdly pretended to swallow it and then came and reported to me. I drove here immediately with the constable, heard my pig in the kitchen, found Beach on guard, and directed the officer to take him into custody and haul him off to a prison cell. At the next session of the bench of magistrates I shall sentence him to whatever the term of imprisonment is that a bounder gets for stealing pigs. I shall have to look it up. I shall be much surprised if it isn't six months or a year or something like that. Nor is that all. You, Emsworth, and you, Threepwood, will be up to your necks in the soup as accessories before the fact. With the evidence at my disposal, I shall be able to net the whole gang. That,' said Sir Gregory, after a keen glance at Lord Emsworth and another keen glance at Gally, 'is how matters stand, and I don't wonder you're trembling like leaves. You're in a very nasty spot, you two pig purloiners.'

He ceased, and Gally shook his head, perplexed.

'I don't get it,' he said. 'I thought I was a fairly intelligent man, but this defeats me. It sounds absurd, but the way it looks to me is that you are accusing us of having stolen your pig.'

Sir Gregory stared.

'You haven't the nerve to deny it?'

'Of course I deny it.'

'You are trying to tell me there isn't a pig in that kitchen? Listen, dammit! I can hear it grunting now.'

'My dear fellow, of course you can. A deaf adder could. But that's the Empress.'

'What!'

'You are surprised to find her here? The explanation is quite simple. It seemed to Clarence that she was looking a bit peaked, and he thought a change of air and scenery might do her good. So he asked Vail to put her up for a day or two, and Vail of course said he would be delighted. That was what happened, wasn't it, Clarence?'

'Eh?'

'He says yes,' said Gally.

Sir Gregory stood for a moment staring incredulously, then he strode to the kitchen door and flung it open, and Lord Emsworth, unable to restrain himself any longer, shot through. Grunts and endearing exclamations made themselves heard. Gally closed the door on the sacred reunion.

Sir Gregory was puffing in a distraught sort of way.

'That's not my pig!'

'Of course it isn't,' said Gally soothingly. 'That's what I keep telling you. It's the Empress. You see now how groundless those charges of yours were. I don't want to be censorious, Parsloe, but I must say that when you go about accusing the cream of the British aristocracy of pinching pigs purely on the strength of a chap like George Cyril Wellbeloved having heard one grunt, it looks like the beginning of the end. If that sort of thing is to become habitual, it seems to me that the whole fabric of Society must collapse. The thing I can't understand is how you ever got the idea into your head that Queen of Matchingham had been stolen. Bizarre is the word that springs to the lips. You must have known that she has been in her sty right along.'

'What!'

'Well, all I can tell you is that I was round at your place this afternoon, and she was there then. I thought I would look you up and have a friendly chat, because I feel so strongly how important pleasant neighbourly relations are in the country. When I got to Matchingham, you were out, so I took a turn about the grounds, just to see how your flowers were doing, and I noticed her in her sty. I'd have given her a potato, only I didn't happen to have one on me. But if you still feel doubtful, let's go to Matchingham now, and you can see for yourself.'

The drive to Matchingham Hall was a silent one, and so was the quick walk through the grounds to the Parsloe piggeries. Only when the sty had been reached and its occupant inspected did Sir Gregory speak.

When he did so, it was in a strangled voice.

'That pig wasn't here this morning!' he cried hoarsely.

'Who says so?'

'Wellbeloved.'

Gally gave a light laugh. He was amused.

'Wellbeloved! Do you think any credence is to be attached to what a chap like that tells you? My dear fellow, George Cyril Wellbeloved is as mad as a March hatter. All the Wellbeloveds have been. Ask anyone in Market Blandings. It was his grandfather, Ezekiel Wellbeloved, who took off his trousers one snowy afternoon in the High Street and gave them to a passer-by, saying he wouldn't be needing them any longer, as the end of the world was coming that evening at five-thirty sharp. His father, Orlando Wellbeloved – '

Sir Gregory interrupted to say that he did not wish to hear about George Cyril's father, Orlando Wellbeloved, and Gally said that was quite all right, many people didn't.

'I was only trying to drive home my point that it is foolish ever to listen to the babblings of any Wellbeloved.

Especially George Cyril. He's the dottiest of the lot. I understand that he's always being approached with flattering offers by the talent scouts of Colney Hatch and similar institutions.'

Sir Gregory gave him a long look, a look fraught with deep feeling. His mind was confused. He was convinced that there was a catch in this somewhere, if one could only put one's finger on it, but he was a slow thinker and it eluded him.

'Ha!' he said.

Gally tut-tutted.

'Surely that is not all you are going to say, my dear fellow,' he said mildly.

'Eh?'

'I should have thought a touch of remorse would have been in order. I mean to say, you have been throwing your weight about a bit, what?'

Sir Gregory struggled with his feelings for a moment.

'Yes. Yes, I see what you mean. All right. I apologize.'

Gally beamed.

'There spoke the true Gregory Parsloe!' he said. 'You will, of course, immediately telephone to the cops that Beach is to be released without delay. It would be a graceful act if you sent your chauffeur down in your car to bring him home. I'd do it myself, only I have to take Clarence and the Empress back to Blandings. Now that she has had this rest cure at Sunnybrae, he will want her back in her old quarters.'

CHAPTER ELEVEN

HAVING deposited Lord Emsworth in his library and the Empress in her headquarters, Gally returned to his car and drove it into the garage of Blandings Castle. He almost collided with another which was coming out with Lord Vosper at its wheel.

'Hullo,' said Gally, surprised. 'You off somewhere?'

'That's right.'

'A little late, isn't it?'

'It is a bit, I suppose.'

Lord Vosper seemed to hesitate for a moment. Then he remembered that this was the man in whom he had confided. As such, he was entitled to hear the latest news.

'As a matter of fact, Gloria and I are driving to London to get married.'

'Well, I'll be dashed. You are?'

'That's right. We both rather shrank from the thought of explaining things to Lady Constance, so we decided we'd just slide off and spring the news in our bread-and-butter letters.'

'Very sensible. "Dear Lady Constance. How can we thank you enough for our delightful visit to your beautiful home? Such a treat meeting your brother Galahad. By the way, we're married. Yours faithfully, The Vospers." Something on those lines?'

'That's right. We shall drive through the silent night, hitting the metropolis about dawn, I imagine. A couple of hours sleep, a quick shower, the coffee, the oatmeal, the eggs and bacon, and then off to the registrar's.'

'It sounds a most attractive programme.'

'So Penny was saying. She was wishing that she and Jerry Vail could do the same.'

'They may be able to ere long. You've seen Penny, then?'

'Just now.'

'I'm looking for her.'

'She's looking for you. Between ourselves, she seems a bit disgruntled.'

'I'm sorry to hear that. What about?'

'Ah, there you rather have me. Pigs entered into it, I remember, but if you ask me if I definitely got a toe-hold on the gist, I must answer frankly that I didn't. But you appear to have been upsetting Jerry Vail in some way somehow connected with pigs, and, as I say, she's looking for you. She struck me as being a shade below par, and she spoke with a good deal of animation of skinning you with a blunt knife.'

Gally remained calm.

'She won't want to do that when she hears my news. Her only thought will be to dance about the premises, clapping her little hands. Where is she?'

'In Beach's pantry. At least, I left her there five minutes ago.'

'Beach is back, then?'

'I didn't know he'd gone anywhere.'

'Yes, I believe he went into Market Blandings about something.'

'Oh? Well, he's back, all right. I was looking for him, to tip him, and finally located him in his pantry. He was having a spot of port with Penny and Jerry Vail. Which struck me as odd, as I understood Jerry had got the push.'

'He had. But he bobbed up again. Well, I'll be running along and seeing them. Good luck to your matrimonial venture. I wish you every happiness.'

'Thanks.'

'You'll enjoy being married. Whoso findeth a wife findeth a good thing. It was King Solomon who said that, and he knew, eh! I mean, nothing much you could tell *him* about wives, what?'

'That's right,' said Lord Vosper.

2

It seemed to Gally, who was quick to notice things, that there was a certain strain in the atmosphere of Beach's pantry when he entered it a few minutes later. The port appeared to be circulating, as always when the hospitable butler presided over the revels, but he sensed an absence of the mellow jollity which port should produce. Beach had a dazed, stunned look, as if something hard and heavy had recently fallen on his head. So had Jerry. Penny's look, which came shooting in his direction as he crossed the threshold, was of a different quality. It was like a death ray or something out of a flame-thrower, and he saw that in describing her as disgruntled Orlo Vosper had selected the *mot juste*.

'Oh, there you are!' she said, speaking from between pearly teeth.

'And just in time for a drop of the right stuff, it seems,' said Gally genially. 'How pleasant a little something is at this hour of the day, is it not, and how much better a firkin of port than the barley-water which our good host takes into the drawing-room at nine-thirty each night on the tray of beverages. Thank you,' he said, accepting his glass.

Penny continued to glare.

'I'm not speaking to you, Gally Threepwood,' she said. 'I suppose you know,' she went on, with feminine inconsistency, 'that you've reduced my poor darling Jerry and my poor precious Beach to nervous wrecks?'

'They look all right to me,' said Gally, having inspected her poor darling Jerry and her poor precious Beach.

'Outwardly,' said Jerry coldly. 'Inside, I'm just a fluttering fawn.'

'So is Beach,' said Penny. 'Say Boo.'

'Boo!'

'There! See him jump. Now drop a plate or something.'

Beach quivered.

'No, please, miss. My nerves could not endure it.'

'Nor mine,' said Jerry.

'Come, come,' said Gally. 'This is not the spirit I like to see. You were made of sterner stuff when we three fought side by side at the battle of Agincourt. Well, I must say this surprises me. Who would have thought that a mere half hour in the jug would have affected you so deeply, Beach? Why, in my hot youth I frequently spent whole nights in the oubliettes of the old Vine Street police station, and came out rejoicing in my strength. And you, Jerry. Fancy you being so allergic to pigs.'

'I should prefer not to have the word pig mentioned in my presence,' said Jerry stiffly. He brooded for a moment. 'I remember,' he went on, 'hearing my uncle Major Basham once speak of you. I cannot recall in what connexion your name came up, but he said: "If ever you find yourself getting entangled with Galahad Threepwood, my boy, there is only one thing to do – commend your soul to God and try to escape with your life." How right he was, how terribly right!'

'He knew!' said Penny. 'He, too, had suffered.'

Gally seemed puzzled.

'Now why would he have said a thing like that? Ah!' He brightened. 'He must have been thinking of the time when Puffy Benger and I put old Wivenhoe's pig in his bedroom the night of the Bachelors' Ball at Hammer's Easton.'

Jerry frowned.

'I think I expressed a wish that that word – '

'Quite, quite,' said Gally. 'Let us change the subject. I've just been talking to young Vosper,' he said, doing so.

'Oh?' said Penny coldly.

'Orlo Vosper,' said Gally, 'is not what I would call one of our brightest intellects, but he does occasionally get good ideas. His latest, as you know, is to drive up to London to-night with that dark-eyed serpent, Gloria Salt, and get married at a registrar's, and he was saying that you were wishing you could do the same. Why don't you? You could borrow the small car.'

Jerry gave him a frigid look.

'You are suggesting that Penny and I should go to London and get married?'

'Why not?'

Jerry laughed bitterly.

'Let me supply you with a few statistics relating to my financial position,' he said. 'My income last year, after taxes, was – '

'Yes, yes, I know. But Penny was telling me of this magnificent opening you've got with this health cure place. She stunned me with her story of its possibilities. It is not too much to say that I was electrified. You may argue that you cannot be both stunned *and* electrified, but I say you can, if the conditions are right. "Stap my vitals!" I said to myself. "I must keep in with this fellow Vail, endear myself to him in every possible way, so that in time to come I shall be in a position to get into his ribs for occasional loans. A young man with a future." '

Penny regarded him with distaste.

'Go on. Twist the knife in the wound.'

'I don't follow you, my dear.'

'You know perfectly well that Jerry has to raise two thousand pounds and hasn't a hope of getting it.'

'Why not?'

'Who's going to give it to him?'

Gally's eyebrows rose.

'Why, Clarence, of course.'

'Lord Emsworth?'

'Who else?'

Penny stared.

'You're crazy, Gally. There isn't a hope. I told you about him and Jerry straining their relations. Don't you remember?'

'Certainly, I remember. That point came up in the course of conversation as we were driving back from Matchingham. I mentioned Jerry's name, and he drew in his breath sharply. "He called me a muddleheaded old ass," he said. "Well, you are a muddleheaded old ass," I pointed out, quick as a flash, and he seemed to see the justice of this. He didn't actually say "Egad, that's true," but he drew in his breath sharply, and seeing that I had got him on the run, I pressed my advantage. Didn't he realize, I said, that it was entirely through Jerry's efforts that the Empress had been restored to him? He would be showing himself a pretty degenerate scion of a noble race, I said, if he allowed a few heated words spoken under the stress of emotion to outweigh a signal service like that. He drew in his breath sharply. "Was it young Vail who recovered the Empress?" his voice a-quaver and his pince-nez a-quiver. "Of course it was," I said. "Who the dickens did you think it was? How on earth do you suppose she got into that kitchen at Sunnybrae, if Vail didn't put her there – at great personal peril, I may add," I added. "God bless my soul!" he said, and drew in his breath sharply. It was one of those big evenings for sharp-breath-drawers.'

Gally paused, and accepted another glass of port. He was experiencing the quiet satisfaction of the raconteur who sees that his story is going well. A good audience, Beach and these two young people, he felt. Just the right hushed silence, and the eyes protruding just the correct distance from their sockets.

'I saw now,' he resumed, 'that I had touched the spot and got him where I wanted him. You have probably no conception of Clarence's frame of mind, now that he has got that blighted pig off his back. Exalted ecstasy is about the nearest I can come to it. I should imagine that you felt rather the same, Jerry, when you asked Penny to marry you and her shy response told you that you had brought home the bacon. You leaped, I presume. You sang, no doubt. You scoured the countryside looking for someone to do a good turn to, I should suppose – it is the same with Clarence. As the car drove in at the gate, we struck a bumpy patch, and I could hear the milk of human kindness sloshing about inside him. So I hesitated no longer. I got him to the library, dumped him in a chair, and told him all about your hard case. "Here are these two excellent young eggs, Clarence," I said, "linked in the silken fetters of love, and unable to do anything constructive about it because the funds are a bit low. Tragic, eh, Clarence?" "Dashed tragic," he said. "Brings the bally tear to the eye. Can nothing be done about it before my heart breaks?" "The whole matter can be satisfactorily adjusted, Clarence," I said, "if somebody, as it might be you, slips Jerry Vail two thousand pounds. That is the sum he requires in order to unleash the clergyman and set him bustling about his business." He stared at me, amazed. "Two thousand pounds?" he said. "Is that all? Why, I feed such sums to the birds. You're sure he doesn't need more?" "No, two thousand will fix it," I said. "Then I'll write him a cheque immediately," he said. And to cut a long story short, he did, grumbling a little because he wasn't allowed to make it larger, and here it is.'

Jerry and Penny stared at the cheque. They could not

speak. In moments of intense emotion words do not come readily.

'He made but one stipulation,' said Gally, 'that you were not to thank him.'

Penny gasped.

'But we must thank him!'

'No. He is a shy, shrinking, nervous fellow. It would embarrass him terribly.'

'Well, we can thank you.'

'Yes, you can do that. I enjoy that sort of thing. You can kiss me, if you like.'

'I will. Oh, Gally!' said Penny, her voice breaking.

'There, there,' said Gally. 'There, there, there!'

It was some little time later that Gally, a good deal dishevelled, turned to Beach. The door had closed, and they were alone.

'Ah, love, love!' he said. 'Is there anything like it? Were you ever in love, Beach?'

'Yes, sir, on one occasion, when I was a young under-footman. But it blew over.'

'Nice, making the young folks happy.'

'Yes, indeed, Mr Galahad.'

'I feel all of a glow. But what of the old folks?'

'Sir?'

'I was only thinking that you don't seem to have got much out of this. And you ought to have your cut. You don't feel like bringing an action against Parsloe?'

Beach was shocked.

'I wouldn't take such a liberty, Mr Galahad.'

'No, I suppose it would be awkward for you, suing your future nephew by marriage. But you certainly are entitled to some compensation for all you have been through, and I think with a little tact I can get it for you. About how much would you suggest? A hundred? Two hundred?

Five hundred is a nice round sum,' said Gally. 'I'll
see what I can do about it.'

3

In her bedroom on the first floor, the second on the right –
not the left – as you went along the corridor, Lady Constance, despite her nasty cold, was feeling on the whole,
pretty good.

There is this to be said for a nasty cold, that when you get
it, you can go to bed and cuddle up between the sheets and
reflect that but for this passing indisposition you would
have been downstairs, meeting your brother Galahad.
After all, felt Lady Constance philosophically, kneading the
hot water bottle with her toes, a couple of sniffs and a few
sneezes are a small price to pay for the luxury of passing an
evening away from a brother the mere sight of whom has
always made you wonder if Man can really be Nature's last
word.

It was consequently with something of the emotions of a
character in a Greek Tragedy pursued by the Fates that she
saw the door open and observed this brother enter in person,
complete with the monocle which had always aroused her
worst passions. Lying awake in the still watches of the
night, she had sometimes thought that she could have
endured Gally if he had not worn an eyeglass.

'Go away!' she said.

'In due season,' said Gally. 'But first a word with you,
Connie.' He seated himself on the bed, and ate one of the
grapes which loving hands had placed on the table. 'How's
your cold?'

'Very bad.'

'Clarence's recent cold was cured, he tells me, by a
sudden shock.'

'I am not likely to get a sudden shock.'

'Oh, aren't you?' said Gally. 'That's what *you* think. Beach is bringing an action against Sir Gregory Parsloe, claiming thousands of pounds damages. Try that one on your nasal douche.'

Lady Constance sneezed bitterly. She was feeling that if there was one time more than another when this established blot on the family exasperated her, it was when he attempted to be humorous.

'Is this one of your elaborate jokes, Galahad?'

'Certainly not. Straight, serious stuff. A stark slice of life.'

Lady Constance stared.

'But how can Beach possibly be bringing an action against Sir Gregory? What for?'

'Wrongful arrest. Injury to reputation. Defamation of character.'

'Wrongful *arrest*? What do you mean?'

Gally clicked his tongue.

'Come, come. You know perfectly well what wrongful arrest is. Suppose you were doing a bit of shopping one afternoon at one of the big London stores and suddenly a bunch of store detectives piled themselves on your neck and frog's-marched you off to the coop on a charge of shoplifting. It happening to be one of the days when you weren't shoplifting, you prove your innocence. What then? Are you satisfied with an apology? You bet you're not. You race off to your lawyer and instruct him to bring an action against the blighters and soak them for millions. That's Beach's position. Parsloe, for some reason known only to himself, got the idea that Beach had pinched his pig, and instead of waiting like a sensible man and sifting the evidence had him summarily arrested and taken off to Market Blandings prison, courtesy of Constable Evans. Beach now, quite naturally, proposes to sue him.'

The full horror of the situation smote Lady Constance like a blow.

'The scandal!' she wailed.

Gally nodded.

'Yes, I thought of that.'

Lady Constance's eyes flashed imperiously.

'I will speak to Beach!'

'You will not speak to Beach,' said Gally firmly. 'Start giving him that *grande dame* stuff of yours, and you'll only put his back up worse.'

'Then what is to be done?'

Gally shrugged his shoulders.

'Nothing, as far as I can see. The situation seems hopeless to me. It would all be simple, if Parsloe would only agree to a settlement out of court, but he refuses to consider it. And Beach wants five hundred pounds.'

Lady Constance stared.

'Five hundred? You said thousands of pounds.'

'Just a figure of speech.'

'You really mean that Beach would consent to drop this action of his for five hundred pounds?'

'It's a lot of money.'

'A lot of money? To avoid a scandal that would make us all the laughing stock of the county? Give me my cheque book. It's in the drawer over there.'

Amazement showed itself on every feature of Gally's face.

'You aren't telling me that *you* are going to brass up?'

'Of course I am.'

Gally, infringing Lord Emsworth's copyright, drew in his breath sharply.

'Well, this opens up a new line of thought,' he said. 'I'm bound to say that that solution of the problem never occurred to me. And yet I ought to have known that you would prove equal to the situation. That's you!' said Gally admiringly. 'Where weaker vessels like myself lose their heads and run round in circles, wringing their hands and crying "What to do? What to do?" you act. Just like that! It's character. That's what it is – character. It comes out in a crisis. Make the cheque payable to Sebastian Beach, and if you find any difficulty in spelling it, call on me. Were you aware that Beach's name is Sebastian? Incredible though it may seem, it is. Showing, in my opinion, that one half of the world never knows how the other half lives, or something of that sort.'

4

Blandings Castle was preparing to call it a day. Now slept the crimson petal and the white, and pretty soon the sandman would be along, closing tired eyes.

Maudie, in her bedroom, was creaming her face and thinking of her Tubby.

Lady Constance, in hers, was having the time of her life. Lord Emsworth, being in no further need of it, had passed on to her his store of cinnamon, aspirin, vapex, glycerine of thymol, black currant tea, camphorated oil and thermogene wool, and she was trying them one by one. As she did so, she was feeling that pleasant glow of satisfaction which comes to women who, when men are losing their heads and running round in circles, wringing their hands and crying 'What to do? What to do?' have handled a critical situation promptly and well. She was even thinking reasonably kindly of her brother Galahad, for his open admiration of her resourcefulness had touched her.

Beach was in his pantry. From time to time he sipped port, from time to time raised his eyes thankfully heavenwards. He, too, was thinking kindly of Gally. Mr Galahad might ask a man to steal rather more pigs than was agreeable, but in the larger affairs of life, such as making cheques for five hundred pounds grow where none had been before, he was a rock to lean on.

Gally, in the library, was having a last quick one with his brother Clarence. He was planning to turn in before long. It was some hours before his usual time for bed, but he had had a busy day and was not so young as he had been. Fighting the good fight takes it out of a man.

He heaved himself out of his chair with a yawn.

'Well, I'm off,' he said. 'Oddly fatigued, for some reason. Have you ever been kissed by the younger daughter of an American manufacturer of dog biscuits, Clarence?'

'Eh? No. No, I don't think so.'

'You would remember, if you had been. It is an unforgettable experience. What's the matter?'

Lord Emsworth was chuckling.

'I was only thinking of something that girl Monica Simmons said to me down at the sty,' he replied. 'She said "Oh, Lord Emsworth, I thought I was never going to see the piggy-wiggy again!" She meant the Empress. She called the Empress a piggy-wiggy. Piggy-wiggy! Most amusing.'

Gally gave him a long look.

'God bless you, Clarence!' he said. 'Good night.'

Down in her boudoir by the kitchen garden, Empress of Blandings had just woken refreshed from a light sleep. She looked about her, happy to be back in the old familiar surroundings. It was pleasant to feel settled once more. She was a philosopher and could take things as they came, but she did like a quiet life. All that whizzing about in cars and being dumped in strange kitchens didn't do a pig of regular habits any good.

There seemed to be edible substances in the trough beside her. She rose, and inspected it. Yes, substances, plainly edible. It was a little late, perhaps, but one could always do with a snack. Whiffle, in his monumental book, had said that a pig, if aiming at the old mid-season form, should consume daily nourishment amounting to not less than fifty-seven thousand eight hundred calories, and what Whiffle said to-day, Empress of Blandings thought to-morrow.

She lowered her noble head and got down to it.

5

In the tap-room of the Emsworth Arms a good time was being had by all. It was the hour when business there was always at its briskest, and many a sun-burned son of the soil had rolled up to slake a well-earned thirst. Strong men, their day's work done, were getting outside the nightly tankard. Other strong men, compelled by slender resources to wait for someone to come along and ask them to have one, were filling in the time by playing darts. It was a scene of gay revelry, and of all the revellers present none was gayer than George Cyril Wellbeloved, quaffing at his ease in the company of Mr Bulstrode, the chemist in the High Street. His merry laugh rang out like the voice of the daughter of the village blacksmith, and on no fewer than three occasions G. Ovens, the landlord, had found it necessary to rebuke him for singing.

Carpers and cavillers, of whom there are far too many around these days, will interrupt at this point with a derisive 'Hoy cocky! Aren't you forgetting something?' thinking that they have caught the historian out in one of those blunders which historians sometimes make. But the historian has made no blunder. He has not forgotten Sir Gregory Parsloe's edict that no alcoholic liquors were to be served to George Cyril Wellbeloved. It is with a quiet smile that he confounds these carpers and cavillers by informing them that as a reward to that faithful pig man for his services in restoring Queen of Matchingham to her sty the edict had been withdrawn.

'Go and lower yourself to the level of the beasts of the field, if you want to, my man,' Sir Gregory had said heartily, and had given George Cyril a princely sum to do it with. So now, as we say, he sat quaffing at his ease in the company of Mr Bulstrode, the chemist in the High Street. And Mr Bulstrode was telling him a story which would probably have convulsed him, if he had been listening to it, when through the door there came the jaunty figure of Herbert Binstead.

In response to George Cyril's 'Oi! Herb!' the butler joined him and his companion, but it speedily became apparent that he was to prove no pleasant addition to the company. Between him and Mr Bulstrode there seemed to be bad blood. When the latter started his story again and this time brought it to a conclusion, Herbert Binstead sneered openly, saying in a most offensive manner that he had heard that one in his cradle. And when Mr Bulstrode gave it as his opinion that the current spell of fine weather would be good for the crops, Herbert Binstead said No, it wouldn't be good for the crops, adding that he did not suppose that the other would know a ruddy crop if he saw one. In short, so un-co-operative was his attitude that after a short while the chemist said 'Well, time to be getting along, I suppose,' and withdrew.

George Cyril Wellbeloved found himself at a loss.

'What's the trouble?' he enquired. 'Have you two had a row?'

Binstead shrugged his shoulders.

'I would not describe it as a row. We did not see eye to eye on a certain matter, but I was perfectly civil to the old geezer. "If that's the way you feel about it, Mr Bulstrode," I said, "righty-ho," and I walked out of the shop.'

'Feel about what?'

'I'm telling you. I must begin by saying that a few days ago Sir Gregory Parsloe said to me "Binstead," he said, "a distant connexion of mine wants me to get him some of this stuff Slimmo. So order a half dozen bottles from Bulstrode in the High Street, the large economy size." And I done so.'

'Slimmo? What's that?'

'Slimmo, George, is a preparation for reducing the weight. It makes you thin. Putting it in a nutshell, it's an anti-fat. You take it, if you see what I mean, and you come over all slender. Well, as I was saying, I got this Slimmo from Bulstrode, and then Sir Gregory says he doesn't want it after all, and I can have it, and if I can get Bulstrode to refund the money, I can keep it.'

'Bit of luck.'

'So I thought. Five bob apiece those bottles cost, so I naturally estimated that that would be thirty bob for me, and very nice, too.'

'Very nice.'

'So I went to Bulstrode's and you could have knocked me down with a feather when he flatly refused to cough up a penny.'

'Coo!'

'Said a sale was a sale, and that was all there was about it.'

'So you're stuck with the stuff?'

'Oh, no. I've passed it on.'

'How do you mean passed it on? Who to?'

'A lady of our acquaintance.'

'Eh?'

Binstead chuckled quietly.

'You know me, George. I'm the fellow they were thinking about when they said you can't keep a good man down. It was a bit of a knock at first, I'll admit, when I found myself landed with six bottles of anti-fat medicine the large economy size, and no way of cashing in on them, but it wasn't long before I began to see that those bottles had been sent for a purpose. Here are you, Herbert Binstead, I said to myself, with a lot of money invested on Queen of Matchingham for the Fat Pigs event at the Agricultural Show, and there, in a sty at your elbow as you might say, is Empress of Blandings, the Queen's only rival. What simpler, Herbert, I said to myself, than to empty those large economy size bottles of Slimmo into the Empress's trough of food . . . '

He broke off. A loud, agonized cry had proceeded from his companion's lips. George Cyril Wellbeloved was gaping at him pallidly.

'You didn't?'

'Yes, I did. All six bottles. A man's got to look after his own interests, hasn't he? Here, where are you off to?'

George Cyril Wellbeloved was off to get his bicycle, to pedal like a racing cyclist to Matchingham Hall, trusting that he might not be too late, that there might still be time to snatch the tainted food from Queen of Matchingham's lips.

It was an idle hope. The Queen, like the Empress, was a pig who believed in getting hers quick. If food was placed in her trough, she accorded it her immediate attention. George Cyril, leaning limply on the rail of the sty, gave a low moan and averted his eyes.

The moon shone down on an empty trough.

6

(From the *Bridgnorth, Shifnal and Albrighton Argus*, with which is incorporated the *Wheat Growers' Intelligencer and Stock Breeders' Gazetteer*).

It isn't often, goodness knows, that we are urged to quit the prose with which we earn our daily bread and take to poetry instead. But great events come now and then which call for the poetic pen. So you will pardon us, we know, if, dealing with the Shropshire Show, we lisp in numbers to explain that Emp. of Blandings won again.

This year her chance at first appeared a slender one, for it was feared that she, alas, had had her day. On every side you heard folks say 'She's won it twice. She can't repeat. 'Twould be a super-porcine feat.' 'Twas freely whispered up and down that Fate would place the laurel crown this time on the capacious bean of Matchingham's up-and-coming Queen. For though the Emp. is fat, the latter, they felt, would prove distinctly fatter. 'Her too, too solid flesh,' they said, ''ll be sure to cop that silver medal.'

Such was the story which one heard, but nothing of the sort occurred, and, as in both the previous years, a hurricane of rousing cheers from the nobility and gentry acclaimed the Blandings Castle entry as all the judges – Colonel Brice, Sir Henry Boole and Major Price (three minds with but a single thought whose verdict none can set at naught) – announced the Fat Pigs champ to be Lord Emsworth's portly nominee.

With reference to her success, she gave a statement to the Press. 'Although,' she said, 'one hates to brag, I knew the thing was in the bag. Though I admit the Queen is stout, the issue never was in doubt. Clean living did the trick,' said she. 'To that I owe my victory.'

Ah, what a lesson does it teach to all of us, that splendid speech!

*Some other humorous
books in Penguins are described
on the following pages*

P. G. WODEHOUSE

This is the third occasion on which five of P. G. Wodehouse's novels have been simultaneously published as Penguins. In April 1953

RIGHT HO, JEEVES

THE INIMITABLE JEEVES

THE CODE OF THE WOOSTERS

LEAVE IT TO PSMITH

BIG MONEY

first appeared in Penguin form, to be joined in July 1954 by

QUICK SERVICE

THE LUCK OF THE BODKINS

UNCLE FRED IN THE SPRINGTIME

SUMMER LIGHTNING

BLANDINGS CASTLE

'Prep school boys at the time of the Boer War first discovered P. G. Wodehouse. By the year of George V's coronation he was an idol of the minority of boys who like some flavour of realism in school stories ... Then, in 1916, he wrote the first of the Jeeves stories ... The once schoolboy cult grew and grew ... Mr Belloc called Mr Wodehouse the best living writer of English. Mr Priestley called him superb, Sir Compton Mackenzie remarked that he was beginning to exhaust the superlatives of his critics, *Punch* observed that to criticize him was like taking a spade to a soufflé.' – A. P. Ryan in *The New Statesman*

STELLA GIBBONS

Cold Comfort Farm

140

When her parents died, Flora Poste found herself – a young and pleasing girl of some twenty summers – possessed of just a hundred pounds a year and no other visible assets. But despite her capabilities she had no intention of seeking a job – certainly not in the accepted sense of the term, for she resolved to make a career of her relatives. There were four possibles. An aunt in Worthing who was 'awfully jolly', a bachelor uncle in Scotland who had to look after himself very carefully, a cousin in Kensington who kept a parrot in the only spare room – and another aunt, Judith Starkadder, who lived in Sussex. It was to the Starkadder family that Flora decided to go. They lived in a place called Cold Comfort Farm, which sounded sufficiently strange and bleak to be really intriguing in its possibilities. For Flora was not simply going to 'plant' herself on her relatives and leave it at that. The Starkadders proved a grim and formidable clan, in all conscience, but vastly entertaining if you decided to do something about them, as Flora did. There was Seth, the younger son, whose prowess as a local Casanova was notorious; there was Uncle Amos, intent on preaching Death and Damnation; there was Mrs Beetle, the char; there was Big Business, the bull, who was penned in all the time – which no bull ever ought to be; there were half a dozen lesser females who were hardly ever seen, and there were others. And brooding in fearful tyranny over everyone was Aunt Ada Doom, who at the age of two had seen something nasty in the woodshed and still felt sore about it. It was this freakish family that Flora went to live with – and to liven up. She did not go in vain.